MAKE MY COFFIN STRONG

William R. Cox

Introduction by
David Laurence Wilson

Black Gat Books • Eureka California

MAKE MY COFFIN STRONG

Published by Black Gat Books
A division of Stark House Press
1315 H Street
Eureka, CA 95501, USA
griffinskye3@sbcglobal.net
www.starkhousepress.com

MAKE MY COFFIN STRONG
Originally published by Gold Medal Books, New York, and copyright © 1954 by
Fawcett Publications, Inc.

"The Kid and the Champ" copyright © 2022 by David Laurence Wilson.

ISBN: 978-1-951473-78-5

Cover and text design by Jeff Vorzimmer, *¡calientedesign*, Austin, Texas
Proofreading by Bill Kelly
Cover art by Barye Phillips

PUBLISHER'S NOTE:
This is a work of fiction. Names, characters, places and incidents are either the
products of the author's imagination or used fictionally, and any resemblance to
actual persons, living or dead, events or locales, is entirely coincidental.

First Stark House Press/Black Gat Edition: June 2022

THE KID AND THE CHAMP
Notes From an Unpublished Encyclopedia
By David Laurence Wilson

Cox said it was easy. I could have begged to differ but instead I just marveled at the bold statement.

When he said it was easy—it was. But in his eighties he had come to believe that perhaps it should have been more difficult. He was so fast, his facility for story-telling so attuned to the marketplace, that sometimes he thought that maybe he hadn't given the art of writing his best shot. He was a master of quantity; quality had been more elusive.

Cox was not a large man but he had a great, expansive presence and a lively intellect. He had accepted the classic definition of a pulp writer. He wrote fast and to order.

In this particular moment it was 1985 and Bill Cox was squinting through the shade of history and discussing his first novel, *Make My Coffin Strong*, a Gold Medal original from 1954, a rewrite of an unsold movie treatment.

In later years three of his novels were reprinted by the French publisher Gallimard in its *Série Noire* series. *Make My Coffin Strong* had been titled *Les p'tits mecs*. In English that meant *The Little Guys*.

"Make My Coffin Strong," Cox said again. "Now, what's that supposed to mean?" He had been appalled by the title selected by Fawcett.

Bill's own title came from the other end of the telescope: The Big Noise.

In 1985 Cox was a boulevardier who could barely get out his front door, down a steep driveway and into the fast-paced lane of traffic that raced past his home like a Sierra cataract. No stop sign, no light, so do you back up or back down?

When I visited I parked on the street below amidst the debris of damaged cars and walked up the hill. Bill wasn't walking the hills anymore.

When you mentioned the name Bill Cox to his peers they chuckled. Consequently, one of my favorite memories of Cox did not come from him at all. It was at the 1985 Bouchercon in San Francisco, the high tea of crime fiction. Bill Gault was there to sign copies of a new Brock Callahan novel and the western writer Tommy Thompson was there by coincidence, on an anniversary trip with his wife. All three had been Fictioneers, members of the legendary writer's club that often met at Cox's home.

Gault and Thompson were imprecise mimics but they were standing near the check-in at the Sir Francis Drake and they both began "doing" Cox, attempting his barking New Jersey accent and a range of gestures that came naturally to Cox, shaking their hands like they were brushing off a coat or clearing smoke, the kind of scene stealing motion that a novelist will use as a cutaway, prompting another line in a page of dialogue.

Gault was short and sporty. Thompson was thick. Cox was neither, but I'd pay a hatful of royalties to see that performance again.

Twelve years later we cut to another literary moment in San Francisco, but this time it was with Ken Kesey—no peer to Cox but nevertheless a writer who could roll up his sleeves for shoptalk. Kesey wrote about the modern west but this day he was on the road from Eugene, Oregon, to the Rock and Roll Hall of Fame in Cleveland, riding in the second edition of a school bus named "Further." Back in Cleveland the bus was going to be inducted.

Kesey had just buzzed past the Palace of Fine Arts with his vehicle's sound system playing "Hit the

Road, Jack," over and over again. Maybe they'd cool it on the freeways and save the noise for the ceremonies.

Like Cox, Kesey, too, was a drum major, and he paused to rhapsodize about the short stories of William R. Cox., the years when Bill's name was always splashed around the newsstands on the covers of pulp magazines. That day Kesey was a fan.

So who was this Cox fellow? And how did he get this multigenerational cheering section?

When I met Cox, his reputation had not yet preceded him, but the signs were there. I had read *Make My Coffin Strong* but hadn't followed up by looking for more of his words. I was taking in the whole great range of pulp and paperback fiction and Cox's voice was but one of many.

It was Cox himself, more than his writing, that spurred the affection from pulp veterans. Cox and his friend Bill Gault were two of the sweetest men to ever gain an irascible reputation.

At this latest and last stage of his life, it was not what Cox did that drew others to him, it was who he was, a charismatic raconteur who was always ready with the last story of the night. He exuded essence and bonhomie. He smoked and drank and was an all-around good fellow.

When health and physical frailty limited him, the party moved home and indoors, where his wife Casey did the heavy lifting, mixing drinks and warming what seemed to be an endless supply of spaghetti sauce.

Bill would say: "Have another drink. You can't fly on one wing," and he would will himself to vigor and the size of that vigor would outlast everyone within the sound of his voice.

At one end of the living room was a statue of the

silent comedian Buster Keaton. When the lights were right, or when you were flying with both wings, the eyes of Keaton might follow you around the room until you bumped into a small bookcase which had been built by Buster. That was where Cox had his novels on display.

"You like pulp writers?" Cox said. "Well, you should have been here last week!"

When the stories were over Cox, too, would be done. Finally he wrote so he could stay alive, stay in the game, have a voice on the page and a story for the conversations.   He was a font of literary gossip.

Women had a thing for Cox, and as long as he was married, they felt safe in his company. But if they were actually married to him ... well, he had been married five times, twice ended by death. Perhaps his greatest romance didn't wind up in matrimony because neither party lined up as single at the same time.

He said, "I may not be a great writer, but I'm a born writer." He didn't brag but he pontificated.

Despite only a small presence on the internet, Cox is credited with over 800 short stories and novelettes, eighty novels and a reported twenty pseudonyms.

The first fiction sale attributed to Cox is "A Teacher of French Grammar," by "Eric James," in *Parisian Life*, October, 1930, which at best is an outlier and maybe even a literary historian's joke.

Cox's own estimate was around 1000 stories, with none of them cut up for serial publication. No one could write every story, in every pulp magazine, but it seemed that Cox had tried, from *Black Mask* to the obscure and pricey *Cowboy Movie Thrillers* (#2, January, 1942). If you've got a computer you can buy the latter for just $474.

Scarce, surely, but you don't have to begin your

reading with the short run of *Cowboy Movie Thrillers*.

Cox also wrote for *The American*, *The Saturday Evening Post* and *The New Yorker*.

In my own collection I have 259 of his stories, many of them copied from the author's own files. Have I read them all? No, but I will probably never run out of stories by Cox, just as probably no one will ever know exactly how many stories he published. He was just too abundant to be sure.

Cox wrote thirty-two stories with a "Kid" in the title, seventeen with a "Champ." Underdog and coming-of-age stories were among his specialties.

Cox wrote fiction for over eighty different magazines, including 30 sports magazines, before the market for short fiction dried up and he began his first novel.

Alphabetically, he begins with "Accounting in Blood," in *Black Mask*, December 1939, the second of his two stories for the legendary crime fiction magazine. Later Joe Shaw, former editor of the magazine became Cox's literary agent.

All this from a career that didn't get rolling until he was thirty-four years old.

Cox was born on his father's family farm in Peapack, New Jersey, but early on the family moved to Newark, where his father, who had tried prizefighting, unsuccessfully, began a business selling ice, coal, fuel oil and firewood.

Cox was close to his grandfather Buchanan, an educated German immigrant and homeopathic physician who had begun reading Charles Dickens to him at an early age.

He skipped grades in elementary school but was not a successful student at Newark's South Side High, though he wrote for the student newspaper and enjoyed sports and poetry.

A helpful English teacher encouraged him to read the stories he had written to the class, tales like "Jason's Triumphant Return" and "The Spirit of the Musketeers."

Cox wrote: "After getting the Golden Fleece Jason and his fifty brave followers set sail in the good ship Argo for the Kingdom of Iolchos...."

And: "The two members of the king's musketeers entered the inn arm in arm, long swords clanking, and jesting loudly. They threw compliments to the maids and ordered wine in loud and jolly voices...."

He was already writing as "William R. Cox," with a fancy, flowing signature, and he thought enough of this early work that he kept it filed until his death, seventy years later.

After many arguments with his father Cox stowed away with a friend on a ship to England. After he was returned he was thrown out of high school. Later he received a general education degree. He enrolled in Rutgers University's extension department and began auditing literature courses at Princeton.

He took on a number of jobs, including work as a welder at a shipyard in Bristol, Pennsylvania. He played on the shipyard's soccer team and boxed in five amateur matches, receiving $25 a fight. He played in a football league for $5 a game.

His first professional newspaper job was as a copy boy for the *Newark Morning Ledger*. He rated a byline by the age of 20 and began a column—"Sports Licks: By the Cat"—for an Italian weekly. By 1920 he was a general reporter for the Sunday edition of the *Newark News*, covering fires, deaths, beatings and other extremes of human behavior.

But there was also pressure to help the family business. During the day he'd work for his father, delivering coal or ice and repairing roofs when the weather permitted. At night he wrote.

In 1934 a notice in *Writer's Digest* magazine led Cox to his first fiction sale, a football story for *American Boy*. Cox immediately submitted several more stories to the publication but was rejected with the suggestion that he send his stories to the pulp magazines.   He sold a track story, "Legs," to Popular Publication's *Dime Sports*. By 1935 Cox was a full-time writer. Eighty-five of his first hundred short stories and novelettes featured sporting themes.

The sales to Popular gave Cox the cash and confidence he needed to leave Newark. He took a train to Tampa, Florida, a town whose chief attraction was the lowest cost of living in the U.S. (Cox had looked it up).

The next ten years in Florida were extraordinarily productive. Cox gave himself a monthly goal of 50,000 words. If he travelled and fell off the count he would try to write 100,000 words each month until he caught up.

On a good day Cox would finish two stories and he seldom did any rewriting. Plotting and character were his strong points but the way he strung his words together—one quick roll through the typewriter and then to market—the language itself could become awkward. "I wasn't the best," he said, "but I was fast. I wrote for the markets, for the money."

Between 1937 and 1949 Cox averaged over 600,000 words of fiction a year. He had as many as five stories published in a single issue of a magazine and claimed to have eight series characters running at once. He reveled in his pace, in the ability to write two or three stories to another writer's one and he'd play games of solitaire on the side as he wrote. He kept meticulous notes on his wins and losses, stories sent, stories sold, and the number of words he was trafficking. At three cents a word those words were the source of a comfortable lifestyle, with plenty of time left over for tennis and parties.

"I don't plot so it's hard for me to describe what I do," he said. "I start with people, a setting and a theme, and I don't know where the hell I'm going. Then it all comes, the characters go to work, the location and the theme starts to work. It's simple. There's nothing to it, really."

He enjoyed the company of intellectuals but accurately described himself as an entertainer.

"To break up the monotony I'd write a fight story, a crime story and a western—in that order," he said in 1985. "My distinction has been my versatility. I can pick up the newspaper, any day, and come up with three stories. In three different genres. I've never had a dry spell in my life."

In 1948 he moved to California, where he worked at Republic Studios on a western series for Dale Evans.

Living at the Malibu colony and later, in Hollywood, Cox began freelancing television treatments and working with the veteran screenwriter "Willie" Lippman on the treatments *No Place Called Home* (an unproduced western purchased for $7,000 by RKO for John Wayne), *Angry Man* and *Tomorrow's Another Day*, the story of a frontier circus. Cox would work on the overall stories while Lippman fleshed out the dialogue in the individual scenes. Several screenplays were left unfinished at the time of Lippman's death.

During 1949 Cox wrote seven screen treatments and 87 short stories. In 1952 he completed only two short stories but had nearly doubled his income by working for the studios. He also purchased a home in the San Fernando Valley and begin working at Universal-International. He estimated that he worked on twenty unproduced treatments at Universal, everything from *Flaming Arrow* and *The Golden Sword* to *Lost City of the Amazons* but his sole credits were for the original stories for *Veils of Baghdad* (Universal, 1953) and *Tanganyika* (Universal, l954).

In 1953 Cox spent several months on *Action in the Afternoon* a live, Monday through Friday western series that was broadcast from Philadelphia. Cox also wrote a screenplay for *Jesse James' Women*, a Panorama Pictures production starring Peggy Castle and the temperamental co-writer, director and producer, Don "Red" Barry. Many years later Cox still fondly recalled the assignment, paid in cash by the side of Barry's swimming pool.

For the next four years Cox concentrated almost exclusively on the television market, also writing two unproduced screenplays, *Horsehide* and *The Gunfighter*, in collaboration with the fantasy specialist Richard Matheson (*The Incredible Shrinking Man*). Altogether, Cox claimed to have written 100 television episodes, a number that is hard to document without taking into consideration the scores of scripts he prepared for *Action In The Afternoon*. Most of his television credits fell into the western category, including several stories for *Bonanza* and *The Grey Ghost*. "The Willie Moran Story" (1957), co-written with Bill Fay for *Wagon Train* is particularly notable, with Ernest Borgnine starring as a punch-drunk boxer.

Another credit was "Behold Eck!" (1963) for *The Outer Limits*.

His greatest satisfaction, perhaps, was his friendship with Buster Keaton, who gave him his favorite definition of plot: "the plot is the clothesline on which you hang the laundry."

Another acquaintance was Aldous Huxley.

Cox's house on the edge of Hollywood was smaller than his home in Florida but his parties were undiminished. One year Keaton showed up for a Halloween event in a ballerina costume. Two more Fictioneers, the writers Robert Bloch (*Psycho*) and Richard Matheson attended as ghouls.

The parties continued into the nineteen eighties, though now his guests were widows and veteran pulp writers on the lean side of their careers.

Bill was at his best when he was stimulated, enthused, and there was a room and an audience for him to perform. When he had the opportunity he'd use it all up, all the energy which he'd once presumed was inexhaustible. But—you know—the show must go on, and Bill was a showman. Always with a cigarette in his hand.

Gradually, and against all odds, Cox had become a writer of westerns, beginning in January, 1941 when his agent suggested the genre could be a wide-open marketplace for him. He began wearing bolo ties.

In 1970, at the age of 69, Cox established yet another career as "Jonas Ward," author of sixteen ubiquitous Buchanan novels in a western series that sold over eight million copies. More recently he had established his own western series hero, "Cemetery Jones."

Writing the Buchanan paperbacks and twenty-five volumes of juvenile sports novels became the bread and butter of Cox's existence though occasionally he also wrote serious, even innovative western novels.

He was proud of *Luke Short and His Era* (New York, Doubleday, 1960), a biography of the gambler Luke Short, and he featured Short in his 1959 novel, *Comanche Moon*.

Between 1965 and 1966, and then again, in 1971-1972, Cox served as president of the Western Writers of America. Now he was a senior spokesman on the writing of the West.

Later in 1985 Cox was hoping to generate some fireworks at the annual get-together of the Western Writers of America. He'd take the lead in rounding up the veterans on the West Coast for a train ride to San Antonio, to "take over" the event. It would be a rolling poker game, an elderly revolution, but somebody had to carry the baggage. I would be along for the ride.

I was clearing my calendar. It seemed that this was going to be the start of a beautiful friendship.

Health did not permit; Cox's extravagant plan stumbled and stalled against the walls of reality and he returned to his next Cemetery Jones novel. He died of congestive heart failure on August 7, 1988, the morning after a dinner with Brian Garfield, a friend of over three decades. An unfinished page was sitting in his old manual typewriter.

The last of his many millions of words were: "He felt a surge of hitherto unknown ambition. He could be as hard and he sure was tougher than Old Man Clanton."

In retrospect, Cox was both a better and more influential writer than the sum of his efforts might suggest to us today.

He had made arrangements for his death. He was cremated and his name added to his parent's headstone in the old cemetery at Peapack, New Jersey, a place which has been surrounded by Newark and really no longer exists. It has become a district instead of a town. The headstone reads: "The cowboy from Peapack came home. He told his story." It was supposed to read "stories" but given the extent Cox borrowed from himself, the mistaken lettering was just as fitting.

R.I.P. Bill Cox (1901-1988).

—March 2022
Portland, Oregon

David Laurence Wilson has contributed to Stark House editions of the crime fiction writers W. R. Burnett, Sid Fleischman, Arnold Hano, Day Keene, Wade Miller, Harry Whittington and William R. Cox. He is also working on an illustrated history of American daredevils and stuntmen.

MAKE MY COFFIN STRONG

For
Lee Fredrick Cox
who retyped every word
and loved it.

1

He supposed there had been changes in eleven years, but walking down Fifth Avenue he could not detect them. More of the men did not wear hats, the women seemed less burdened with habiliments and walked with easier stride. But the noise was as great, the odors were as strong, the cops as big, the show windows as garish—and the lean girls still carried their hatboxes and hustled to their appointments with cameras.

It was early fall and his deep tan was not particularly noticeable among the returned vacationists. He had managed to buy a ready-made blue suit with accessories to match. He carried the Homburg the salesman had insisted upon, envying bareheaded men on their lunch hours who swung along empty-handed. He had always hated carrying anything in his hands when he walked.

He was taller than most New York men, and broader, yet he was not an outsize. He fitted well enough, he thought, despite the years abroad. The inner difference was not apparent even to a close beholder. It was extremely important that he should be undistinguished; he had thought about it a lot since the news of Sam's death had come to him.

Sam Goulding had first shown him New York, long ago, before the war, and it had been fun. Things always had been fun with Sam, because of the sentimental gentleness, the profound belief in life just for the living that comprised the soul of the little old horseplayer. These things Steve Galloway had loved in Sam, and this was the reason he had returned to New York.

He crossed Forty-second and a young girl with slender legs and ankles to turn a Moslem's eye skyward almost ran into him. She looked at him fleetingly, half-smiling a hasty apology, and was gone. Steve gazed after her a moment, shrugged, and went on. Plenty of time for that. Plenty of time to use the things Sam had allowed him to find out for himself.

The lions still looked broodingly down their noses in front of the library and the pigeons still maculated their stone skulls and this was pleasing. He had never admired the lions.

He thought some more about Sam and wished he could rid himself of the deep-seated guilt that gnawed at him because he had not thought subjectively about the old man for years. Had he returned a year ago, Sam might still be alive. He had planned to come back, every year he had made plans. Always there had been something.

Last year it was Saudi Arabia and the oil deal into which he had walked, blind lucky as usual where there was money to be made. Before that it was the small house in Sydney where the games had almost tilted the roof. Before that it had been Honolulu and the girl with green eyes and the dice table he had owned through bribery of the proper authorities. Before that it had been the Army and the opportunities presented to a sharp lad with cards.

Now Sam was dead and he had to see Lou Moscow. It was bad to think of Sam dead at sixty, that healthy small man with the happy grin who had raised Steve Galloway.

He turned east on Forty-second and the tempo changed near Grand Central, people scurrying, buses tangling traffic as they turned west from Park, sober-faced men arguing with their hands as they hustled along, a cool, dusty wind blowing down the canyon of concrete and metal. The sky was never as blue or as sunny on the side streets, he remembered.

He found himself increasing his pace.

No use wasting time on regrets, he thought. Sam was dead and soon he would know and then he would take steps. It was—it was something to do. He had chased money and its components far enough and long enough, stretching his luck, the luck that seldom failed him. He needed something in which to fasten his teeth, he was growing irritable and restless and at thirty-five he was beginning to look backward at what had happened to him. Like an old man. As Sam had never done.

He found the building and went into the lobby and looked at white-lettered names on a black board. He went to the elevator bank and a man snapped a gadget like a cricket and several people surged forward and he let himself be shoved, disliking it, realizing that this was one thing that had kept him from New York, this physical contact with the millions. He got off on the eleventh floor and walked down a corridor around a corner to a small office bearing the sign "Moscow, Hittleman, Nevers, Attys."

When he was twelve Sam had first brought him here and made a small joke for an orphaned boy. "Hittleman is dead and there never was a Nevers." He had added, "But Moscow ain't a city in Russia, it's a shyster in New York." Steve went into the dingy reception room and faced a blonde girl with the general outlines of an inverted cello.

She was a girl of medium height but everything else about her was almost embarrassingly extravagant. She wore a loose sweater, but it wasn't loose enough. She wore a skirt tucked into a nineteen-inch waistline, but it seemed scanty from there on down. Her flat-heeled shoes should not have pointed up exquisite anklebones, but they did.

Her eyelashes were fringes for eyes that were peculiarly slanted and probably green, Steve thought, trying not to stare. He said, "My name's Galloway. I don't have an appointment, but I think Mr. Moscow will see me."

"Mr. Stephen Galloway?" she asked coolly. Her voice was like that of a boxer hit too many times in the larynx, but smoother.

"That's right."

She said, "You can go in, Mr. Galloway." She pressed a buzzer, walked to the door to the inner office and waited a moment, then opened it and stood aside.

Steve went past her and felt, rather than heard, the door close behind him. He shook off a surprising feeling of being on the defensive as he said, "Hello, Mr. Moscow."

Louis J. Moscow looked at him from behind a cluttered old oak desk. He was a lean man, ageless, dry-skinned, rumpled, myopic. "Hello, Steve."

"It's been a long while." Steve sat on a straight chair, put his hat on the desk. It was as if things had never changed since that first day Sam had brought him here. "I guess you didn't expect to see me."

"I expected you." Moscow seemed to be waiting for a lead in order to counterpunch.

"Everything's the same except that vision in the outer office," Steve said. "You never were a man for getting excited."

"Why should I be excited? Because you turn up?"

"Look—what's the matter with me? I thought we were friends, at least in a business way," Steve said. "I came here on business."

Moscow leaned back, brushing cigarette ash from his lap, tilting his head to look over the bifocal lenses of his horn-rimmed glasses. "You're late. We buried

Sam six months ago."

"And I got the news three months ago. I had to clean up a deal, book passage, travel from Saudi Arabia to New York," said Steve. "What do you want from me, blood?"

"Twenty-three years ago Sam brought you in here. He was not a wealthy man, he lived on the thin edge of a shaky world." Moscow's voice was hard. "He made provision for you to go to school. He took care you didn't want for anything. He went short plenty of times so you'd have the best of it."

"Who knows that better than me?"

"You go into the Army. That you couldn't help," Moscow went on coldly. "You get out of the Army, you got something cooking. We get a letter once a year."

"I never was much for writing letters." Again he was on the defensive.

"We get a few checks." Moscow fumbled in a drawer, took out a bankbook, tossed it at Steve. "You'll find them accounted for. The only expenditure is for Sam's funeral. I took great pleasure in making it cost two thousand bucks."

Steve leaned forward, knocking the book aside with his index finger. "You can keep the rest for your fee, you goddamn shyster. And you can stop lamming into me about Sam. He wouldn't if he was here. And you can go to hell."

He got up and reached for the Homburg. Then he paused, looking down at the lean, angry man behind the desk.

He replaced the hat. He sat down, crossed his knees. He said quietly, "All right, Lou. You loved him. I was thoughtless—I goofed as far as Sam was concerned. Now let's talk business."

There was a long pause. Steve lighted a cigarette,

waiting.

Moscow said, "What business?"

"About Sam. A crumby short-carder drifted into camp and before I threw him out he said things were wrong at the end."

Moscow said, "What kind of wrong?"

"Before Sam was murdered."

"You mean about the horse?"

"Yes."

"Things were wrong. Damned wrong."

"Damnit, I want to know," said Steve.

"Why?"

Steve looked incredulously at the lawyer. "You mean you think I won't do something about it?"

Moscow tipped his chair forward. "I'm out of smokes. I was just going to ask Virginia to get some for me."

Steve handed over his pack. "That girl outside?"

Moscow found a long holder, fitted a cigarette into it. "Sam brought her here three years ago. Her father was another one of them like yours, only he lasted longer. Sam always had to have some kid to worry over. Her last name is Butler and keep your hands off her."

"So that's why she acted like I was poison." Steve nodded. "She knows all about me."

"To her, you're a heel."

"So I'm a heel. Look, Lou, all I want to know—what happened to Sam?"

"He finally got a horse," said Moscow. "A good one."

"That's bad? All his life, he wanted a good one."

"He rated it along. Flaming Arrow. How he loved that nag!" Moscow shook his head. "Never could see it. A horse—an animal. But to Sam it was his life. He had a couple of others—platers. Nothing. But

Flaming Arrow—it was a thing to him."

"So Sam had a horse."

"He was smart, you know. Not many people knew about this horse. Small tracks, a jock barely an apprentice, Legs Murphy, a no-good little jerk. But Sam loved kids and Legs was a kid. They played the Florida back country—Tampa, like that. Charlestown, they win a couple, just for cakes. Sam was building."

"Sure, for the big one," Steve said impatiently.

"For the Derby," said Moscow. "Sam dreamed. He came up to Belmont and dropped Flaming Arrow into an eight-horse thing out of his class, just for the experience. Legs had his orders—let the horse run, but don't try anything."

"Nothing wrong with that. It's been done since Apollo ran against the sun," said Steve. "What happened?"

"Flaming Arrow won the race," Moscow said deliberately. "And died in the barn right after they gave it the saliva test."

"What happened?"

"They found that someone had slipped Flaming Arrow a goofball. Big enough to shoot him home first and to kill him. A dumb job, pulled by amateurs. What could they figure?"

Steve said, stunned, "They figured Sam did it?"

Moscow nodded. "Or Legs Murphy, which amounts to the same thing. They pulled Sam's colors, barred him from the tracks."

Steve sat a moment, thinking about it, about Sam's lifelong dream of the horse he would someday find. The little man must have been pretty close with this Flaming Arrow; he had never fooled himself too much about horseflesh.

He asked, "What about Legs Murphy?"

"Disappeared."

"The cops, what about the cops?"

Moscow said slowly, "You got to understand how Sam was killed. Legs had already gone. Sam was drinking it up a little. You know how he was—nothing serious, just a little slump when things hit him."

That was correct. Booze had never been a problem to Sam. Only horses.

"They picked him up on First Avenue, near Fifty-second Street. It looked like robbery and homicide. His rock was gone."

"First near Fifty-second. Around the corner from Dead End," Steve muttered. "Yeah. I knew that rock. It was in and out of hock so often it had grooves worn in it."

Moscow said, "So there was a wave of muggings at the time and the cops lumped it in with the run-of-the-mill stuff. Sam's publicity had been bad and they knew he was on a bender and they filed the case. You can't hardly blame them."

"You don't agree."

"No. I had a call from Sam. He was cold sober. He said he had a lead on the horse thing. I talked to him the day he was killed."

Steve thought some more, about the gentle, happy Sam trying to clear himself by detective work, fighting to get sobered up and make sense, calling his lawyer, then getting skulled before he could make a move. Fresh anger was building on the embers of the smoldering flame that had begun with the news of Sam's death. He forced himself to deliberate.

He said, "You must have some ideas. How do you figure it, Mr. Moscow?"

The lawyer tapped a pencil against his fingers. "Money was down on Flaming Arrow all over the country. Every bookie not in the know was slaughtered. Right around here the money was spread evenly. That's all I know."

"One of those syndicate deals," said Steve slowly. "They move in, pick a sucker, make the kill, move out."

"You ought to know. You were raised in the business."

"Six months. The bastards could have killed each other off by now."

"Easily, they could have."

"I'll have to find out." Steve touched the bankbook again. "Keep this for operating expenses. Draw me up a power of attorney so if anything happens to me you can handle everything. Make out a will." He paused, then grinned. "Split my estate between you and the girl outside until further notice."

Moscow ground out his cigarette. "I'll do no such thing. You leave that girl alone."

"Draw up an agreement that I'm never to mention it to her," Steve said. "What the hell, I've got nobody. She was Sam's kid—who else would I leave it to? An orphanage? Nuts to that. You do like I say and stop making like a boss."

Moscow asked, "And what is the size of this estate you're making so much about, gambler boy?"

Steve picked up the hat. "I'll send you all the papers on the oil deal in Saudi Arabia. They said it would be well over a million. There'll be taxes for you to figure out. See you later. I got to start looking for trouble."

He took a moment's satisfaction from the amazement on the lawyer's face, then made his exit as though on cue. That had been another of Sam's teachings—knowing when to get off stage. In the outer office he paused. The girl looked at him without expression.

"I'm not stopping to argue with you now," he told her solemnly. "Check with Moscow. I'll call you later."

"I'll be busy later," she said flatly.

"That's what you think." He flourished the Homburg and left.

Pretty flamboyant, he thought, going to the elevators. You and your million, your lucky million that you parlayed from a drunk's conversation and a gambler's bankroll into an oil well. Big stuff, real big, and Sam six months in his grave. Bring Sam and his horse back with your million, let me see you try that. Or follow a stale trail to get to the people responsible for his death and wind up where? In the chair for a killing? Just because you got away with a couple of self-justified killings in far lands, don't think you can do it in this country.

Yet, as the story of Sam's ending sank deeper into his consciousness, he wanted to kill. Slowly and hurtfully he wanted to kill someone, to take him apart, piece by piece. An eye for an eye, a tooth for a tooth—and a few fingernails plucked by hot pincers to pay for the broken dream of a kind old man.

That's the way it is, Galloway, he told himself. You never had a mother to bring you up right. You're a slob, never a mother since you were twelve. Why, you bum, your mother was a swell dame out of burlesque and you remember her as well as you remember Sam. She was the very best kind of mother a kid could have, quick with a buck, quick to anger, quicker to forgive. Your old man was just like her and he was crazy about her and about you and that's why it was the first of your million lucky breaks that Sam knew this, took pity on you, gave you every chance in the world.

You've got your reasons for what you're going to do.

2

The first thing was to get out of the hotel and establish himself in an apartment. He bought the *Times* and made a few calls and walked around Central Park South and by noon on Saturday he had found an apartment for only slightly less than his left arm per month. It had everything he needed for the front he wanted. Three bedrooms, three baths, and daily maid service. A doorman big as Atlas and with a crooked gleam in his eye. Self-service elevators to stave off nosy operators and petty blackmail. An enclosed fire stairway leading to a basement garage. And a den.

The den was big enough for a six-handed poker game. The bar was in the corner, out of the way. There were pictures on the wall, mostly horses like Man O' War and Citation, and in a corner just for kicks several colts in a blue-grass pasture. Yes, the den would do fine.

Saturday noon he was moved in. He ate lunch out of his newly stocked double-door refrigerator, enjoying the manufacture of a jelly omelet and coffee black as his Homburg. He looked in the yellow section of the directory and found that the Businessman's Midtown Gym was on the Avenue of the Americas near Fifty-ninth, and this floored him a moment, but he called the board downstairs and they informed him that La Guardia had flipped his lid and allowed Sixth Avenue to lose its hallowed name in mistaken hemispheric patriotism, but that nobody paid any heed—it was still east of Broadway and people still called it "Sixt'."

He walked, digesting his light meal, happy in the autumn sun. He found the entrance to the gym and went upstairs and into a large, well-lighted loft fitted with everything to make the tired businessman even more tired.

There were half a dozen men puffing at various pieces of apparatus. In one corner there was a businesslike squared circle, complete with taut ropes and swinging corner stools. Steve nodded and looked around for Socker Cane.

The big man was directing a corpulent gent toward the rubbing room at the rear of the gym. He looked just the same as when Sam had staked him at Hialeah twelve years ago. He wore his slightly bunched ear and his scarred brows and twisted nose with the patient air of a man who knows he is not beautiful and couldn't care less. His blond hair was cropped close, his shoulders were square, and his back was straight as a board. He looked forty and was fifty-two. He saw Steve, hesitated, started forward, paused in disbelief. Then he roared, "You come back! Hiya, boy! Hiya!"

They shook hands and Socker's left fist pounded Steve's shoulder. The big man boomed, "You're in shape, huh? Wanta go a couple rounds?"

"With you, any day, you bum," said Steve happily. It made him feel inordinately good to have someone welcome him without cavil. "Can we talk first?"

There was a small office, well appointed, with framed photographs of celebrities on the walls. Steve sat in a deep chair and looked at a shiny print inscribed "To Socker, who could hit. Jack Dempsey," and shook his head.

Socker grinned. "Sure, I signed it myself. Jack wasn't around."

"He wasn't around when you were his sparring partner, either," Steve said. "You swatted at him, he wasn't there. How many times did he k.o. you in training?"

Socker said, "From him, who minded?"

"Where's Greb's picture?" asked Steve.

"That dirty sonofabitch."

"Sam always said he was the best."

"That freak."

"Sam said he could have beaten Dempsey."

Socker glared. "Did you come up here to argue with me or to find out about Sam?"

Steve dropped his teasing air. He lighted a cigarette, looked at the glowing end. "Moscow called you, huh?"

"No. The hell with Moscow."

"The girl, then. Virginia Butler."

"She's all right. You won't mess with her, will you, Steve?" The big man seemed to be pleading. His brow was furrowed; he looked like an unhappy gargoyle.

Steve wagged his head, marveling. "What's this with me? Have I got glamour or something? Everybody tells me, lay off Virginia Butler."

"It ain't you. It's her. She's got an effect on men. And she—she don't exactly hate the idea."

"But you older characters want to keep her pure and innocent." Steve laughed. "O.K., Socker, O.K. Now tell me your story about Sam and what happened."

"They goofed his horse, the stewards slammed him, he got clobbered and died," said Socker sadly. "You got the story from Moscow. It's straight. Moscow's all right."

Steve looked around. "Nice place you got here. For a horse player. You're supposed to die broke, you know."

"Mortgaged," the big man said glumly. "I hit a crazy parlay, set this joint up. Ain't had a winner since."

"I hear you get a lot of mains for customers."

"There's some high players around." Socker grew cautious. "They know me from the tracks, see? Some of 'em remember 'way back when I played tackle for Steve Owen. Some of 'em saw me box—the older ones."

"Any of them remember you were a private eye?"

Socker said uncomfortably, "Leave us not go into that. It was only a spell with the Pinkertons. It wasn't serious."

Steve said slowly, "You've been a lot of things, Socker. One thing you never were. Crooked. You say you got a mortgage here. How much?"

"Ten gees."

Steve said, "I might lift that for you."

"I'd only plaster it again when I hit a losin' streak," Socker said without enthusiasm. "This way the bank won't give me no more. I got to take it easy, see? Maybe it's better this way."

Steve said, "I want Legs Murphy."

"I ain't got him."

"I want to go from him to the contact man. Then I want the man behind the contact man."

"Steve, this is somethin' I don't know about."

"I believe that. I just want you to help me find whoever is responsible for Sam's death."

Socker sat quietly for a long moment. Then he said, "Steve, you know how I felt about Sam. He staked me often enough. He was a doll. He was the best. But this business—I don't know."

"Scared, Socker?"

"Not exactly. Only—well, Sam's dead. Nothin's

goin' to bring him back. What's the use of opening a can of beans?"

"Sam brought me up. I'm peculiar. I want to know the whole score."

"What you gonna do when you find out something?"

"How about letting me worry?"

Socker hesitated. "What you want from me?"

"You know people. You know the tracks and I don't even want to know them. You've got a good spot here for learning where Legs Murphy might be found. I can trust you."

Socker looked at the picture of Dempsey. "You still play a little cards, Steve?"

"If it will help, I'll be glad to play a little cards."

Socker said, "There's some people hang around here. One of them is a real nice guy. Name of Jack Barr. Square gambler. Maybe you ought to meet him."

"All right."

"This guy is a main. Lives uptown in a neighborhood where he was raised. Funny kind of guy."

"Important?"

"On his own. No big connections, except the cops. He knows a lot of cops."

"You mean he's not with a syndicate?"

Socker nodded. "Nobody knows any connection between you and Sam. It's too long ago and you went away—nobody could figure it. But if you start askin', it'll be a tip-off. So maybe you better start by gettin' with the high players, like Barr."

"You'll check Legs Murphy?"

Socker sighed. "This I don't like. Everything tells me I should leave this strictly alone."

"But you'll play?"

"I'll play."

Steve took out his checkbook. He wrote in it. He tore out a pink slip and handed it to Socker. "Ten thousand dollars. When the deal is completed I'll sign it."

Socker put the check into his wallet with great care. He said, "That's good enough for me." His face wrinkled into a carefree grin that utilized every muscle above his shoulders. "Come on, I'll give you a locker and sell you some stuff."

There were a couple of men getting dressed in the locker room. They looked curiously at Steve as Socker introduced them. "Pal of mine—been away."

One was named Charlie Goode, a big fellow with bulky shoulders and close-set eyes. He had a most pleasant manner, almost ingratiating. The other was called Sid November, which was not reasonable. He was reminiscent of the Near East, a barrel-bodied, hairy fellow with liquid brown eyes and an air of self-importance that Steve found incongruous. They both welcomed Steve to the club with offhand cordiality and continued to adorn themselves with most expensive haberdashery and suiting.

Steve stripped and donned an elastic supporter, shorts, white wool socks, and rubber-soled leather gym shoes, provided from Socker's retail supply counter. He threw a towel around his brown shoulders and nodded to the two men as he went toward the gym.

Socker, stripped to tights, was in the ring with big gloves and a couple of head guards. Steve jumped over the ropes and took a pair of gloves. In Saudi Arabia he had kept up his boxing to kill time, and in the Army he had skipped a lot of irksome duties through his ability to box. It had also helped distract authority from his activities with dice and cards. To the brass a gambler was a certain type, a jock strap another. They could not conceive of a man who could be proficient in both categories.

Socker chuckled in Steve's ear, "Watch Barr get interested. That's him with the skip rope."

Jack Barr was shorter than Steve, but weighed about the same. He was very fair, with freckled skin and a pug nose. His jaw was round and strong, his gaze direct. He skipped rope like a professional pugilist, deftly, without apparent effort. He turned himself now, looking up into the ring, slowing the tempo of the looping rope.

Socker turned back to Steve and said, "O.K., keed, let's see what you forgot."

They sparred. Socker didn't move much. He wheeled easily, picking off leads, countering lightly. Steve stepped around him and lazily poked out a left. Socker caught him with a right cross that almost tore his moorings loose. He heard the big man's light laugh.

Instinctively Steve swung back, covered. He dug in close and let Socker clout his elbows and head. He got his bearings back, eased off. He feinted a left, threw an overhand right.

Socker caught it on the side of his jaw. He went down on his haunches as though someone had blackjacked him.

He stayed there, shaking his head. Then solemnly he began removing his big gloves. "Too old," he complained. "No reflexes. I seen it, but what can I do?"

Steve said, "You shouldn't have clipped me."

Socker winked one eye. "Maybe Jack would like to try you. Jack tries out all the new guys. Jack's our cop around here."

Barr dropped the rope and bounced into the ring.

He was laughing heartily, from his belly. He held out his hand.

"I'm Jack Barr. Anybody who can hit Socker with a sucker lead is a pal of mine."

"Steve Galloway. Glad to meet you." He could feel Barr's firm grip through the padding of the twelve-ounce glove. "Want to go a round or two?"

"About two," said Barr. "How do the pros go ten, fifteen?"

Steve watched Barr put on the gloves, expertly, from long practice. "People don't know what it takes."

Socker finished with the lacings and came over to Steve and examined his gloves. In a quick whisper he said, "He was a pro."

Steve kept his expression blank. He went back to a corner, leaned there. He liked Barr at once. There was an enthusiasm, a friendly air that the man wore like a mantle, attractive on sight. But there was something going on here and Socker had tipped him.

Goode and November had come from the locker room. The other men in the gym were lounging, drifting toward the ring. Steve saw Goode nod in answer to something November said, saw one of the other men lift an eyebrow, look squinting into the ring, shrug, and nod. No one needed to announce that bets were being made.

He looked at Socker, who held a stop watch. The big man said, "Two three-minute rounds?"

"O.K. with me."

Barr was no longer smiling. His brow furrowed, his blue eyes were gray. Socker said quietly, "Time, gentlemen."

Steve came out with his hands high. A whirling fury swept across the ring at him. Barr came with both hands winging, hooking for the body.

Steve side-stepped. His left snapped down at the shorter man. He prodded, trying to keep Barr off balance. He succeeded only in part. A swinging glove slid upward, slapped against his ear so that bees seemed to swarm inside his head.

He moved right, then left. He cocked his right, watched a moment, ducked a left, and pulled the trigger. The big glove met Barr solidly, drove him across the ring and into the ropes. An amateur would have dropped his hands then, but Steve followed across to where Barr was already bouncing back to the attack. He shoved the other man off balance, sent a dipping right behind the ear. He led with the overhand right. Barr staggered, looking respectful. Steve hit him with a calculated right cross on the chin.

Barr fell in close.

Steve tied him up, whispered, "You want to kill the bets?"

Barr said, "They got a right."

Steve said, "O.K."

They sparred tamely to finish the round. They rested when Socker gave them the word. Steve looked down at the gaping men on the gym floor. Sid November looked slightly unhappy, Goode was smiling. Socker called them out again.

Barr discontinued his rushing tactics. The man could box, Steve knew very well. They went around too fast for men of their years who were not in strict training, and both felt the pace.

Suddenly Barr increased the tempo. He had got a second or third wind. Steve met the attack with all the skill he could command. He slipped a left, rolled with a right. He bent at the waist to get leveled off at the smaller man. He set his heels.

Barr came with a hook. Steve pegged it. Steve's right followed over Barr's left.

Barr stumbled, his feet tangled for a brief instant. Steve held a punch in mid-air, a right from over in Jersey. He poised, waiting for Barr to regain balance.

"That's enough," Socker said, stepping between them, snapping his watch. He looked at Steve, at Barr. "Barr landed most punches. Galloway hit harder."

Barr was biting at the laces of his glove, panting, his face reddened from punches. He managed to gasp, "Don't be a chump. You know as well—as I do." He drew in air, grinned. "Let the long-shot gamblers win. I bet they got three, four to one."

Socker nodded. "Galloway wins."

The men on the gym floor said nothing. Sid November took money from his pocket and gave it to Charlie Goode, then they left together. Barr stripped his second glove, watching them go. He said absently to Socker, "Good old Sid. He believes in me. Loyal to the end."

Socker said, "I got a fat-guy class comin'. You mind?" They drifted together toward the lockers. The remaining customers came in and Barr introduced Steve all around. They showered. When they came out, Barr said, "I'd like to see you sometime. You going to be around town for a while?"

"For a while. Doing anything for dinner?"

"I've got a business date." Barr hesitated. "Well—sometime, maybe. That's some right hand you got."

"How many bouts did you have?" asked Steve.

Barr's eyes twinkled. "Ten or twelve. Sixes and eights. I wasn't conning you about ten or fifteen rounds."

"I never went over six," Steve said. "Mostly in the Army. You were Navy."

Barr said ruefully, "Every smart guy knows a

Navy fighter."

"Hookers. You're all hookers."

"Funny, ain't it?" Barr picked up a Homburg hat identical to Steve's. "It was fun, Galloway. We'll try it again, for grabs."

"Any time." Steve finished dressing. He picked up his hat and started out. The fat men, a dozen of them, assorted, were coming in. He waved to Socker. "Call you tomorrow."

He went out onto Sixth. The afternoon was waning and people were all about, busy at week-end preparations. He was not a man to suffer loneliness, but suddenly he realized he had nothing in the world to do with himself. Nothing that he wanted to do, anyway.

That was pretty stupid, he told himself. He was young, healthy, and wealthy, and this was New York. He had only to walk toward the Plaza, go into a fashionable bar, and keep his eyes open. Results were guaranteed anywhere in the world.

Maybe that was it, he thought. It had worked for him so often that nothing of anticipation was left. The same tired routine, the same amount of money spent, the same result. He wasn't knocking it, he hastily assured himself, he hadn't reached that stage. He was merely wishing it could be different for once.

A cool breeze slapped his still damp brow. He put on the Homburg and turned to look for a cab. He stood on the curb for a moment, trying to adjust the hat to a comfortable angle.

It did not fit. He tried it again, took it off, stared at it. The salesman had been very particular about it. A cab wheeled to a stop and he crawled in, giving his home address, still examining the hat.

Initials were perforated in the sweatband. They were J.E.B. He studied them a moment, then light dawned. He remembered Jack Barr going out of the gym with a Homburg in his hand.

He turned the hat over, feeling the expensive sheen of its nap. There was an inscription, "Custom Made by Fowler," and a Madison Avenue address. He asked the driver, "What kind of shop is Fowler's on Madison?"

"How should I know?" snapped the cabby. "Could I buy a shoelace in that neighborhood?"

"Drive me over there," Steve said.

"You wanted to go to Central Park South," the driver said accusingly.

"That's right."

"Now you want to go to Madison."

"I'm eccentric."

"Go here, go there," muttered the cabby. "Nobody knows what he wants. Nobody knows nothin' anymore."

He was a small man with a dented nose. The identification card gave his name as Sol Mintz. He crouched low behind the wheel, driving with insolent skill through the harrowing Saturday afternoon traffic. He slid the cab between a delivery truck and a chauffeur-driven Rolls Royce. He sneered at the uniformed figure behind the wheel of the Rolls and said, "Them foreign cars. Crazy for 'em. Everybody. Big thing, foreign cars. Nobody knows nothin' no more."

"You got ulcers, Sol?" Steve asked him mildly.

"Big thing, ulcers. Everybody's got ulcers. What's so great about ulcers?"

"I never had ulcers." Steve was beginning to enjoy this.

"So don't tell me about ulcers." The light changed and the cab leaped like a willing animal, beating the traffic, crossing Fifth. A uniformed policeman stepped

tentatively off the curb, restraining suicidal
pedestrians, and Sol Mintz nearly took off his heel.
"Traffic cops get ulcers. The jerks. Too good for
'em."

"Why should traffic cops get ulcers?"

"Occupational disease," Sol Mintz said grandly.
"Nerves. All the noise. You ever hear so much noise?
I was inna Battle of the Bulge. It was quiet,
compared."

"You don't like it?"

"Like it? Are you kiddin'? What are you, a wise
guy or somethin'?"

"Just looking for information," Steve said humbly.

"Nobody likes it. Everybody hates New York.
And you know why? Noise. The big noise. That's this
town. Big noise!"

"I'd noticed."

"You noticed. That's a laugh. Lemme tell you
somethin', bub. You stick around this town. It'll
getcha. Like it gets everybody. Noise. Cabs, trucks,
whistles, trains, planes, subways, people ... noisy.
Real noisy. You ever been on Fifth on a Sunday?"

"Not for a long while." He remembered walks
with Sam along the quiet avenue many Sundays gone.

"Quiet-like. You think. No traffic, nothin', No
people. Nice, you think. But listen. Underneath. You
can hear it. Noise. It's there."

They turned north on Madison, barely missing
two old women and another profane cab driver. Sol
Mintz leaned out and used a few rich four-letter
words, cut sharply in front of a hesitant coupe, and
braked. He glanced at the meter. "A buck will get it."

Steve said, "With the tip, that is."

"Certainly with the tip," said Sol Mintz. "You
think I don't know you ain't from here?"

Steve gave him two dollars and said, "Buy yourself

some earplugs, Sol." He got out of the cab. Something made him hesitate. He turned and Sol Mintz was regarding him with shrewd, deep-brown eyes. He said, "I live on Central Park South. It's quieter there. Maybe I'll be using you again."

The cabby nodded. "I got two, three guys like that. Call Madison five-four thousand if you ain't in a rush. The route man's a hep kid." He was gone in a whirl of exhaust fumes.

Steve grinned to himself, turned, and looked across the sidewalk. A discreet window was chastely lettered "Fowler's." There was one hat in the window, one shirt, and one tie. Very high-class. He made his way through the people hurrying north and south and entered the shop.

There were no customers in the cathedral hush of the place. The light was ample, but cleverly indirect. Almost none of the merchandise was on display. The walls were lined with cabinets of dark wood and against one of them a girl struggled on a ladder, taking down cardboard boxes and placing them on a glass-topped counter. It was a long stretch from cabinet to counter. As Steve moved closer on a deep carpet she overreached and a box of men's lavender shorts spilled to the floor and she almost fell.

He stepped past the counter and reached up his hands. He felt firm hips in his grasp as the girl struggled for balance on the ladder. He saw long, slim, tapering legs in sheer nylons as the muscles moved under his hands. Then the balance was gone and the girl fell in his arms.

He set her down and said, "Think nothing of it. You wouldn't have done more than break an arm." He looked hard at her. "On second thought, think a lot about it. You might have been killed. I have probably saved your life."

She had high cheekbones and skin that was unbelievably smooth and lovely. She had exquisite brows, drawn straight now, and a mouth that looked as if it belonged to her and not Elizabeth Arden. She looked vexed and amused at the same time, which became her. She said, "My father, the king, would properly reward you, sir, were he available."

"I ask no recompense save your smile." He had to release her then, because she seemed about to squirm and he did not think even this girl would squirm becomingly. He looked at the lavender underwear with aversion. "You risk your life and limb in a strange cause."

"Markdowns," she said thoughtfully. "We've never tried to run a sale. Edgar is against sales."

"Edgar is Mr. Fowler?" He put the hat on the counter next to the underwear.

She shook her head. "I'm Fowler. Fay Fowler."

"Oh? You own this establishment?"

"And make a fine buck out of it," she said. She had retreated a step and was leaning on the end of the counter, her aplomb restored, her smile friendly but impersonal. "Now how much would you pay for these French broadcloth shorts of doubtful hue? Tops, I mean."

"I wouldn't own them."

"I was afraid of that." She dismissed them, giving him her full attention. "So what can I do to make you happy?"

He didn't want to tell the truth. "I came about a hat. I bought one just like this." He proffered the misappropriated Homburg. "Mine is not so sleek, not so grand to the touch. Your name was in the band of this one, so I came to find out how you make them so good."

She took the hat from him, turned it over, nodded.

"You've met Jack."

"Jack? Jack Barr?"

"My best customer," she said. "How did you—Oh, I see. You had one like it. I'll bet he's having a fit. He loves hats."

"I always preferred women," Steve murmured. It got him nothing. She tapped the brim of the hat on the counter, coolly surveyed him. He said, "However, I suppose if a man loves hats, he loves hats."

"You want one like this?"

"You make them yourself?"

"Certainly not. A man in Danbury makes them to order. By hand. One hundred dollars retail."

"Nobody can be that crazy about hats," said Steve.

She shrugged. "You'd be surprised. Running a shop like this teaches a lot of things about men. Jack Barr wouldn't pay over five dollars for a shirt, but hats at a hundred are nothing."

"Me, I'm a shirt man," said Steve.

"Custom made? About thirty dollars, monogrammed?" She moved to the cabinet, took out a box. "This is just a sample of the material and cut. You'll want all white."

He indicated the tumbled boxes. "And shorts to match. No monograms, please."

She brightened. "That's a test question I throw in. Maybe I'm glad you saved my life, after all. I'm against monograms, too."

He took off his coat, extended his arms. "Measurements," he commanded. "A dozen white shirts, two dozen shorts. Pick me out some socks, too. Move, woman!"

She bowed in pretended humility. Then she called, "Edgar!"

From the rear of the store a man moved out of the

dimness. He was almost as tall as Steve and wider. He had blond hair extravagantly waved, and in his obtrusively conservative suit he was reminiscent of a dandified undertaker's assistant, highest class. When he came close, a measuring tape languidly dangling from one large hand, he smelled faintly of sandalwood and soap. He said, "Shirts, Miss Fowler?" He lisped.

Steve took a long step back. He saw Miss Fowler grinning maliciously behind the effeminate clerk's shoulder. He braced himself and stood quite still.

After a second or two he was grinning. It was calculated strategy, this impact of the hulking pansy on a predatory male intent only upon making passes at the proprietor.

Edgar was calling off cabalistic numbers in his blurred sibilants and moving around behind Steve. The girl bent over a pad, making notes. She stood hipshot against the end of the counter in a posture that gave evidence that she was not dependent upon a girdle. Steve wondered how she kept her garters up. He supposed he should know, but he had been away from American girls too long.

He said, "I need shoes, too. I've just got back from Saudi Arabia and all my things are foreign made."

"Shoes across the street—pal of mine." She dug out a card. "Suits at Jablonski's. We get a commission if you mention us."

Edgar finished and stepped back, frowning a bit. "Blue or gray in suitings," he pronounced. "We can sell you weskits. Vari-hued, Tattersalls—you *must* have them this season. And cravats. My, Miss Fowler, won't he just *gurgle* over the new line?"

She said, "He will, he will. Thank you, Edgar."

Edgar tiptoed back to the dimness. Steve looked after him, nodded. "Perfect," he said. "If he doesn't fall in love with one of your customers and elope."

She said, "He already has. But he came back, repentant. Tell me, sir, where did you meet Jack Barr?"

She was making up a sales slip. Steve watched her hands, the long, sensitive fingers. He said, "At Socker Cane's gym."

"He meets more people there. Half my trade comes from Cane's," she said lightly.

"My name's Stephen Galloway." He gave her his address. "I'll give you a check for the full amount now."

"Why do people trust us like that?" she marveled.

He put on his coat, picked up the Homburg, suddenly began thinking about the things she had said about Barr. "If I leave his hat here, could you return it to him?"

"I was going to suggest it," she said promptly. Their eyes met and hers did not falter. They conveyed a plain message.

"I was afraid of that," he said seriously. "And I liked that guy on sight, too."

"Everyone likes Jack on sight."

Steve hesitated. She smiled at him in the most friendly fashion and it encouraged him. "He said he had a business date tonight. Could I offer myself as a substitute for dinner?"

Without equivocation she nodded. "Better you than Edgar. I love Edgar, but his conversation is sometimes—abstruse."

"You say where and when. Remember I've been away."

She considered. "You want to dress up?"

"If you can stand looking at a Parisian dinner jacket."

She shuddered, but agreed. "All right. Just so I can

wear a new thing I bought in a weak moment." She
paused, looked frankly at him. "This is because
you're acquainted with Jack—and because he plays
too much poker at night. Call for me at
One-twenty-three Beeckman. About eight?"

"I think this may be fun," he said judiciously.
"Real good fun."

Madison Avenue looked brighter, friendlier. He
walked briskly across the street and bought four pairs
of shoes, one to wear with the dinner jacket. He still
had time and Jablonski's was nearby.

Jablonski, to his delight, had a small ready-made
department for just such emergencies. He found a
dinner jacket not so fanciful as his Paris version, a
black tie, and a soft shirt. Jablonski sold him six
hundred dollars' worth of suits to be delivered and
Steve was a happy man.

He went home and made a single Martini in a
shaving mug he had carried around the Orient for
that purpose, his sole inheritance from his father. It
had forget-me-nots embossed upon it and the silver
initials M.X.G. He felt enormously eager and excited,
as though it were the eve of an important anniversary.

He sipped the icy drink, trying to shake himself
into a more temperate mood. He was being silly, like
a schoolboy, and besides, she was Jack Barr's girl, she
had plainly let him know. He didn't even know her,
only the feel of her hips and the way she had of
looking derisively but kindly at a stranger, as though
she knew him, all about him, and approved of him.

He had known other women like that, but always
they had been kindly professionals of one sort or
another. Like Sadye, the international spy, most
successful of her kind, always able to make a man feel
safe and comfortable. Or Marise, who ran the brothel
in Cairo with such enthusiasm that all the

good-looking men asked for her rather than her girls. And got her.

He made himself another quick one and decided to take a hot tub bath before his shower.

3

That cab driver had made him supersensitive to the sounds of the city, he thought, and now the liquor and the swift movement of the evening had heightened all his senses to a point where discretion must be struggled for. They were in the Roosevelt Grill, of all places, and Guy Lombardo's noise alone had not changed in his absence, indeed had not changed in two decades and a half. They danced a long set, through the carefully measured pacing of the Lombardo genius, wherein no one tires or grows bored with the varied rhythms.

It was midnight and he was enchanted. In an evening gown she proved not so slim as she had appeared in the shop. She was one of the rare ones, perfectly fashioned in every joint of bone structure, overlaid with flesh like expensive velvet, colored to satisfy the eye of the most meticulous painter. Her beauty was not overwhelming; it was quiet, satisfying, almost insidious. He thought of Jack Barr, whom he had met so fleetingly, and had liked, but the alcohol he had consumed lapped against his resolution.

He ordered more brandy and looked across the small table into her eyes. "Thanks for bringing me here. This is unchanged, this is home. Garish, noisy, corny, but definitely home."

She gave him her easy, natural smile. "A special sort of raucousness. Good for getting acquainted. Coincidentally, there's another reason for coming here. You'll have to believe that there were two."

"I'm inclined to believe what you say," he said gravely. "I'm going to be nosy about your other reason in a moment. But first I want to give you a chance to tell me it's none of my business about you and Jack Barr."

She sobered, dropping her eyes. "That's the second reason. The game is upstairs tonight. He called me earlier. He wants to meet us here for a drink."

"I guess I'm answered." He watched the waiter put down the large snifter glass with the brandy floating in its bottom. Always he had to be careful with alcohol. He had a low tolerance for it. Probably the gambling had prevented him from giving it more leeway; he never touched it when he was in a game. Now he wanted to ask more about Barr, learn the exact status of Barr and the girl, pin down every detail in order to adjust himself to the situation. Because he wanted the girl, he wanted her more than he had ever before desired a woman.

She said, "Since you came into the shop I've been thinking. Please be flattered."

"I'm flattered." It was difficult not to say more. He revolved the spot of brandy in the glass, brought it to his lips, did not drink.

"I've been attracted to men before. Long ago it hurt several of us. I've learned better."

This was something he had not speculated upon. Surprise drove him to ask, "You've been married?"

"Once. It didn't work. Then—other things." She looked at him hard. "The drinks are getting me. I'm answering unasked questions. Pretty silly."

They had been drinking casually since dinner at the Chambord. He strove for restraint. "You're not silly and I wanted to ask questions and I would have. I usually don't. But I would have."

"Funny about the attraction between some

people." She shivered. "Well, we grow up. Maybe I had better tell you about Jack."

"I was going to ask."

"Yes, you were going to ask. It's funny, all right." Again she paused, sipping the brandy, and now she did not look at him. "Came the time, after the war, when things were all black. Not gray, not merely dull. Black. No money, no nothin'. You know?"

"I've seen it."

"It was not fun."

"It's never fun."

"Jack came along. I was selling in Macy's Basement—handkerchiefs, gloves, men's things. He had the idea for the shop. He set me up."

He thought about it for a moment. "Not an apartment—a shop."

"Exactly. He's a nice guy, you see."

"Gives you a chance to make it for yourself. Sure, I see."

"He lets me repay him. Out of profits."

"Yes, I see that, too."

"Business arrangement," she said proudly. She lifted her head and he noted the firm set of her chin. "Jack has imagination and he has guts. He's a gambler—you know that."

He could laugh, then. "You never asked me what I do."

It stopped her dead. He could read shock, then disappointment greater than he could have imagined she would feel. "You too?"

"Since early childhood, when I found I could beat the kids at marbles," he said.

"You and Jack," she murmured. "Maybe I'm doomed to it. If I like 'em, they're gambler types. It's probably Freudian."

"You dislike gambling?"

"How can I?" she asked helplessly. "A couch doctor would probably learn that I adore gambling in all its forms. It seems to me that I have no love for it, but I'm wrong. I must be wrong."

He felt thoroughly sober now. He said, "I think Jack and I are going to be friends."

"You'll be bosom buddies," she said wearily. "I know it."

The subject of their thoughts appeared at the entrance to the big room and peered about, saw them, came briskly among the tables. Steve arose, smiling, and shook the solid, strong hand. Jack Barr sat down and beamed upon them both.

"This is a thing, now, ain't it? How about this guy, Fay? Does he get around fast? Clips me on the chin, clips a date with my girl, all in half a day."

Steve said, "Don't think it hasn't been charming."

"I like him." said Fay. "Do you like him, Jack?"

"I got to like him. He can lick me."

"That, too?" She shook her head, sniffing the brandy. "This man should have stayed in Saudi Arabia."

Jack looked sharply at Steve. "Oil?"

"I got lucky. Parlayed a wad of stake money into a gusher."

"Oho!" Jack shifted his scrutiny to Fay, raising his brows. "This man talks like he's hep."

"Go on, take him upstairs, put him in the game," she said. "I can take a cab. Toss me aside like a broken blossom."

Jack said, "I'll put him in a game. But not tonight. From now on, this is my party. I quit winners."

"It's always your party. But who invited you, my friend? We have a date, Steve and I. You said a drink—to thank him for bringing in your hat. That's all, brother. You buy us a drink and you blow." She was so nearly serious that for a moment Steve's hopes rose to a new high.

Jack Barr said easily, "I think Steve will invite me. You want to go home? We'll take you. There are a couple of broads right down the street from your place—you know Clarabelle and Isabel?"

She turned to Steve. "I can't win."

"It's a man's world." Steve beckoned the waiter. What could he do but play along? he asked himself. When a man you like joins forces with you to tease a woman, you have to go along. It was a game played throughout the land, its rules unwritten but well known to both sexes. Abroad it was not like this, but he remembered the dictum from years gone by. From now on it was a threesome, everything for fun.

Some fun. Since eight o'clock he had been getting to know this girl, trying to make her know the best side of him, seeking the truth of her relationship with Jack Barr, feeling that unnerving attachment to her that meant he could fall in love if he were allowed. Now it was a party and Jack Barr was wired in there so strongly that it would be he that took her home and kissed her and held her in his arms, and Steve would know this, the moment of its happening, while he was wending his way across town to Central Park South and his overfurnished, opulent, goddamn lonely apartment.

Jack was saying, "We can blow this joint after this drink. I know a hot-piano boy who can break your heart. Are you a hot-piano man, Steve?"

He acknowledged the truth: All stay-up people are hot-piano fans. They frequent the after-hours spot where hot piano flourishes, and it becomes a part of them, he thought. He remembered how Sam had loved Fats Waller, how Fats would beam and wave his gin glass when Sam came in and began buying for the house. He hoped Fats and Sam were somewhere up yonder together, with plenty of booze and a beat-up piano burned with cigarette butts.

He made himself study the brash, happy-talk man who was Fay Fowler's love. Barr meant to him quick ingress to circles where he could learn the things he needed to know. Socker Cane had pointed the way. It was a lucky thing and maybe his luck was going to stand up again. It always had, and this looked like another break. If Barr was on the level, he could be helpful, and if he was a square gambler merely on the surface, like 99 per cent of them, he would be even more useful.

The man was tough, slangy, yet far from illiterate. Probably Fay had made him read a book. Fay was educated above the average girl, of course. Probably they had been very good for each other. Steve felt himself joining in the fun as they paraded from the Roosevelt; he had not thought he could.

4

He awakened at ten, with a terrible taste in his mouth and his head buzzing and lumps in his stomach. Hangovers were another part of his alcoholic curse. He struggled into a white silk burnoose that served as an excellent bathrobe and made the kitchen. He poured himself a whisky glass full of Fleet's and drowned the bitterness of it in frozen orange juice. He fumbled his way back to the bedroom, then remembered to call Moscow and give him the address and phone number. He returned to his pillow and slept until noon.

The morning papers lay outside his door, and when he was fully awake and had forced down some scrambled eggs and coffee and toast, he turned the pages, looking for something to do on Sunday. Actually he had no desire to move out of the apartment. He came to a page marked "Television Programs." Television was something he had never known.

He opened the doors of the big radio-phonograph and discovered a twenty-one-inch bulging surface attached to a switch that said "On" and showed a number. Idly he twisted it. Sound leaped at him and lines whirred incredibly upon the bulge and then a picture formed and he ducked at gunfire as horsemen rode hard and others pursued them, firing. It was a movie, he gathered, a horse opera from Hollywood, and not new. He twisted the dial and got a snowy nothing, then a church service to which he listened for a while, letting the sonorous voice of the preacher lull him. The choir sang a hymn and it was one that he knew, a marching song that Sam had hummed from time to time when things were bad and Sam had one of his occasional flings at religion.

He had discovered television. He picked up the newspaper and scanned the program listings with interest. He found the proper eye level and viewing distance and planted a comfortable chair and some tobacco and a big ash tray and loafed, smoking, watching, listening.

Soporific, he decided. "Omnibus" came on and that was better, a lot better, but somewhat pretentious. The master of ceremonies was erudite and spoke too beautifully and there was an air of righteous smugness, but still it was good stuff. He forgot to be lonely.

But when the telephone jangled he jumped halfway across the room, because the image of Fay Fowler formed instantly in his mind's eye. Only she had the number, he thought. It must be ... And then he was totally amazed to hear the low-pitched accents of Virginia Butler. "Steve? Are you going to be at home this afternoon?"

"Why—uh—yes."

"I'll be up to see you."

She hung up before he could say more. He went back to his chair and scowled at the television set. Moscow talked too much to the girl. Moscow was a sucker for her, he had sensed that from the start. Sam had been a sucker for her, too, and Socker Cane. Moscow must have given her the phone number and address within the last two or three hours. Maybe he had told her that she was temporarily heiress to his money. He thought about that and decided that Moscow wouldn't tell her that. The old shyster wouldn't want her to be disappointed if Steve changed his will—a will that hadn't yet been signed, anyway.

He went to the shower and felt a little better after a bath and a shave. He doused himself with aftershave lotion and combed back his stubborn, close-cropped hair, and the apartment buzzer sounded and he let the girl in.

She was wearing a fall suit of gabardine, fawn-colored and crisp, and a blouse with a tiny black bow tie caught with a small diamond pin. Her hat was a wisp of nothing, and becoming.

She sat and looked at him and he gave her a cigarette and asked, "What will you drink?"

"Bourbon and water," she said in her husky, low voice. She accepted the drink, took a good slug of it, put it down with care in a glass coaster he provided, and continued to stare at him.

He said, "Moscow should keep his mouth shut."

"I made him talk. He always talks to me."

"He talks to you, Socker talks to you. Sam talked

to you."

"People do. Maybe because usually I don't say much." She seemed indifferent to this allusion to herself, in a manner that caught his interest. She seemed detached, that was it, he decided. She was a side-liner, a spectator at the party, possibly of herself. Few people are thoroughly objective; it was a quality he had no opinion about.

The silence grew uncomfortable as she took another good-sized swallow of the drink. She finished it before she spoke again.

"You're going after the mob that finished Sam."

He sighed. "All right, all right! Tell me what you know."

"I don't know anything. Except Legs Murphy. I knew him, of course."

"Where is he now?"

"I wish I could tell you."

Steve made two drinks, deciding he would have to try one in order not to make her feel uneasy. He suspected that she was belting them, in order to overcome her admitted disinclination to confide in anyone. He brought them in and sat opposite her on a hassock. Her legs were exquisite. The girl's body was simply unbelievable. He moved restlessly, recognizing the lure of sexuality that she exuded so naturally and with such insouciance.

He said, "You'd better keep out of it. Those mobs use women for leverage when things get tight. I may put them where they'll be looking for a handle."

"Mr. Moscow says you're a hard case. He says you could kill a man, that you probably have."

"Moscow's a sharp character except where you're concerned."

She nodded. "I had the wrong idea about you. I came up here to tell you that I'm sorry. And I don't want to stay out of it."

"You don't know anything that will help," he said impatiently. "As I say, you might be a hindrance."

"You'll need a girl. To go around with. If you could trust her, you'd be ahead." She looked at him. She took another drink. There was a slight film over her slanting green eyes.

He said, "That's a strange angle."

"You don't know anyone in New York. I'm insurance for you." She did not urge him, she let it lie on the table between them. She looked at him unblinkingly. "That's the way it's going to be, Steve. I thought it out on the way over here."

"Does Moscow know you're here?"

She shook her head. "Mr. Moscow knows nothing about me outside his office. Sam guessed, toward the end, but Sam was big. Socker—maybe he knows a little."

"Guessed? Guessed what?"

"That I'm not a simple, sweet child, the darling of sweet elderly gents," she said blandly. She sipped her second drink with more confidence.

"This is a switch," Steve muttered. "This is really different."

"I'm different." She nodded.

"All right. You've got me. I'm interested," he said. "At first glance I thought you were a dumb broad with stuff she didn't know she had."

"That proves you weren't thinking," she said coolly. "How could a girl like me get to be my age without knowing? You think there aren't teachers every place you look?"

"You can tell Cousin Steve," he said wryly. "Was it a real gone love affair? Can I help pick up some pieces?"

"It was Legs Murphy when I was fourteen" was

the shocking reply.

He came to his feet flushing. He was angry with himself, but more for being shocked than for any other reason. "The hell you say!"

"Don't blame him." She shrugged. "I was precocious. He was convenient."

"I'll be damned!"

"It's not nymphomania," she told him, as if she were discussing a case history out of Krafft-Ebing. The detachment he had noted in her was never more apparent. "I don't think I'm oversexed—much." She tilted her glass, still looking at him. "I never discussed this before, except with a psychiatrist. It was time I did. You came home at the right moment for me. On account of Sam, I can talk to you."

"This I believe." He had to get hold of himself. She was being honest and it was unfair not to respond in kind. Sam had caught himself another Tartar. First Steve, then this one. Poor Sam! Only Sam had enjoyed it. He was such an off-beat character himself, he had been happy with his two odd orphans.

She said, "I take spells, I guess. Like a man. Then Providence sends along someone. You see, I'm basically against one-night stands, that sort of thing. So it's always an affair. Only I can never bring myself to marry him."

"Probably all for the best," he assured her. "You might go on getting urges."

She nodded. "I thought of that. It's a problem. Frankly, it's a very big problem. Very big."

Sincerely he said, "I can understand that. Leaves you very little security."

"I have almost no friends. People don't understand. Social events bore me. I need direction—an aim. That's why you've got to let me help you in this business."

He made a last attempt. "It may be dangerous, you know."

"I hope it is," she breathed. "That would help. It would help a lot."

She had relaxed under the release of confession. She re-crossed her knees and his temples throbbed a bit. He changed his seat and thought for a moment. Then he smiled at her.

"You'll excuse me for being dull," he said. "This is—a bit unusual. I'm not easily stunned, but you did it, Virginia. You know what Moscow and Socker said to me about you?"

"They probably told you to leave me alone. What can they know?"

He said, "I think you've told me enough of your problem. Let's take it from there, shall we?"

She waited before replying. "You're a bit like Sam, at that. Yes, I think we can take it from there."

She arose and took off her hat and the jacket of her suit and put them carefully over a straight chair. She moved to the divan and arranged herself comfortably without the slightest attempt at coquetry. She said, "You talk. About where you've been and why Sam didn't hear from you and everything."

He was doomed to talk to her; he was no different from Sam or Moscow or the other men. The hours went by and the whisky in the bottle went down. She became hungry and told him that there was a delicatessen nearby, Cohen's, which provided meals for such as he, and Steve called them and had supper sent up, steaming pastrami and sour pickles and apple strudel and tea with lemon.

He talked through the meal and she cleaned up, all her movements brisk and economical. She walked with decisive firmness, he noted, and her hips swung without exaggeration. Yet the sex drive was there; he imagined the kind of man who would note it immediately and take advantage of it. Sex as a thing, he pondered, dissociated from every other thing, emotion, warmth, spirit. Only that wasn't it; never had he met anyone more complicated than this girl. She had used sex in an abstract manner, but it had hurt her and puzzled her; witness the psychiatrist, the desire to cleanse herself by talking.

She said finally, "I was going to hate you. On account of Sam. I'm glad I decided to come over here and talk."

They were both on the divan and the fences were down. It was dark, but neither moved to turn on a light. He said, "You're very perceptive. Go ahead and tell me about me."

"You've had it," she said, nodding vigorously, with more animation than she had displayed yet. "Too much luck. Too many easy things. Even the gambling—you always win. That's no good."

"It'll do me," he laughed, but he saw the germ of truth in what she was trying to say.

"Like me. You need an aim. This business about Sam will help. It'll help us both. You can see that."

He was not so sure, but he was committed. He knew one thing: To back out now would be negation, and he was in no position to accept that in himself. He said, "Maybe."

She was silent again. They had continued to drink, and after last night his resistance was low. On the surface the liquor did not have any visible effect upon Virginia. For a long time neither of them spoke. The dimness blanketed them. His glass was empty but he did not move to make another drink. He thought of Fay Fowler.

Was she with Jack Barr, as he was here with this strange girl, alone in the evening? Was she in Jack's arms? He felt a small pang at the idea, but it went away quickly when he looked at the outline of the profile of the girl beside him. He put out a hand and touched her arm.

She said without looking at him, "Yes."

In the bedroom he learned that it was a dainty garter belt that kept up the stockings of girls without girdles.

5

Monday was dull, dreary. When Steve awakened, the girl was gone. He lay looking at the ceiling, not liking himself, feeling nothing of pride. It was almost noon. He forced himself out of bed, bathed and dressed, and walked around to Socker Crane's gym.

The big man met him, dragged him into the rubbing room, closed the doors, stripped him, and put him on the table. Muscular hands well-oiled began prodding.

"I had a bad week end," Steve said. "I can't drink."

Socker shrugged. "Who can? Guys with big livers can drink. For a while. Nobody can go the limit with John Barleycorn."

That was straight from Sam. "John Barleycorn," that was his expression. Steve asked, "You had a chance to learn anything?"

Socker said, "Legs is alive."

Steve felt his body go tense. He was thinking of a fourteen-year-old girl now, and a punk jock, a double-crossing jock. "Where is he?"

"His mother lives over in Jersey. Near Newark, a country kinda place, they told me."

"Who told you?"

Socker shook his head. "I shouldn't even be askin'.

Never mind who or where."

Steve said, "I'll go over there right away. If I can get my hands on Murphy, I'll learn the rest."

Socker kneaded a shoulder with skill. "Steve, you better get a license to tote a gun."

"If I start carrying a gun I won't ask for a license. Too many people get to know about it."

"It would be better to have a license. Gives you standing with the cops."

"I don't use guns."

Socker said, "Maybe you'll have to."

"Maybe I will. But not yet."

"You oughta apply for a license," Socker insisted gently.

Steve thought for a moment. The rubdown was stirring the sluggish blood in his veins. He said, "You think there's a big mob behind Sam's trouble?"

"It was a smart operation."

"If I start stirring it up, they'll come after me."

"They wouldn't want trouble."

Steve said, "I expect you're right. But no gun. Not now."

"What you got against protection?"

"Guns go off. Sometimes when you least expect it. I know about guns, all right. Don't worry about that."

Socker nodded. "Maybe I get it."

Steve said, "You get it. No guns until it's necessary. Then we get them without serial numbers and ditch them."

After a moment Socker said, "You sound like you had mob experience yourself, Steve."

"Look at it this way: If I wanted to squawk to the cops, I'd go about this another way. I'm not much for hollering cop, Socker."

The big man said no more. There was a faint

frown on his face as he finished the workout and Steve showered. He had an address written down when Steve was ready to leave. He said, "I'm in it with you now. But I won't say I like it."

"I don't like it, either," Steve told him. "If Jack Barr comes in, tell him I'd like to sit in a game, will you?"

"You made a connection with Jack?" Socker was pleased.

"After you put me in there it was easy." He stalled a moment, then asked, "You know his girl?"

"Fay Fowler? Everybody knows her. That's a real great one."

"I met her."

"Jack's goin' to marry her." Socker sounded impressed. "He's been plannin' on it for months now. He couldn't do better."

"She wasn't wearing a ring."

Socker looked sharply at him. "Hey!"

"She's a great girl," Steve said calmly. "We went out together. We met Jack after the game."

Socker said, "You're movin' fast. Maybe you ought to slow down a little, boy."

"It's no good when I slow down," Steve said. "No good at all. I keep thinking about Sam. I should have come home sooner."

"Yeah. You should have come home sooner."

"I'll go over to Newark," he said. "I'll call you if there's anything hot. You need expense money, Socker?"

Socker grinned. "I got my bets down for today."

Steve laughed. He could never understand horse players. The daily urge that was like a disease had never touched him, despite his upbringing by Sam.

He called Madison 5-4000 on an off chance and got the right starter and downstairs a half hour later he was climbing into the cab driven by Sol Mintz.

"Newark? That's gonna cost ya, hey. I can't take no chances on gettin' stuck without a fare comin' back. Ten bucks, plus what's on the meter. Whatcha wanta go to Newark for? This is a place to go, Newark?"

He was tooling the cab through crosstown traffic, heading for the Lincoln Tunnel. His driving was uncanny. Trucks boomed, but Sol scuttled beside them, passed them, ducking in and out like a bug in a potato patch.

Steve said, "O.K. I've got ten bucks."

"Plus. You're gonna need me around Newark."

Steve looked at the address Socker had given him. "I want to go to a place near Nutley. Cross Gardens."

Sol Mintz said disgustedly, "Nutley. That ain't Newark. That's 'way north of Newark. People don't know nothin'. Lemme see that paper."

Driving with one hand, he read the address. He shook his head solemnly. "You're a greenhorn, all right. Some other driver, you'd go through Newark, out to Nutley, and back again, the hard way. This here place is onna Passaic."

"The river?"

"Cert'ny the river."

Steve asked, "How come you know so much about Jersey?"

The little man did not answer for a moment. Then he said, without pride, "I was born there."

"Then why did you move to New York, if you hate New York?"

"Who asked to move to New York? My old man moved here. What's with New York, it's so bad?"

"It's noisy," Steve said gravely.

"All right, it's noisy. You know any place ain't noisy where a cab can make a dime? Whatta you want from me?" He wheeled past a hesitant motorist, swung toward the tunnel entrance. Sol Mintz set his mouth in a straight, firm line, refusing conversation. He was the most cantankerous individual Steve had ever met, but the over-all effect put him in a good humor. He was also an excellent driver, and Steve relaxed, thinking about Sam and Legs Murphy and what he would say to the ex-jockey when he caught up with him. He did not want to beat up a jock-sized character, but if he had to, he would. In the Orient he had learned subtle ways of beating up a man so he would talk.

In a surprisingly short time they were in New Jersey, turning off the main road down toward the river. Rutherford with its factories and oil companies along the water, then the outskirts of Nutley, and they stopped for directions and Sol Mintz shook his head and drove on a narrow macadam road to a sharp curve, bent onto it, and slowed.

"Goat Town," he said. "You wanta go to Goat Town awready?"

"Just go where the paper says," Steve told him. "Don't be a snob."

"Snob, shmob," said Sol Mintz indignantly. "Inna Bronx maybe there's garlic, cabbage, like that. But no goats!"

"I haven't seen a goat," Steve told him. "Is that the house?"

The cab stopped. "Further and more," said Sol Mintz angrily, "over yonder is a city dump. You smell it? You think I want to sit here smellin' a city dump?"

"You'll get used to it in a little while." Steve got out of the cab. The house was alone on a narrow dirt street on the edge of nowhere. Within forty square miles ten million people lived, but Legs Murphy chose the neighborhood of a dump, acrid with smoldering fires and rolling smoke.

It was not an old house, either. Probably prefabricated, he thought, going up a concrete walk to the porch. Square as a box, but with curtains at the windows and a geranium in a pot. He rang the bell.

The door opened almost at once. He found himself under the scrutiny of a wispy woman about five feet tall, gray-haired, attired in a clean house dress and an apron, wearing small, stubbed shoes no larger than a child's. She said, "Oh. I thought you was the special-delivery fella. I don't want to buy nothin' today." She started to close the door, hesitated, then looked more closely at Steve, or rather at his clothing, he thought. She swallowed hard and asked in a small voice, "Who sent you here?"

"Nobody sent me. I'm looking for a young man known as Legs Murphy."

"You ain't no cop." She was trying to reason out something, he thought. "What you want with Brad?"

He said, "I just want to see him."

She spoke through her attempt to think, to reason. "Brad ain't here. He ain't been here."

"Since when hasn't he been here?" Steve smiled reassuringly. "An old friend of his sent me."

"Socker Cane," she said, nodding. "I heard he was lookin' for Brad. But he ain't here."

"I'd like to talk to you," Steve said. "Can't we sit down?"

For a moment she seemed about to refuse. Then she slowly moved back and allowed him to enter.

Something was disturbing her, something more than his unexplained visit. He thought about that, looking around the neat room, at the holy pictures on the walls, the cheap but hardly used furnishings. He said to kill time, "Nice little place you have here, Mrs. Murphy."

"The insurance money," she explained. She glanced toward a group photograph on a table and he looked at the grim faces of two Celtic young men in uniform.

He said, "You lost them?"

"Korea," she said tonelessly. "Mike and Pat. Brad, he didn't get in."

Steve said, "But surely Legs could take care of you. He did all right there for a while—until last year."

"He did all right while he stuck to Mr. Goulding," she said. Then she was frightened again. "He told me to say nothing about that. He told me there might be trouble. Who are you?"

"My name's Galloway. I knew Sam Goulding years ago. I'm thinking about buying a horse or two."

She said, "Brad can't ride no more."

Steve ignored that. "Will he be home soon, Mrs. Murphy?"

She had been twisting the end of the apron, looking out of the window. "Would you like a touch of beer, Mr. Galloway? It's kinda early, but I like me beer in the afternoon."

He said, "I'll send the cab for some beer." He went out past her protestations and gave Sol Mintz some money. The cabbie snorted, but turned around toward the macadam river road and departed. Steve went back to the house, slowly, looking about to see if there was a possible place for Legs to be hiding.

Mrs. Murphy had coldly sweating bottles of beer on the table, the photograph of her dead sons in the background. She poured the beer into clean goblets and handed one to Steve. She was, he thought, lonely and not sure of herself, but she wanted to talk to someone. He sought some means to encourage her.

He indicated the photograph. "Tell me about Pat

and Mike."

"Mike and Pat," she corrected him. "Mike was the oldest. It don't sound so much like an old Irish joke that way."

She drank the beer slowly. He waited patiently. The cold beer tasted good.

She said, "They were big boys. Took after their father. Brad was for my side, you see. They played football and baseball, everything. Mike had a year in college on a scholarship."

Carefully ignoring her revealing reference to Legs, he asked, "So they both went into the Army?"

"First Mike. Then Pat. Brad stayed home. You never saw Brad?"

"No."

"He's all legs. Five feet six and a hundred and one. He was always—strange."

"Because he was smaller." Steve nodded.

"That's what makes me wonder. If that was it." She pondered.

Steve said, "I'd like to see him. Brad. I'd give him some money."

"He don't need money." This puzzled her more than anything, he saw. "He just seems to want to hide since the trouble." She looked hard at Steve. "You know about the trouble." It was a statement, not a question.

"I knew Sam Goulding long ago," he repeated.

"I want to do right by Brad. No matter what he done, I want to do right by him. I'm his mother. I got to do right by him."

Steve leaned quickly forward. "What did he do?"

"I don't know. But he don't need money and he don't work. I shouldn't be tellin' you this, Mr. Galloway."

He had a flash of insight. "You're afraid Brad has

done something wrong and that he'll hurt you. Disgrace you—and his brothers."

"What can he do to them?" Her voice was quiet.

She finished her beer. The small amount of alcohol seemed to affect her, and she spoke quickly, in a different tone, sharp, incisive. "Mr. Galloway, I don't know you, or why you're here. You ain't the law, no law dresses like you. Maybe I ought to be scared of you. Maybe I'm wrong. But I'm telling you, something is wrong about Brad. Since the trouble he's been two ways. Above himself, and below snake level. Like I told you, he's never been one of us. One of the family. He's hard and mean, always proving how tough he is. My grandmother woulda sworn he was a changeling."

Steve nodded. "Yes. I remember about changelings."

"You're Irish too, and maybe that's why I'm talking to you." She was now unable to stop. "Brad went away with the horses and for a while I thought it was all right. Sam was all right, wasn't he?"

"Yes. Sam was better than all right."

"And in the end Brad done something. I don't know what. But he couldn't ride no more. He come home and hung around. He got his mail in a box at the post office. He had some money. Not a lot, because he wouldn't of stayed here if he had enough to go away. He paid me twenty dollars a week. He lived in this house like a boarder. Mr. Galloway, it's queer for a son to act like a boarder. Be like a boarder. But that's how he was."

Steve said, "When will he be home?"

She wagged her head slowly. "I don't know. He's been gone since Saturday. No word, nothing."

"I wonder if I could see his room."

She hesitated, then got up and wordlessly led him

to a small, square room, painfully neat, nearly bare. She opened a closet door and showed him clothing hanging empty, long-legged trousers, ridiculously short jackets. She said, "He was wearing a windbreaker and Levis and those cowboy boots. Everything else is here."

There was a small table with drawers in it. Steve went to it, opened it. It was bare, without even a scrap of paper.

She said, "Like always. Just nothin'. I've looked."

"That's strange."

"You think he ain't a strange one? Things I could tell you, when he was growin' up—" She broke off. There were tears in her eyes. "You got an understandin', Mr. Galloway. It's the Celt in you. You know I ain't blowin' a whistle on my son. You know I wouldn't go to the police if he never came back. It ain't that. It's just—he never was one of us, and it's queer, his going like that."

"Two days," said Steve thoughtfully. "Well, who can tell? Maybe he'll turn up. Saturday, was it?"

"Saturday afternoon he went for the mail and didn't come back."

"Has he got a girl friend?"

She shook her head. "Not Brad."

"Did he have any friends hereabouts?"

"Not any place in the world that I know."

They went back into the living room. Sol Mintz pounded on the door and brought in a case of beer and took it into the kitchen. He came back into the room and hesitated, looking at Steve. Then he put the change from twenty dollars on the table and left. Steve did not pick up the money.

He said, "Mrs. Murphy ... I'm sorry."

"Thank you, Mr. Galloway." She managed a tired smile. "I didn't do Brad no harm talkin' to you?"

"No. I imagine he creates his own trouble."

"Yes. He does that." She seemed to debate with herself. "Should I worry more about him? Can I make myself worry about him that never cared for a soul, who hated his brothers and his dead father?"

Steve said, "You know best about that."

"You think I'm a bad mother, Mr. Galloway?"

"I think you're an honest, decent, sensible woman, more sensible than Brad deserves," Steve said impulsively. "More mothers should be like you."

She glanced once at the photograph of Mike and Pat and said, "I'm not so old. I got livin' to do. The good Lord hates a quitter."

He said, "I won't lose touch with you, Mrs. Murphy. If you hear from Legs—Brad—here's my telephone number and address." He wrote them down, put the slip of paper next to the loose money on the table. He touched the money and said, "Buy yourself something, will you?"

"I will," she said, and smiled widely for the first time. "And Mr. Galloway, if you need me, call me."

She meant that, too, he thought, going down the walk to the cab. Some mother, Legs had. Some rat, Legs Murphy.

As if Steve had cued him, Sol Mintz said sharply,

"Rats! Lookit 'em! Packs of rats!"

The cab was at the end of the narrow street, where Sol had pulled it looking for space to make a U turn. They were at the edge of the dump. Steve followed the direction of Sol's pointing finger and saw them, a dozen of them.

There was a pile of rubbish and the rats were worrying it. Their fierce activity was repellent. It was like a nightmare, and he started to tell Sol to turn around.

Then something clicked in his mind, and he was

out of the cab and running. He snatched up a stick, and when he came close he struck at the scrambling rats, knocking one a dozen feet, sending them squealing hideously away.

He stared down at a boot protruding from the heap of rubble. It was a Western boot with a rider's heel. The leg of the Levis showed where the rats had uncovered it. There were nasty little marks of teeth in the inch of white flesh.

He turned and went back to the cab. He said dully, "Sol, can you take this stick and keep the rats away? Or do you want to go for the police?"

"You crazy? What's with this? Cops, in Jersey? Get inna cab and let's scram outa here!"

"If it wasn't for the rats I'd do just that," said Steve. "Take your choice, Sol."

Sol said, "Can I call from Mrs. Murphy's house?"

"If you want to tell her I've just found her son," Steve said.

6

Socker Cane came to the apartment on Saturday after the inquest with a bundle of newspapers. He said, "They don't make you as anybody who knew Sam Goulding, anyway."

Steve poured bourbon over ice. Socker added water from the carafe and sat scowling at the horse pictures in the den. Steve said, "Those damned rats. I couldn't leave him to the rats."

"It wasn't good, though. Never mind the cops. They bought it that you knew the other Murphy kids inna service. It ain't the cops. It's whoever knocked off Legs."

"You started asking about him last Saturday. That same night they shot him."

Socker said, "He was in touch with them. They were payin' him off every week by mail, the old lady tipped us to that much. Five'll get you fifty he was puttin' the bite on them for more dough."

Steve nodded. "Then when you started asking, they figured he might start playing both ends against the middle."

"So they eliminate the middle. Namely, Legs."

Steve said, "It proves they're still operating. That part I like."

"It proves they knew I was askin' around. That part I don't like," Socker said.

"Where did you ask?"

Socker said evasively, "Just around. Some odds and ends of people."

"We'll have to start eliminating. Make a list of the calls. I'll hire a private detective."

"No good. I been a private eye, Steve. There ain't one in the country can go against a real mob. Forget about peepers. This one is on us."

Steve sat and sipped his drink and thought about it. The co-operation of Mrs. Murphy had prevented the police from tying him in with Legs. He wondered if the levelheaded little woman knew more than she had told him. She had displayed little grief at the loss of Legs, but then, she had no reason to love her youngest son—the suspected changeling. When things cooled off he would see Mrs. Murphy again.

He said, "If they know you were asking about Legs, they'll be watching you for another move. Don't make any. Give me that check and I'll sign it."

Socker took out the pink slip, looked at it. He shook his head. "The corpus of Legs Murphy ain't worth no ten grand." He tore the paper carefully, put it in an ash tray, touched a match to it. "Besides, I ain't about to turn up with no hunk of dough. People get real nosy when a horse player turns up with ten gees. Just forget about it, Steve. In fact, why don't you forget the whole thing?"

"Because a crooked jock gets bumped off?"

"Because it ain't a thing you can beat," Socker said gravely. "Because it's cop business. What do you want with this kinda play? You got everything Sam woulda wished for you."

"Sam didn't get what I wished for him," said Steve. "If I'd come home, maybe he would have had it."

"A Derby winner?" Socker wagged his head. "Flamin' Arrow wasn't it. Just a good colt, a game colt. Like when Legs fed him the goofball he run out his heart."

"And Sam's heart."

Socker moved his bulk uncomfortably. "All right, all right. How you goin' to find out who killed Legs?"

"I'm not going to try," Steve said. "That's the police's job. I'm going to stick around and see what happens. You can forget the whole deal, Socker."

"That's the trouble with me," mourned the big man. "If I could forget it I'd be very happy. That's been my trouble most of my life. Gettin' into things I can't get out of. Why you think I keep playin' the horses? I keep thinkin' I can beat it. I know I'm wrong, but I keep thinkin' I can do it."

Steve said, "All right. You're in. But for a while let's both lie low. Let's see what the cops turn up."

"The cops'll turn up just what the coroner's jury said. Death at the hands of person or persons unknown. This was a mob kill, Steve. Legs was keepin' a mob secret. They figured he might peddle it to a higher bidder, so they stopped him. They did it quick and neat and clean. Cops can't do nothin' about it."

"That's a hard thing to say."

"Look, pal," Socker said patiently, "it ain't like a citizen got shot inna head. Legs was one of 'em. Why should the cops worry about him? Sure, they'll keep a lookout for any mob stuff for a while—but nothin'll happen. This was a hit-and-run murder, done by experts. Maybe by some Detroit guy they flew in and out quick-like."

"Not that quickly. No, Socker, this was a local job. The time element proves that. Let it rest for a while. Now, what about that list of calls you made?"

"No."

"No what?"

"First, I wouldn't put it on paper. Second, some of these characters are pals of mine."

"It's the best way to get a lead," Steve argued.

"I'll handle that end," Socker said.

Steve unlocked a drawer in the table. He took out crisp, new bills, counted to five hundred. He handed them to Socker. "That's the expense dough. No arguments. I won't ask about the calls again, but if you need me, or want to tell me, you know I'll be around."

"You'll be around the gym," said Socker. "Because if you ain't, people might think it's funny."

"I'll be there."

Socker asked, "Is there another way outa this trap?"

"Push the button to the basement and go out the service alley."

Socker said, "I don't figure they're watchin' me. But it could be." He unfolded his length from the chair and Steve walked to the door with him.

"Take care of yourself." Steve frowned. "I'd hate to think I got you into a jam."

"If they come at me, let them worry." Socker

eased out the door. "I'm cautious, but I ain't exactly scared. Much." He winked and was gone.

Steve went to the telephone and called Lou Moscow. He waited for the connection, drumming his fingers on the table. He had not seen Virginia since Saturday. Her voice, warm and husky, impersonally gave the firm name. He said, "This is Steve Galloway."

"Oh." There was a brief pause, then she said almost in a whisper, "I read about Legs Murphy. Why didn't you call me?"

"Good reasons," said Steve. "I'll ring you at home later."

In her natural accents she said, "Yes, Mr. Galloway, you can talk to Mr. Moscow now."

The lawyer snapped at him, "What's this business about Legs Murphy? You want to wind up in jail?"

"So long as I don't wind up in a shroud," Steve said. "How much do you know about rackets, Lou?"

"Nothing at all."

"Lou, how do you expect to get to heaven?"

"Legs Murphy knew about mobs."

"You're frightened?"

"I'm frightened."

Steve sighed. "O.K., shyster. Be seeing you around." He hung up. He did not blame Moscow. He would not have blamed Socker if the big man had quit. He probably had an unsuspected hole in his head, or he'd forget the whole thing himself. The promptness of the elimination of Legs pointed a plain moral.

He started at the ring of the telephone bell. He picked up the instrument and a hearty voice said, "Galloway? You jerk, what's the idea of getting mixed up with cops? I thought we were going to deal a few."

"Hello, Jack. It was just one of those things. You think I enjoyed it?"

Barr laughed. "If you've washed off the cop smell, there's a game tonight. Cooper House, Fifty-third Street. Room Ten-forty-five."

"Good! About nine?"

"We'll be three hours started by nine."

"I'll be busy until then."

"O.K., nine." He paused, then said seriously, "I guarantee the game, Steve."

"Suits me."

He hung up.

He sat a moment, knowing what he was going to do, wondering if he was making a mistake. He had spent the days since Monday avoiding a showdown with himself, aware that he was postponing it, unwilling to come to a decision.

He got up and went into the bedroom and selected one of the suits from Jablonski's and matched his tie and socks with care. He donned the Homburg and moved nervously about, finally pausing before a mirror.

He saw a lowering, dark face, not handsome, with tight corners to a grim mouth, deep-set eyes under straight brows. It was the face of a stranger; he had not looked at himself so in the mirror for years. Introspection was new to him.

He jerked himself out of the apartment and took a cab and rode over to Madison Avenue, afraid that if he walked his determination would weaken. He went into the shop and removed his hat and put it on the counter.

Fay Fowler came from the dimness at the rear of the store with unaffected pleasure in her smile. "Well, Mr. Galloway! Where have you been?"

"Don't you read the papers?"

"Not if I can help it."

"I went over to Jersey to look up a couple of boys I knew in the service. I ran into a murder."

"You ran into a what?"

"I found a dead body."

"Oh, no!" she said. "How terrible!"

"It wasn't fun," Steve said. "Inquest—all that."

She said, "A fine homecoming! I'm sorry, Steve."

"Think nothing of it. I came in to order a couple of hats." It came out lamely, as though he had memorized it badly. He added, "And handkerchiefs. We forgot them. I'm always running out of them."

"All men do." She nodded. "What else have you been doing?"

"Er—nothing," he said. "I'm seeing Jack later." That was another remark he could have left unsaid. He was all conversational thumbs around this girl.

"Another game," she sighed. "What a bore."

"Well, we could have dinner together. I mean—Jack wouldn't mind, would he?"

She picked up his hat, examined the sweatband, turning it in her long, graceful hands. Without looking at him she said, "If he did, there would be a small war."

"Look, I don't want to cause any ..." He stammered like a schoolboy.

"You and I," she said softly, looking at him now, "liked each other on sight. Jack wouldn't try to do anything about that even if he cared."

He took a deep breath and regained control of himself. "Sure. I'm acting like an idiot. You'll have to stop doing that to me."

"You mean you don't always act like an idiot?" She arched her brows at him.

"I came in here to buy," he said severely. "Hats. Handkerchiefs. I don't want any chicken arguments out of any broad."

"Yes, sir. Indeed, sir," she answered briskly. "Hats. You want Edgar?"

"No. Just a couple of hats. I can't go around wearing this black thing all the time. And on handkerchiefs I like monograms. You pick them out. Where do you want to eat?"

"Tim's?"

"Tim who?"

"You don't know Tim Costello? But you haven't lived! Third Avenue at Forty-fourth," she said. "Seven o'clock."

"A gray hat and a brown one?" he asked her.

"I'll ask Edgar. He'll check with Jablonski. You can't be too careful about these things. Edgar shocks easily."

"O.K. Seven, then." He waved the hat at her and managed to get out onto Madison without any further gaucherie.

The effect she had upon him was just short of demoralizing. He admitted it freely to himself, walking toward Fifth Avenue. Since he had met her she had been in the back of his consciousness at all times. Even when he had been with Virginia, he thought, and was ashamed.

Especially when he had been with Virginia, he insisted grimly, determined not to let himself off the hook. And that was damned foolishness, because Virginia demanded all of a man's concentration. He was not making the mistake of thinking of her as a chippy or a nymphomaniac. Virginia had compulsions, but who hadn't? He refused to hide behind the double standard. There was nothing wrong with Virginia. The only trouble was Fay Fowler.

It was only four o'clock. He turned on Fifth and

went into the Pierre and ordered a drink at the bar. He sat over it, ignoring the minked women of the cocktail hour, delving into himself with sharp queries.

Coming home, learning about Sam, meeting Fay, beginning his search for those who had killed Sam had altered him somewhat. He had to learn how much. It didn't matter why. He knew enough to face change when it occurred, to welcome it, examine it. He had schooled himself in such discipline when he had become aware of his gift for gambling. It was one thing to make wagers for money and another to throw his life, or any part of it, into the pot.

He was investigating himself as well as Sam's killers. The law, as such, had meant little to him, save that life was more comfortable and less complicated when it was observed. He had formulated his own law for living, basing it on day-to-day convenience. Now he wondered if it would not be better if he carried his problem to the legal authorities and allowed them to avenge Sam through investigation of the Legs Murphy killing. If he could do this without involving Socker ... But at once he knew that he could not. Once he began to talk, he could help the police only by telling all he knew.

Anyway, he liked it better without the cops. He had a long-standing neutrality toward police. He had stayed out of their path and they had not bothered him, When it had been necessary to bribe them, in the Orient, he had done so and they had played as fair with him as possible. In the United States he had so far had no dealings with them. Sam had set this pattern for him many years ago. "Fuzz is somethin' we always got with us. It is strictly for the square johns. Us people, we just stay away from fuzz. They no make trouble for us, we no make trouble for them."

He had a second drink and his ear picked up a discussion between the bartender and two of the men at the bar about the professional football situation. Steve had played a lot of football in college with modest success and he felt an urge to see the pros perform. He listened carefully and made a mental note that the Los Angeles Rams were six-point favorites over the Giants in an exhibition to be played on the following afternoon at the Polo Grounds. Just in case he might make a bet.

Just in case? Didn't he always make a bet? He wondered if he could enjoy a sporting event without having some small wager upon it. He doubted it, nor did he care one way or the other.

7

The Cooper House was a most respectable apartment-hotel. On the tenth floor Jack Barr surveyed the opulent furnishings with pleasure, grinned at the green-baize round table set incongruously in the center, and asked Freddy George, "Everything set? Ice, service, cards?"

Freddy George was a thin, fair young man elegantly attired, who was older than he at first appeared. He was blue-eyed with colorless lashes and brows. He said, "Jack, I never get a chance to talk to you. We got to slow down this merry-go-round."

Barr lit a cigar, then nodded. "Guess you're right, Freddy."

The slight man moved closer, frowning. "This Galloway. He was over in Jersey. He was asking about Legs. He's an old pal of Socker's. Socker was asking about Legs. Galloway makes like a lover boy with Fay. He buddies up to you. He wants in the game tonight. How can you buy this fellow?"

Barr said softly, "You're too smart to ask questions like that."

Freddy relaxed, nodding. "Sure. Only I had to check. I've had four men watching and checking on Galloway."

"I think he's clean," Barr said flatly. "He knew the Murphy boys in the service. Socker found out Legs was their kid brother and began asking about him for Steve. He's a high player and packs a roll that cries for action and I liked him and led with my chin."

"You like a lot of people," Freddy said sympathetically. "I understand that, all right"

"And a lot of people I don't like."

Freddy said worriedly, "Jack, you got to get over this idea of pulling out."

"We've been over that." Barr scowled, moved restlessly.

"Buying into legit business is O.K.," Freddy insisted. "They all do that, all the big ones. But you can't pull roots without killing the plant."

"You've said that so many times. I'm getting bored with it." He knew the man's loyalty, amounting to devotion, but he felt a surge of impatience. He hated to be told that he could or could not do anything. "Set up your bank. They'll be here any minute."

He picked up a deck of cards, aware that Freddy was sullenly resentful at being cut off in his plea. He sat at the table, shuffling the new, slippery pasteboards, laying out a hand of solitaire. His hands were wide and strong and capable, but not deft with the cards.

He had proved he could do anything within reason, proved it the hard way. From boyhood he had been a leader. Freddy knew—Freddy was one of the kids who had followed from the beginning.

At first it had been because of poverty. They had swiped bundles from delivery trucks because the ERA had been humiliating, degrading—doling out prunes and potatoes and no meat for gravy, prying, suspicious, badly organized, politically controlled. The parents loathed the grudging but needed charity. The kids took action.

Hymie the Fence had bought the stuff, and from good-natured, sloppy old Hymie they had learned stuns, pinochle, and finally the game Barr took to his heart, poker. It had cost him the loot from many a raid to learn as much about poker as Hymie could teach him.

His mother had protested, but then Pop got killed on the docks in a riot and there wasn't much left for Mom to do or say. Young Jack was the head of the house, after the custom of the neighborhood, and therefore the boss.

Hymie had connections and Jack was leader of the kid gang. It had to work out, and it did. When the neighborhood bookie found that the Barr boy never played the horses, he let him take some bets. The next step was a tip on a basketball game that, he shuddered now to remember, he had accepted as gospel, borrowing to get money down on it, unsuspecting of the twenty-four happenstances that can upset such a fix. Young Jack had won twenty thousand dollars that sunny afternoon.

A partner then, and the bookie died and Barr took over and Freddy came along and they moved up fast. He did not dwell on other events. He had never liked the necessary violence, the double-crossing, the build-up of suckers, the disposition of beefs. He had been quick with his fists and the few professional bouts had been fun—but killing was never a good thing.

It was all over now, thanks to Kline and Cassidy, who had quit the game early to go on the police force. Barr had seen to their promotions and they took care of things. They were good cops, and honest, too. Cassidy was religious and spent a lot of time lecturing Barr about past happenings, exhorting him to get out of it and live like a citizen should. He and Kline took care of Barr only. They were fine, tough, smart boys.

Freddy was smarter. Freddy had done time in the reformatory and while there had become a reader of books. He studied a lot now, checking civic events against the world in which he moved, scenting trouble before it began, balancing his knowledge of the past against the trends of today. Freddy did not believe a man could pull out of the rackets and make it stick.

Barr stared at the cards without seeing them. Freddy might be right. But he had to make a try. There was only one reason.

He wanted to marry Fay. He had never dreamed of marrying Hilda, or Pat, or Gussie, or any of the others. Only Fay. He wanted kids and half the year in Miami and enough business to occupy him, and Freddy around to help and a home in Westchester. He, Jack Barr, who had never moved out of the old neighborhood, wanted these things so hard he could taste them.

He shook his head. A woman can do just about anything to a man, he thought, if she's the right one. He looked up and caught a glimpse of Freddy's worried face as the buzzer sounded.

Sid November came in with Charlie Goode. On their heels came Dan Slidell, a Rochester gambler, an illiterate with a large diamond ring and a dollar cigar. Barr put away the cards he had been using and rose to greet them.

November looked about and asked, "Where's the

fresh meat? Where's Galloway?"

"He'll be around later." Barr tried to refrain from hating the man.

November said, "Who is this Galloway? How come you to import him?"

Freddy looked up from banked chips. His voice was cool and hard. "Nobody brought him in. He knew Socker Cane from 'way back. He's loaded and he's a poker player. What do you want, Sid?"

"Nothing. I don't want a thing. Only this Galloway I don't like."

"Then you'll be glad to top him," Barr said.

"I got a funny feeling about him," November persisted. "You remember the last time I got that feeling? You remember Glisson?"

Barr said sharply, "Never heard of any Glisson."

November showed his white teeth. "O.K., Jack. Only I got that feeling."

The oily fat man could always make Barr feel unclean. It would be an hour now before he could forget the cheater Glisson and what had happened to him. He fought down his hatred of November; it was no good to carry emotion with a card game.

He wished he were out of it now. He wished he could wrap it all up and throw it into the East River and go with Fay to Europe and forget it all. He had the money.

He ran into the blank wall that always stopped him. He did not have the money. Not enough. He needed a million. It was the goal he had set and he never paused short of a goal. He did not quite have a million in spite of desperate efforts during the year since he had met Fay Fowler.

Soon, though, he assured himself. Soon he would have it. When he sold the numbers, unloaded the houses of prostitution, and cashed in the last of the junkie operation, he would have it. Meanwhile, poker was relaxing and could help toward the goal.

They began to play.

8

Virginia at dinner at Bergolotti's with Lou Moscow. She was very quiet, even for her, and the lawyer brooded through a long, excellent Italian dinner. Finally he remarked sulkily, "Steve Galloway is no good for you, none at all."

She started, her eyes widening. "I wasn't—I mean, how did you know I was thinking of him?"

"That's right, be honest." Moscow smiled thinly, rubbing a dry hand over his thinning hair. "You'll always be all right as long as you're honest. It's your great virtue, a natural gift, I expect." He added slowly, "Then there was Sam."

"Yes, there was Sam." The combination of a queer straightforwardness and Sam's teachings, she thought, and Moscow saw it clearly enough. She knew she was different from other girls. In lots of ways she was different. She said, "What's bad about Steve Galloway?"

"Selfishness," Moscow said promptly. "Egoism. Sam could never cure him of it. He always knew very well what he wanted and grabbed for it. He owed Sam everything in the world, but there were things going for him abroad. So he never came back to check on Sam."

"He sent money." She knew she should not be defending him. She was always careful with Moscow, fully aware of his shrewdness and insight, and if he knew about her he would be hurt. She did not want Moscow hurt because of her.

"Money! Did Sam want money? Did he ever touch

Galloway's lousy checks? You know better than that,
Virginia."

"I know a lot about Galloway. Through Sam. He
talked about him, you know."

"What Sam said was not the truth. Sam had to
love everyone who was close to him. That was Sam's
way. He idolized that boy."

"Why do you hate him?" Virginia asked.

Moscow squirmed. "Hate him? You can't believe
that I hate him. What's the matter with you tonight,
Virginia?"

She put the tip of her spoon into the spumoni,
then withdrew it and placed it alongside the saucer.
She knew what was the matter with her; she wanted
to see Steve.

This was the first time. Since Legs Murphy,
huddling in the haymow, frightened but eager,
learning the ecstasy even then, sensing her destiny, she
had never known longing for a particular man at a
particular time. She corrected herself: She had never
known this kind of wanting.

She said, "I ate too much and the spumoni's too
rich. Let's go, Mr. Moscow. I think I need some
sleep."

"Are you catching cold, child?" He fussed like a
hen, aware that it was stupid, that she was capable of
taking care of herself and of him too, but unable to
prevent himself from fussing. He paid the tab and
bustled her into a cab and drove with her the few
blocks to her apartment, on Sullivan Street. When she
got out and smiled her good night he sank back into
the taxi and snapped at the driver, angry with
Virginia, himself, Steve Galloway, and the world. He
was an old man and he hated being old.

Virginia's living quarters were on the second floor
of an old tenement that had been refurbished at great

expense during the transition of the Village sector from Bohemianism to its present state of convenience to the workers of the city. There were a tiny but decent bath, a kitchenette, and a large, high-ceilinged living room with a deep and luxurious day bed that had cost a considerable sum. The furnishings were simple but adequate, almost severe in their low-keyed colors and conservative design.

She had few feminine foibles. She had many books and she had read them, including all the standard psychological works. She was curious about people; mainly she was curious about herself. She was too well balanced to wish to change and too intelligent to think that she might succeed without disaster. She merely wanted to know.

At first she had been afraid that there were too many male hormones in her, but a little study had convinced her that the opposite was more likely to be the case. Further delving had brought her to the amazing conclusion that she was normal. The trouble, if any, was more likely to be with other people, with society.

She had reluctantly and after long cogitation decided that the old man who invented it all was correct. Sex was the mainspring. She had a lot of sex. Freud had been hardest of all to read, and maybe she hadn't understood him completely, but he was the guy who had finally made sense.

She went into the bathroom and looked at her face. It was flushed. She began tearing off her clothing and in a jiffy was under the shower. She stayed there a long while, soaping and resoaping. Cleanliness was a fetish with her and the cool water had its soothing way. When she towelled she was relaxed again and could think objectively about Steve Galloway.

She made up the luxurious bed and arranged the

pillows and the reading light Socker Cane had given her. She held Steinbeck's *East of Eden* in her hand, rereading it, trying to understand the woman of evil who crept through its pages, wondering where Steinbeck found her and how much of her could ever have existed in one being.

She put the book down. The sex urge was gone, but she still wanted to see Steve, to ask him if he had read the book, to talk with him about it. She had always been completely self-sufficient, even before Sam's murder. This was something new.

She tilted the lamp, thinking of Sam, then of Socker and Lou Moscow. They had all tried to protect her. Their help had been more important than they knew, and for startlingly different reasons. She had learned to evaluate men, to use them, and to keep free of entanglements.

Both Socker and Moscow had warned her about Steve. She wondered if it was only because he had been away so long and they feared him as a stranger. Strange that they should know instinctively his attraction for her. Unless Socker and Moscow suspected her.... But she couldn't believe that. She had been utterly circumspect.

She remembered the last time, with pleasure. It had been springtime and the man was young and lean and virile. She had taken her vacation in New Jersey and the beaches had been warm and the water cold and the man gay and generous. He hadn't even known her real name. It had been a good three weeks.

Since then nobody had attracted her until Steve. She pressed her hands against her face, stifling remembrance of Sunday and its aftermath. He would never know, she swore, how she had come home and walked the floor, half scared, half exalted. He would never know how nearly she telephoned him, how she wrote and tore up a dozen notes. She, Virginia!

Sam had always said in his blunt, lighthearted way, "Save it for the guy who'll appreciate it, baby. Morals ain't anything, but bein' clean is a lot."

Damn Sam! She couldn't have saved it because she wasn't built that way and she had thought nothing much of that part. What hurt was that with Steve she was too expert, she knew too much, she had no blushes, no trepidation to make him tender and solicitous. Bounce into the pad, Virginia, wiggle for the man. So it's very nice, but what does it mean?

"Hoist by your own petard, Virginia," she said wearily. Another of Sam's favorite expressions. Go to sleep, Virginia, and what a hell of a name that was to hang on you!

9

When Steve entered the apartment the five men were already immersed in the half-drugged, half-impatient state of poker players. Introductions to Slidell and Freddy were murmured. He sat between them and Barr grinned.

"Dealer's choice, Steve. Whites are twenty, reds fifty, blues a hundred. The blacks go for five cees and the golds a grand. Table stakes, of course."

Steve nodded, buying a thousand dollars' worth of chips. It was a game the players could make as strong or as weak as they chose. Stud would be expensive, but he was looking for action. He was prepared to lose the first thousand learning the game.

November said, "All right, let's go, let's gamble." He looked at Steve without expression, measuring him.

Steve shrugged, recognizing the animosity, returning it with interest. Goode seemed relaxed,

Slidell was an old head, Barr was quietly intent on the contest. Freddy had the secret of detachment, always a valuable asset to a card player.

The excitement grew slowly in him always when he sat in with a new crowd. He had spent hours drawing cards, folding them in, watching, estimating the caliber of the competition. He had always been a percentage player and had profited thereby.

Actually, competition excited him only when more than money was at stake. He knew to the thin white one how much each poker hand was worth; this he had learned as easily as the alphabet and at about the same time. He touched the first draw hand, dealt by Freddy, and looked at November and smiled. It was stupid to try to beat any one man in a poker game, but given the opportunity, he knew he would take vast pleasure in tapping out the glowering fat gambler.

He edged his hand and saw three hearts, seven through ten. Goode opened for a hundred. November played, Barr folded. Slidell went along. Steve had no knowledge as yet of what constituted a strong opener and decided to learn this and other things.

"Raise." He shoved in three blues.

The dealer did not play. Goode chuckled, "Beginner's luck," and matched the play. November sulked but came in. Slidell shook his head and dropped.

Goode and November both took three cards, so it had been a weak opener and play. Steve said, "Two tickets."

He discarded the useless spades and, without glancing at the draw, ground the pasteboards together. Goode winced and said, "Check to the two-carder."

November nodded agreement. Steve fingered

chips. "Two hundred?" He made it a question, as though begging that they call him. It was an ancient trick, the only question being who would keep him honest. None minded losing the two hundred, of course, but pride runs deep in the poker player and calling to keep the game on the level is twice as stupid as to allow a man to run a bluff.

On such a narrow ledge does the gambler walk, thought Steve. He watched November. The swarthy man hesitated, then shook his head and said, "Steal it."

Steve raked in the small pot. As he did so he managed to get a chip under his hand and flip it over with seeming awkwardness. He quickly returned the cards face down, but not before everyone had seen the three hearts—and two unpaired black ones.

No one spoke, but November's eyes flashed and Steve had trouble repressing a grin. Here was a man who could be irked.

The game went on. Barr was running in good luck. In two hours Steve was a thousand ahead, but Barr was better off. Slidell and November were the losers, with the others just breaking even.

Barr was a sound poker player. Goode was luckier, but weak. November was daring and shrewd, but temperamental. Slidell was average, but in hard luck. Freddy played like a house man, right up to his vest.

They built up to the pot that every such game breeds when the players are right. It was stud, with time running out, the dawn beginning to crack through the Venetian blinds. Steve dealt the hand, calling for stud, pushing his luck a bit while it was riding high. His face card was a jack and no other jacks showed. November was high with the ace. He bet a hundred and everyone played.

On the second round November received a king. He said flatly, "Five hundred."

Paired up, thought Steve. In a six-handed game he would not bet like that unless he was paired. Steve should fold right now. Then Barr saw the bet and Slidell stayed and the others were rattling their chips. It was the big one. He would have to peek at his hole card.

He did so and found another of the aces. He flipped in a black chip and saw Freddy and Goode do the same.

He knew that either small pairs were out or aces in the hole were epidemic. He dealt again.

November drew a trey. Still he was high. He growled, "Let's separate the men from the boys. Two black ones."

He had to have something, Steve thought. Barr was fingering his chips, staring at the queen and nine before him. Everyone had drifted away into his poker-think world now, leaving a void in the room, as though the six were wax figures in a museum.

Barr put in his money. Slidell sighed, followed suit. There were now a jack and a king showing for him. That meant he had equal to November twice, with the hole card of the fat man probably a king. He should not be in the hand.

Being in, he saw November's bet. Freddy and Goode, with smaller cards, still had to hang on, hoping November and Steve would kill each other on the high tickets.

Each card fell into silence with a small plop now. Freddy paired sixes. That could mean three of them, Steve knew. Goode did not pair. November drew—a deuce. Barr drew a nothing and Slidell the same.

Steve dealt himself, unbelievably, beyond gambling reason, the ace of spades.

Without hesitation, as high man, he said, "I tap."

He had more chips than anyone else. He had a perfect right to bet every man his limit and run out the cards without further tilting, letting each man in for his percentage. That it did not sit well on Sid November was something he expected.

November snapped, "That's a hell of a bet."

"I like it," Steve said.

"You let the peddlers in."

"They could come in anyway for what they've got in front of them," Steve said gently. "You think anyone's dropping out?"

"It's a sucker bet," November said darkly.

"For all your chips," Steve pointed out. "You want it bigger?"

"I want the game played right."

Barr said, "How about dealing?"

November's face flushed. "Don't butt in on me, Jack, when I got something to say!"

It was Freddy that moved back from the table about two feet. Barr merely turned and stared at November. Steve felt lightning strike about the room, saw Goode pale, saw Slidell grin in a sickly fashion without moving.

November tried to meet Barr's eyes. He made it for a moment, full of rage and bitterness. Then he dropped his gaze and said quietly, "All right, deal."

It was anticlimactic. The money on the table represented a small fortune to the average man, but the falling cards were of minor importance now. A challenge had been met, Steve realized. Events pended, their meaning greater than any a poker pot could represent. He looked down at the ace he had dealt himself, knowing that November had only kings, that any two pairs around the board were not good enough, that the pot was his. He was more interested in the impending trouble. He dragged in the pot and felt November's hot eyes upon him.

November said, "Some friends you got, Jack. Guy deals himself three aces in six-handed stud. What was he staying on, to draw out on us like that?"

Steve pushed back his chair and arose. As Barr started to speak he cut him off with a head shake. He said to November, "You think I'm dealing seconds? Or bottoms?"

November lifted one eyebrow. "Are you kiddin', Galloway? Barr guaranteed you."

Barr looked at Freddy. "Was he dealing anything, Freddy?"

"Certainly not. He was making his ace-jack stand up," Freddy said. "Then he got the second bullet."

Barr said, "You heard him, Sid."

November shrugged. "Check me out. I got enough."

Barr got to his feet then. He was on November's left, looking straight at him. "You said something about butting in. Like you were very important and I should be quiet when you speak."

"You were ignoring me," said the big man. "I was trying to register a complaint, like, and you wouldn't listen."

"All right. Now you can complain. Start in," Barr said.

Freddy looked unhappy. Goode looked startled and afraid. Slidell began backing away, toward the door. Steve watched them all, knowing what had to happen.

November said, "Now I got no complaint. Now it's all over. Galloway won the pot, didn't he?"

"Never mind Galloway. This is my game, Sid, I set it up. You know the rules."

November's temper flared. "Rules, he says! Who

makes the rules? You make 'em. Where did you get the right? There's plenty of us sick of you and your rules, you know that, Jack? Little Caesar Barr! You've been warned!"

Steve could have predicted the exact moment it would happen, the spot upon which the first blow would land. In the gut, then a follow-up smashing against the fleshy jaw. No marks, no blood, no broken bones. Just a quick washup of a beef.

November went down in sections, half conscious but helpless with pain. Barr looked at him and said, "That's for thinking. Keep on going the way you have been lately and there'll be more." He turned to Goode. "Get him out of here."

Goode protested, "Geez, he's going to be sick."

"All right, the hell with it," Barr said. "Freddy, cash in. Slidell, I guess you didn't see or hear anything."

The man nodded, biting a cigar. He took the money for a few chips he had stored away in his pocket and left. Freddy counted out a wad of bills to Steve.

Barr was putting on his coat. He said to Goode, "I'll pick up the tab for the room. Let him stay as long as he wants. He's been looking for this. Nothing against you, Charlie."

He nodded to Steve.

Steve had already donned his jacket. He walked over to where November was retching. He said without emphasis, "You can get me any time for anything. Check it out with Socker Crane. I hope you look me up."

Then he joined Freddy and Barr and they left the apartment.

They had little to say, going into the dawn-washed street. There was a black Cadillac El Dorado, and

Freddy got behind the wheel. Barr was bemused and
Steve thought he detected something like alarm and
resentment in Freddy.

Steve said, "I'd rather walk home. Clear out the
cobwebs."

Barr grinned at him. "Cobwebs you ain't got. Say,
I've got a box at the Polo Grounds. What about the
football game tomorrow?"

"I was going to buy a ticket," Steve said. "What's
the line?"

"The Giants and six. I'm taking it," Barr said. He
sighed. "I shouldn't. I'm an old Giant fan. Imagine
me, a fan, the way the Giants have been doing."

"Give me a grand of it?"

Barr said, "Like hell. I may be a fan but I'm not
that stupid. I'll give you a hundred of it."

"O.K."

He watched the Cad pull away. Freddy was silent,
hunched over the wheel, disapproving.

Steve moved into the hush of early morning and
thought about what had just occurred. It wasn't only
the poker game and November's antipathy for him,
he realized. There was something else. There was
some connection between Barr and November,
something far more important than these desultory
poker meetings. Barr was too smart to slug a man
without great provocation.

The connection could be something interesting, he
decided. November handled money like a big
operator, with contempt. So did Barr and his man
Freddy. Money was counters in a game to these
fellows. Cheap. And if money was cheap, life could be
cheap. It was men like these that could lead him to the
killers he sought.

He thought he might take Barr into his confidence
later. He liked the man, liked his toughness and

directness. And if Fay was going to marry him, he had to be all right.

Whoa, Galloway, he told himself. What kind of figuring is this? Pretty damned silly. How Sam would howl at such a naïve line of reasoning!

Anyway, he did like Barr and he would follow along and learn what he wanted to know sooner or later.

Meanwhile he was walking and the city was quiet and calm and he could sleep until noon and tomorrow was another day and he was several thousand dollars richer. It was several blocks before he became aware of the rumble of the subway beneath the paving, the hushed noises of a million different stirrings. Sol Mintz had been right, the noise was there. It was always there, the big noise.

The Cadillac rumbled across town, adding its hissing to the muffled morning noise. Freddy said, "You know you shouldn't have hit him."

"I had to," Barr said simply. "Stop and think."

"You can't pull out like that. You know his tie-up."

"It's the only way to do it," Barr said calmly. "You're smart, Freddy. But you're not tough, real tough. Get this is in your head: If you give an inch to those people, you're dead. You got to make them respect you every second of the day."

"Sure," Freddy said. "I agree. So we rod up and bring in Eddie and Hotspot and then Cassidy turns on you. Then we wind up in a shoot and those that don't get killed get the chair. I admit you'd get those people busted up along with us. That you can do. But is this an ending we can fall in love with?"

"We don't rod up. We leave Eddie and Hotspot out of it. Nobody fires a shot or uses an ice pick.

November asked for it tonight. You think the word won't be out? Goode talks. Slidell will drop a word to his broad or someone. Everybody's got someone he talks to, always remember that, Freddy. This just gives me another reason for wanting out. Mugs like November with the big mouth. Incidents in quiet games. I don't like it, I get out."

"They'll never let you. They'll think of something. Too many things have happened, we've been in on too many deals. They'll never let you out."

Barr suddenly chuckled. "O.K., Freddy. You worry about it. No use both of us fretting."

November was very thoroughly sick. He ran water in the basin, dipped his face into it. He examined the spot where Barr's fist had landed, found only a slight bruise. He pulled out his shirt and peered at the thick, hairy belly exposed to the merciless strong light. There was a red spot already yellowing. It would be sore for weeks.

He stood a moment, clinging to the edges of the lavatory bowl, almost ready to vomit again. The rage was debilitating, surging through him so that he quivered from shoulders to knees.

When he had recovered he adjusted his clothing, ran a comb through his thick hair, and went into the sitting room: Charlie Goode was waiting.

He walked up to Goode and without warning slapped his face.

Goode's fist clenched, he crouched a little, starting a punch. He stopped it short, caught his breath, stepped back toward the door, his eyes narrow and shifty, his mouth slack. "What was that for, Sid?"

"You don't know? Where were you when I was getting clobbered?"

Goode said, "Too close to Galloway. You saw

him and Barr in the gym. If I made a move I'd have been flat on my ass, and you know Freddy carries heat. What the hell did you want, a war?"

November said, "Yeah. I want a war. I don't like to be hit. I don't have to be hit. Not by Barr, not by anyone."

Goode sullenly watched him, saying nothing. November walked to the table, shoved it petulantly, turned and glared.

"You're chicken, Charlie."

"All right, I'm chicken."

"You been doing real good with me. You never had it so good."

"So?" Goode's voice was low, toneless.

"You been riding a nice wave. Like tonight, did you lose anything tonight? Like hell you did. They clouted me for plenty but you wind up better than evens. Well, O.K., Charlie, you can blow."

"I played the cards they dealt me." Goode shrugged. "O.K., Sid. So I blow."

November was smiling now. "You know what that means, Charlie?"

"I know what it means."

"You don't show anymore."

"I don't show."

"Not at Socker Cane's. Not anyplace."

Goode bit his lip until blood came. "Yeah. O.K."

November laughed, pleased. "You haven't got it, Charlie. You'd like to take a sock at me. But you don't dare try it."

"O.K."

"You're chicken and you're through. You don't make a bet where I know about it, because nobody'll handle your markers."

"You can do it to me, Sid."

"You ain't going to beg?" November mocked.

"No. I know the score," Goode said.

"That's all you do know," November sneered. He looked around the room, his equilibrium completely restored. "So Barr picked up the tab, so I'll use the joint. It's a flop for the night and maybe I can rustle up a broad. One broad, Charlie. Just for me."

Goode said slackly, "Have a good time, Sid." He picked up his hat and went to the door. He paused, a hand on the knob. He said, "And Sid—you looked awful silly when Barr let you have it. Real silly. Like an old cow sliding on the ice."

He went out quickly and closed the door. November took one step, then stopped, staring at the spot where Goode had stood. His red tongue licked at his upper lip. His jaw was hurting again and his belly felt empty and queasy. He cursed savagely and went back into the bathroom.

10

Sunday noon the telephone rang and Steve reached for it, coming awake without pain because he had not drunk anything the previous night, congratulating himself.

Virginia's voice said, "I'll be right over."

She hung up, a habit she had, evidently. He started to call her back, scowling. Then he yawned and stretched and rolled from the bed and into the shower. It would be pleasant to have someone around while he ate breakfast, he thought. He shaved with care. He caught himself whistling and shut off the sound, recognizing the anticipatory implication, admonishing himself for it.

To lie with Virginia and think of Fay was worse than unfair. It was debilitation of the mind. It was unmoral. It was surrender to the sorriest of frustrations. That it had been practiced untold billions of times by men and women made it the more humiliating to him.

He dressed for the ball park and began cooking scrambled eggs and very crisp bacon and strong coffee, and Virginia appeared promptly. She joined him, setting the table, deft and capable as in everything she did, nearly silent, smiling without coquetry or guile, eating with a healthy appetite.

She wore a tweed suit and a fresh blouse with a narrow ribbon at the collar and looked utterly beautiful. He had not thought of her as beautiful, excepting her body, but now he was conscious of skin soft and fine, of coloring without cosmetics. He asked abruptly, "Don't you wear make-up, Virginia?"

"Lipstick and powder," she said. "I sleep a lot. Good for the skin. I also bathe. I sleep nude. I like to eat, as you can see, and I drink too much only on occasion. I'm real healthy. I don't care for frilly underwear. Seldom wear any." She looked at him gravely. "Next question."

"I didn't mean to be personal," he said sulkily.

"It's all right," she said.

"I'm going to the football game," he said.

"With a girl?"

"With Jack Barr."

She said, "The gambler? Then you're onto something?"

"Certainly not. Barr's been very nice to me. I may meet some of the people we want to get at through him."

She said, "Stop talking down to me." She gathered up dishes and took them to the sink. Her lips were as he remembered. He managed to jerk his gaze from them only with effort. She said, "I'll go to the game with you. It'll be a start."

He started to protest, then an unworthy thought occurred to him and he grinned to himself. "That's a swell idea. Barr has a box. It'll be all right." He frowned. "But don't mention Moscow. We don't want to leave any loopholes. Someone may know that Moscow was Sam's lawyer and tie in the Legs Murphy business."

She rinsed the dishes but did not attempt to wash them and he found himself liking this. She was not pretending to be the housewife type. She said, "Please, Steve, treat me like a grownup. You know I wouldn't mention Mr. Moscow. I'm doing a lot of thinking about Sam and about Legs and what must have happened. I've been going through some old accounts I kept for Sam, trying to find a clue. I thought maybe today we could drive over and see Mrs. Murphy—but we can do that another time."

He looked at her and sighed. "I'm sorry if I seem stuffy. I shouldn't, around you. Sam brought us both up right, God knows. Get your hat and I'll fill you in on last night."

He told her about it on the way to the Polo Grounds. She listened in grave silence, nodding occasionally. When he had finished, she said, "Sid November. He's been around a long while. Sam knew him. He's wired in with the syndicate."

"What syndicate?"

"The big one," she said. "The one everybody talks about and nobody knows anything about."

"What do you know about it?"

"Nothing. Only that it exists. November is in it. Barr is in it."

He said, "Barr is not in it. Socker told me Barr is independent."

"That only means that Barr has his own territory," she insisted. "He couldn't operate if he wasn't in it. Sam knew all this."

"Don't tell me Sam was in it!" he said scornfully.

"Sam's dead. If he was in it he wouldn't be dead."

He stared straight ahead. It was impossible for them to speak about Sam without sharing pain. It was, he admitted, a bond between them. He touched her hand and she responded gently, acknowledging the gesture as it was intended.

He looked at her then and she smiled like a small girl, tentatively, her eyes shining with unshed tears that were for Sam and for herself and probably for things Steve would never know. He said, "I'm glad Sam found you."

She said directly, "Later, Steve. Tell me that later."

The urge welled up in him then and he was helpless to prevent himself from wanting her. He was glad he had postponed it, he was aware that it was inevitable and that he was fortunate to have it coming later, something to which he could look forward through the pleasant early-autumn day. He continued to hold her hand until they came to Coogan's Bluff.

When they found tickets at the proper window and entered the ball park, he felt the first twinge of conscience. He had brought Virginia along so willingly for one purpose, to show her off to Fay. Last evening at dinner he had sensed a diffidence on her part that had made him unhappy. He had wondered if Fay were using him to make Barr spend more time with her. He had wondered a lot of things, none of them progressive in his relations with the girl. He had jumped at the chance to retaliate and he was using Virginia unfairly. It occurred to him that the word "unfair" in regard to his dealings with Virginia occurred rather too often.

He bought a huge chrysanthemum from a vendor and pinned it on the tweed jacket and smiled at her childlike pleasure and took her arm and held it firmly, seeking Jack Barr's box.

He saw the eyes of both Barr and Fay widen at sight of Virginia, and he introduced her as a girl whose family he had once known and felt peculiarly masculine pride as they wordlessly confirmed his good taste. The teams came on the field and a roar went up and he was back into the madness that is American football.

In the excitement of the kickoff Fay leaned close to him and whispered, "Friend of the family, my left foot! Where did you get that adorable sex pot?"

"Lay off," he muttered, but again he was proud.

"You and your fickle city ways," Fay jabbed at him.

He looked at her and she was more than half serious, he thought. "Think Jack would swap?"

She turned abruptly away from him.

It was puzzling. He gave his attention to the field, but he could not shake off the feeling that Fay was annoyed at him. Jealous? Ridiculous, Galloway, he scolded himself. Maybe she'd like to have two men dancing attendance, as what woman doesn't, but only in fun.... But there had been something ... He was sensitive to reactions and he had felt something when she spoke which he couldn't analyze.

There was a hydrant-built Number 11 on Los Angeles with arms like logs who could throw a football a mile. He looked up the name—Van Brocklin. He remembered Sammy Baugh, but he could not remember whether the Texan was any better than this West Coast flinger. Only Sammy could run, and this boy was molasses-slow.

A colored end named Boyd ran like a frightened buck and Van Brocklin threw one and forty thousand people stood and howled. On the goal line, ball and man came together in a perfect fluidity of motion that was all the grace and thrill and emotion of the great sport and the New York fans cheered as loudly as though the Giants had scored the first touchdown. The Rams converted and Steve remembered that he had given six points and now had his margin if only Los Angeles could maintain it.

Barr shook his head disgustedly. "They should've kept Steve Owen. He had Tunnell covering Boyd like a tent last year."

"You mean Steve isn't with the Giants anymore?"

"The game got away from him," Barr said unwillingly. "Too many new things—sliding T and all that. Steve stuck with his own A formation too long." He broke off, staring.

A party had entered the adjacent box on the perimeter of the first gallery of the park. There were two women in mink, then two well-dressed men. Then there were Sid November and a small blonde girl scarcely out of her teens, who clung to the fat man and laughed too gaily, off key. November looked over, his chin raised, eyes half lidded. He said coldly, "Hello, Jack."

Barr nodded, affecting indifference. But he was angry to the bone, Steve knew.

The two men with November made a point of staring at Barr, forcing recognition. Barr got up and walked around, joining them, sitting between them.

Fay said dryly, "Mr. Big and Mr. Next Big. Ossie Lebella and Al Bogardus. Have you met them, Steve?"

"Syndicate biggies?"

"Name them and you can have them. Friends of Jack's."

"I thought Jack was independent," he said innocently, carelessly.

"He will be," Fay said softly. "He's got to be."

There was excitement below and everyone watched the Giants try to run through a green Rams line. Poole sent in Tank Younger and the Giants fumbled and Paul recovered for L.A. Steve's bet looked better all the time.

November was staying out of the conversation in the next box. It was evident to Steve that Barr was not too happy with what the other two men were saying. Fay had stopped pretending to look at the game and was frankly eavesdropping.

Steve looked at Virginia. She was watching the three men in the box with rapt attention, but she was concealing herself from them and from November by nestling close to Steve. She whispered, "I can read lips. Remember Deaf Bob, Sam's hostler?"

He nodded. "Jack's arguing with them."

"They're telling him he can't quit," she said. "He's saying he's willing to pay off anything fair, but he's quitting. Lebella said something about last night.... They're talking about you, Steve!"

He waited, watching the Rams use the split T.

She was saying, "Steve, they're suspicious of you. November put in a big beef that you and Barr were ganging up. Barr is trying to convince them that it's not true."

"He can save his breath," Steve said. "I'd love for them to come after me."

"Then you're foolish," she said sharply. "These are upper-bracket men. They own killers by the dozen."

"That's Prohibition stuff," Steve said. "I thought Dewey cleaned up all that mob stuff."

"It was Turkus and Murder, Incorporated," she sighed. "You've been away a long while, Steve. This is different. This is quiet and well organized and powerful right up to Washington."

"Let it be. I only want the ones that killed Sam," he said.

She was silent. He felt the tension in her. He looked at Barr and the others, saw Barr rising, excusing himself, his face still unsmiling, not offering to shake hands. In his ear Virginia whispered, "Steve! Just at the end they mentioned Legs!"

"What did they say?" he demanded.

"Something about you and Legs. I couldn't get it all. They're suspicious of you and Legs is in it."

Steve eyed the two men. Mr. Big, Ossie Lebella; six feet tall, thin, middle-aged, swarthy—one punch would hospitalize him. Mr. Next Big, Al Bogardus; medium-sized, colorless, narrow-shouldered, loud necktie—a real nothing character. It was difficult to believe that they were dangerous.

He knew they were. Otherwise Jack Barr would not be flushed, stifling anger, possibly a trifle nervous as he returned to Fay's side, lifting his brows at her, shrugging off unasked questions.

Fay said in a low voice, "They didn't have that box last year."

"Or this," Jack said, his voice choked with rage. "They bought it out to be next to me. They'll wish they never saw it." He stopped, glancing at Steve and Virginia, who were pretending vast interest in the game.

Los Angeles scored on a long run by a bowlegged back called Skeeter Quinlan and Virginia said in Steve's ear, "Your luck is holding up. It's a good thing we came here today."

Steve nodded and the picture of Sam rose in his mind's eye, Sam dead with his skull bleeding on a sidewalk near Fifty-second Street. He managed to steal enough looks at those in the next box so that they registered firmly as identities he would never forget. He noted that November's blonde was higher than a kite on marijuana or worse. He began planning, sitting there, forgetting Fay for the moment, forgetting everything except the vengeance he had sworn to have.

A wild yell went up as a husky youth in a Giant jersey scrambled twenty yards to a touchdown. Barr said, "That Gifford is the greatest Giant since Mel Hein!"

"They need three more of him today," Steve said. "The game has sure changed since my day."

Barr seemed to have recovered his spirits. "You played football? What school?"

"Trinity," Steve said without thinking. He could instantly have bitten off his tongue. Why couldn't he have denied his college years? Why didn't he deny football? What stupid vanity compelled him to be proud of his limited athletic career?

Barr said only, "They must have a hell of a poker course there, wherever it is."

Steve directed the conversation back to the Giants and the Rams, but he was uneasy all through the remainder of the game. When the last whistle blew he was a hundred-dollar gainer, and promptly offered to buy dinner. He was neither surprised nor disappointed when Barr begged off.

The cessation of play seemed to have dimmed the gloss of both Fay's and Jack's personalities. They departed, unsmiling, in the wake of the party in the next box.

Steve lingered deliberately, pretending preoccupation with Virginia, flirting openly with her, covertly watching. He perceived November's ill-hidden triumph, the lordly attitude of Lebella and Bogardus; he sensed Barr's restless resentment, which barely concealed rebellion. Fay was lower in morale than Jack, he thought, her shoulders drooping, face averted, as she picked her way toward the exit.

At his side, Virginia said, "I still think we should see Mrs. Murphy."

"How about tomorrow night?"

She hesitated, not looking at him. She knew what he was thinking now and she was making a small effort to resist. "We could hire a car and drive over there right now."

"Do you have a license to drive?"

"Why, no."

"Neither do I." He laughed. "I'll see about getting one tomorrow."

"All right." She looked directly into his eyes. "All right. Do you want to buy me dinner first?"

He protested, "Hey! Take it easy! I'm going to feed you, wine you, and woo you."

"All right," she said listlessly. "Whatever you say, Steve."

He was uncomfortable all through the meal at Gallagher's, the movie she wanted to see, the ride to her apartment. He hesitated at the taxi, started to tell the driver to wait. She pressed his arm, shook her head.

She was smiling then, the somber humor evaporated. He dismissed the cab and went up the stairs with his blood singing in a way that astounded him.

In the delightfully luxurious bed he lost himself, forgetting all else but the girl in his arms, unaware now of artifice or of anything but delight. When he thought of it later he knew that somehow it was different from the first time, but he dismissed this as something to do with alcohol.

Virginia knew better, with her powers of self-analysis. She had surprised herself by a new submissiveness, an abandonment of art in favor of pure emotion. It was, she knew, dangerous for her, because it was putting all her eggs in one basket.

Which again brought her back to Sam, his homely expressions, his love for her and for mankind. As she drifted into sleep her memory clicked and, dozing, she saw a picture of the smiling old man and his little loose-leaf notebooks from the five and dime, but she could not recall having seen the last of these, a red-covered one, among his effects at the police station.

Tomorrow, she thought, she would check this.

11

Fay Fowler detested the Uptown Political Club and all its denizens. The building was stiffly new, with an overdone ladies' lounge in green imitation leather and chrome. The women were cheap or worried or worn, matching the room in discomfort. Sid November's blonde was named Kitty and wore perfume that could not quite cover the reek of the butt she produced and promptly lighted for a last few puffs.

Jack was upstairs in a meeting and Fay had no idea how long it would last. She could walk out, of course. She almost did walk out when the blonde went at her marijuana. She stayed only because she knew Jack would need her.

She kept fighting the memory of Steve Galloway and the girl at the Polo Grounds that afternoon, and the strange way the girl had regarded Steve from time to time. What was her name? Virginia.

Virginia, hell, she thought. A high-powered sex machine, without a flaw. Nice, too, with a quick, ready smile and few words. No small talk, no girl talk; she was the sort Fay usually liked at once. All business, and the business was Steve.

And what the hell business is it of yours? she asked herself. Your man is upstairs fighting with some really dangerous people. Your man wants to take a million dollars and go with it to far places with you. He has done everything you ever asked of him, even this. If anything goes wrong he can and probably will get killed for it. You made your bed and you can damn well lie in it with Jack Barr and be grateful it's not that spineless husband of yours or the others that promised and did nothing. Jack's a man, all man, and you have every reason to know it and appreciate it. You were doing fine with it until Steve came along.

So you're not accustomed to the Kittys and the Lebellas and the Freddys. You were upper middle class in Montclair, you wanted to teach and the war got you into a marriage and you could have gone back home when it broke up, but you were proud. What happened to that pride when you realized that sex had become a habit and you were too frightened to remarry and you started doing the wrong things? You were on your way to becoming a lady-like tramp when you met Jack and he fell in love with you, really in love.

She looked at Kitty, who was all of nineteen and already a tramp with marijuana roaches in her purse and all hell stretched ahead and not the wit to know hell when it encompassed her. Kitty said, "Sid's real cool, y'know?"

"Is he?" She restrained a shudder at the thought of the hairy, greasy, fish-belly-white body of November.

"He gimme this." Kitty showed a bracelet set with semiprecious stones, running halfway up her plump arm. There was a dark-blue bruise beneath the bauble.

"Did he give you the bruise, too?" Fay asked ironically.

Kitty shrugged. "I wouldn't know. I was a little high, see? The tea had me floatin'."

"He gets you the tea?"

"Look, I don't need nobody to get it. I've known the place to get it for years!" Kitty laughed, off key. "I been on it since I was fourteen."

So what have you got to lose? thought Fay. November is so depraved that he's gone past the deflowering of virgins and wants only the hopped-up young veterans.

And then she felt emptiness in her with the knowledge that in such as Kitty lay part of the fruits of Jack's activities. The junkies were bred from the tea addicts. Prostitution, robbery, murder—all adjuncts of the rackets, with gambling the king; to be in it meant embracing all of it.

So he was upstairs fighting to get out. She could forgive him the past, that was easy. He had never asked her of yesterday's happenings.

If she could only forget Steve Galloway and the way he had looked at her and touched her and danced with her and smiled at her, if she could push it aside, she could manage. She had to have strength because Jack needed her strength. Jack was her man.

She said it again, almost aloud. Jack was her man.

Upstairs it was smoky in the small room and Jack Barr was angry. He said, "Don't come at me. I've told you before."

Lebella and Bogardus were quiet men. They were utterly undistinguished, colorless, businesslike. They smoked cigars and collaborated like twins, with psychic mutual understanding. Their strength lay in their calm, judicial approach to the problem at hand,

WILLIAM R. COX 113

Barr knew, and he fought to maintain control of his anger.

Lebella said, "We're not coming at you, Jack."

"Then get him out of here." Barr gestured contemptuously toward Sid November.

"He works for us," Bogardus said mildly. "You know us—on the level. Out in the open. Sid's got something to say."

"Let him say it and get out," Barr snapped. He added sneeringly, "Or is he so big he sits in with you guys?"

Lebella smiled. "Now *you're* coming at *us*, Jack. That ain't the way to do business and you know it."

Bogardus said, "Sid, you better get it off your chest."

November came into the strong light of the shaded lamp above the card table. His heavy features lighted with malice, he spoke respectfully to Lebella and Bogardus, ignoring Barr. "Jack brings this Galloway into the game, see? I don't like the way he handles himself. Galloway, I mean. Maybe I got out of line a little, I'll admit I was sore. Jack clobbers me." He choked on the last words.

Lebella said, "We'll skip that."

November said, "O.K., I had it coming. Only I don't like it. So I begin checkin' this Galloway. Like he was over in Jersey. Nosin' around. Said he knew the older Murphy boys in service. O.K. Only they was in the Navy. Galloway was in the Army. They was in the Atlantic Fleet. He was in the Pacific!"

Lebella said to Barr, "You see? It was Legs he wanted."

There was a small silence. November breathed hard, started to go on, stopped. Lebella was looking at Barr.

"All right," Barr said. "He knew Legs."

"He knew Socker. Who brought him to you?" November raised his voice until it squeaked, facing Barr now, triumphant. "He knew Socker and Socker knew Legs and Socker knew Sam Goulding!"

Barr leaned back out of the light, looking at the ceiling. He had to think now. Sam Goulding? What did it all mean?

November was not finished. He said, "Maybe I'm a dumb cluck. But I know how to plug. I had Goulding's will examined in the courthouse. He left a little dough. He split it. Between a broad named Virginia Butler and Steve Galloway!"

That was the bomb, then. Barr had played too much poker to show it, but he felt the impact.

Lebella said gently, "Guess you made a mistake about Galloway."

"Yeah," Barr said. "Guess I did." The girl this afternoon—she was Virginia Butler. Oh, yes, he had made a mistake, all right. And he had liked Steve—still did, in fact. A real guy, a lot of fun, a hell of a gambler.

Lebella said, "No harm done yet."

"He's gonna snoop," November said. "The Goulding thing was put away real good. But Galloway is gonna snoop."

"That's right," Lebella said. "You see, Jack, in a way it's good you got to playing with Galloway."

"Yeah." Barr made an effort. "It's good Sid dug up all that dope on him. It was a real good job."

November looked at him suspiciously. "O.K. Thanks."

Barr said flatly, "But he wasn't pulling anything in the poker game. You loused up on that. And you got too tough, Sid. Too big."

There was a moment's silence. November took a deep breath to end it. He mumbled, "O.K., Jack.

Forget it."

Lebella said, "Now that's the way to do business. Something happens, iron it out in the open, forget it. Right?"

Barr said, "I'll buy it."

Bogardus purred, "But about this other matter, Jack. You can see it now, can't you? How we feel about it?"

They had taken away his guns. How could he get out now? He had brought Galloway into it and he had to stick. He had to watch and be ready to take Galloway out of it. The responsibility was his. Getting out clean was all right, they would have allowed it in the end because they were slightly afraid of him. But there was a nicety of conduct that he must observe.

Lebella put it into words. "You wouldn't want to leave anything dangling, Jack. It ain't ethical."

He scowled at them. "You're right. I'll make a deal with you."

Bogardus said cheerfully, "Sure you will. You've always been clean, Jack. I know the deal you'll make. Don't we, Ossie?"

Lebella nodded. "Take care of Galloway. Make sure the Goulding thing ain't dug up. We'll buy your territory at a fair price. You blow town and live like you want. Is that kosher?"

"You're going to leave November on it?" Barr asked.

"Sid's done such a good job, we figure he better stick with it," Bogardus said frankly. "He's organized pretty good for investigation. We'll keep you up on everything."

The tension was easing off. Barr stood up, apologizing, "My girl's waiting. I guess we know the score."

"Sure, I knew we could get together." Lebella

looked puzzled. "One thing, Jack. This Galloway. He ain't a cheater—how come he wins all the time?"

Barr laughed for the first time that day. "Gentlemen, every once in a while a guy comes along, he can do no wrong. You know? He's hot all the time. If he's a good gambler and he's got this heat in him, you can't beat him."

"Can't do wrong?" Lebella was fascinated. "You mean not never?"

"That's what makes me feel so bad about Galloway," Barr said. "I was hoping to be around to see how long it could last."

Bogardus interposed, "Look, Jack, we don't want anything bad to happen to Galloway. Not if we can help it. You'll work along that line, huh? Only if he gets too close to anything."

"We never *want* anything to happen to anybody," Barr said.

"That's right," sighed Lebella. "You're so right, Jack. We got to keep that heat off us, is all. Look, me and Al have to go to L.A. on something. You check with us, huh?"

At the door Barr turned to them. "Am I in charge? Or is Sid?"

"It's sort of split," Lebella smiled. "You're on Galloway, Sid's taking care of other things. It'll work out, Jack."

He went down the stairs with a dark-brown taste in his mouth, a slight quiver in his knees, his hands slightly unsteady. They did not trust him. He wanted out and he made a mistake with Steve and they were putting Sid on him to keep him honest. And they had all the horses, they had a thousand men to do their bidding, and they had wires running through the cops all the way to Washington.

He was tough, he had always been tough. But was

he tough enough to get away with this? He almost ran to the ladies' lounge, beckoning Fay, getting her out of there.

On the sidewalk two figures loomed. He looked up into the wide, florid features of Cassidy as he greeted them. Kline smiled, a lean man, sardonic, but Cassidy was hearty and happy to see him. They were in plain clothes and both looked well barbered and prosperous. They undoubtedly were going in for a pay-off from Lebella.

Cassidy said, "Hear you are takin' a trip, Jack. You know how glad I am. Will I be dancin' at your wedding?"

Barr said, "No one if not you, pal. See you later."

He almost dragged Fay to where Freddy waited in the car, the radio playing soft and low. He shoved her in while the motor coughed into life, held her hand tightly while they drove to her place, around the corner from the shop. He sent Freddy away with a short word, led the way into the apartment, closed the door, locked and chained it, and went to the portable bar and poured two stiff ones.

She said, "It was bad?"

"It wasn't good."

"You mean you can't—you can't get out?" Her hand shook so that she spilled a little of the drink.

He looked at her sadly. He said, "Galloway."

"Steve? What about him?" She put down the drink and folded her trembling fingers. "What has he to do with it?"

"Everything." He was boiling inside. He had been so close, he had felt it in them, in their eagerness to throw it at him, to compromise with him, that he could taste freedom. Now there was a net around him, he was floundering, his only outlet a rage against the world. "The bastard is connected somehow with—something that happened. You wouldn't understand that part. Anyway, Steve is on the snoop."

"But how does that affect us?"

"I brought him in, sponsored him. I got to take him out."

"Take him out? What does that mean?"

"Just what it says. I can't quit until I make sure he won't cause trouble."

She shook her head as if recovering from a blow. "How could Steve cause us trouble? Why, he's fond of us. Really fond of us. Both of us. Steve's clean."

"You wouldn't understand," he repeated dully.

"I understand you've let them beat you again." She picked up her drink, her hands steady again.

With her alone he could let down his defenses. He begged, "Don't make it tougher than it is, baby. I almost had them. It was in the bag. They were scared, baby, scared of me and Freddy and knowing what we might do. Then this thing."

He dropped alongside her on the couch, slumping. No one else saw him like this, she knew, not ever. Her sympathy stirred, she touched his hand. He clutched at her.

She asked, "Can't you tell me all about it?"

"There's nothing to tell. I got to stick until Steve is through with his snooping. Socker is in on it, too. November and his crowd will be watching every move." He faced her, his eyes darkening. "I could get out, all right, baby. I could put you on a plane. I could kill November and do a Brodie and join you in South America. Maybe the cops wouldn't even know it was me, maybe we'd stay clear of heat. But we wouldn't dare ever come back. And I haven't got the kind of dough for that. Not the way I want to live."

"Kill November?" She shook her head. "No, Jack. You can't do that. He deserves anything bad that happens to him, but you can't kill him."

"I won't," he said. "You know I won't."

Again the wave of sympathy engulfed her. She put her arm around his lowered head. "It's bad, Jack. I hoped ... Well, it's bad. But you'll come through. You always have."

He turned toward her, one hand beneath her breast. His eyes lightened, he grinned. "You believe it, don't you, baby?"

"We've agreed and you keep your word," she said. "What else can I say?"

"We'll get out of it. I got to make a couple scores and I need the pay-off money for the territory. I'll think of some way to get Steve out of it. I don't want Steve hurt, either."

Her breath came a bit quicker. "Of course you don't. Steve's your kind of guy."

A tiny frown was between his brows. His hand tightened on her. "That's the kind can hurt you, knock you off balance. The guys you like."

She asked puzzledly, "But what is it that Steve is prying into? What happened? He just got back to this country."

"An old gambling thing," Jack said evasively. "It happened a long time ago. Too complicated to explain."

"Steve doesn't need money. Why should he bother?"

He moved restlessly, but did not decrease the pressure on her breast. "I wouldn't know, baby. All I can think of is that I love you. I've never loved anyone but you, never. You know that, don't you?"

All his strength and all his weakness were clear to her. She had been a long while realizing that the weakness was there, beneath his physical courage and his drive to succeed and his gay humor. Probably no one knew it but her, because he truly loved her and exposed himself to her without restraint.

It was a twisted thing and it could be good, she knew. He was all male, he was so much stronger than most, with all his frailty. Was it his fault that the skein of his life had weakened him in a certain manner? Could he have been a cop, like Cassidy, a truck driver or longshoreman like the other boys of his neighborhood beginnings?

She felt warmth rising in her, familiar, soothing while it tingled. He had the other hand on her thigh, gently testing, because in love-making he was gentle in approach always, seeking her response. She moved to let his hand rest comfortably, enjoying his stroking fingers. He could have been a gangster, a corner peddler of dope, a pimp, like others of his gang. He had taken what advantages had been offered and he had risen to the top. He was in the end, a man.

She kissed him and her lips parted and he was lifting her, carrying her to the bedroom with practiced strides. It was their favorite entry into love-making, a Sabine abduction, when the woman was willing beneath her pretended outrage. She laughed and scarcely recognized her own voice as she struggled a bit in the darkened room, while he roughly removed her blouse.

As she went dizzily into his arms, she had a sudden, appalling thought of Steve Galloway. She fought it with all her strength, but it would not go away.

It was still with her when it was over and Jack was sleeping beside her, his arm curved protectively about her, his breath misting against her shoulder.

12

Virginia made an excuse not to go to lunch on Monday. She watched Lou Moscow leave the office and her brow puckered. She thought of the things she had not told Steve, wondering if she were wrong.

Better to be wrong than precipitate, she hoped. It was her habit to be deliberate in all things. Moscow had been good to her since Sam's death. She sat a moment behind her desk, thinking of the kindnesses, the small things that came of understanding and tolerance and knowledge of the world that had been Moscow's contribution.

Then she thought of his repeated warnings about men and his eyes upon her so often when he thought she did not suspect. She knew what his thoughts were and why he did not put his hands upon her. Only his age and his awareness of his shortcomings as a romantic figure had restrained him. He was no different than those against whom he had so fruitlessly warned her. She arose and quickly went into his office.

While she searched, really knowing where she would find anything not meant for her eyes, moving with that quick certainty that was part of her health and her vitality, she thought wryly and ruefully that she should not weigh against Moscow what she welcomed in Steve. No sop to her conscience, then; she was doing what she thought would help Steve and that was that. Keep it on the level, Virginia, face the facts.

She found the key first. It was in the locked drawer that she knew how to open with a bobby pin. She went to the safe, worked the combination, located an old-fashioned box, and the key fitted it.

She had thought to buy a red notebook in the five

and dime. She removed Sam's red-covered notebook and substituted the other in case Moscow should take a look. On second thought she fetched a pen from the desk and scribbled in the new book, copying Sam's scribbling hieroglyphs as best she could.

She replaced everything with meticulous care. She put Sam's notebook in her purse and put on her hat and jacket and went out to lunch.

The day was hot and the sound of the city battered at her, but she was scarcely aware of it. She was thinking of Steve and of the little red book in her bag, which connoted less than reluctant betrayal of employer and friend. She was also thinking of the woman she had met yesterday, Fay Fowler.

Nothing ever quite escaped her. She had been able to read Fay's lips when she whispered to Steve. She had known immediately that there was a bond of some sort between them. She had also recognized a possible formidable rival.

Rival for what? Her lips curved with humor and a man stopped dead, staring at her. She flicked him a smile of negation and entered a malt shop and found a lone stool at the end of the counter. A youth sipping coffee looked slantwise at her, resumed his perusal of *Variety*, swiveled in a perfect delayed take for another look. She turned her shoulder to him and ordered a tuna-salad sandwich and a chocolate milk, contemplating a thick wedge of lemon-meringue pie on the shelf of a glass cage, wondering if she should order it in advance lest someone beat her to it.

Rival for Steve, of course, she resumed. She refused to have another woman chiseling in at this time.

Rival for his hand in marriage? She laughed at herself, and then in a moment she did not laugh.

Up until now all she had recognized was the

strong thing that ran through her when he was in the vicinity or when she could conjure him up in her mind. This she had known with other men, but not to such a degree, nor had it mattered. This she had now to examine.

Other women, she had gathered in her small experience with them, did not exercise in these matters much logical thinking. They merely allowed their femaleness to function. With her it was different; she had to think.

She had tentatively decided that marriage was not for her. Never had she considered a man as a companion of the future. There was no image within her of a man who would be her husband and to whom she would be wife.

She had to acknowledge that Steve had affected her more deeply than anyone else she had ever known. It could be a bad thing. She was fully aware that he was not "in love" with her.

She smiled at her old mental habit of putting "in love" in quotes. She decided against the pie. She would see Steve later, and better to have hunger in the stomach than in that other, adjacent sector of the viscera; a girl had to learn not to force a man to bed too often, whatever her wanton desires, she admonished herself.

As for marriage, nnnyeh! As for Fay Fowler, let her beware. She had a man, and Jack Barr seemed adequate for any woman. If Fay wanted to play around, if she had a touch of Virginia's own elasticity, let her play in someone's else back yard.

She wondered what it would be like to be married and have the right guaranteed by the social structure, to be jealous and protective of one's uxoriousness. It worked both ways, she decided, and she might not favor the other side of the coin.

She had to smile again at her thoughts and the boy put away his *Variety* and was beginning to breathe hard, so she finished her drink quickly and walked back to the office, feeling not one jot like a female Benedict Arnold, feeling only like a healthy girl with a clear, active mind who was going to have dinner with a man most desirable.

Steve remembered that noon that he had promised not to stay away from Socker's gym. He carefully washed and dried the old shaving mug, loth to trust it to the cleaning brigade, put it in its place, thinking of how Virginia and he had sipped from it, naked, laughing like fools. She had a knack of unloosing all inhibitions that was altogether charming; he had never enjoyed a girl more.

If she only had the intangibles that he imagined in Fay Fowler, he sighed. If she only weren't so—He sought the word for her. Not trampish, he hastily admitted. Not dirty like some women, dirtier than men in nastier ways, none of that in Virginia. He could not categorize her; the phrase eluded him. It was just that a man wanted something more than a willing, practiced woman in his bed.

Instantly he was ashamed. By what standard did he criticize Virginia? And by what right? Why should he attempt a deprecatory description of her? Had she not given freely, with no strings attached, whatever he asked? Why was it wrong that she should also want it?

A few weeks from the Orient and you're thinking like a damned New York bond salesman, he told himself. He stomped out of the apartment and over to the gymnasium.

The gym was deserted except for Socker and a tow-headed young man of lower middle height, who were sparring in the ring. Socker paused, nodded meaningfully at Steve, then resumed.

The blond youth moved with amazing speed, displaying shifts and counters without actually hitting Socker, using shoulder feints and varied swift leads, combining punches in flurries of action. Steve watched, open-eyed, until Socker ran out of breath and quit.

Steve said, "Hey, who is this boy?"

The boy glared at him. He had small, pale eyes and his mouth was a slash. As he looked at the tough, scarred face, Steve's memory stirred.

Socker said, "Meet Sailor Hock."

Hock shrugged, raised pale brows at Socker, moved toward the dressing room. Socker dragged Steve in his wake, saying, "This boy is from Pat Paule, out West. His record says twenty out of twenty-two with both losses reversed by k.o.'s."

"Only twenty-two bouts?"

Socker snickered. They entered the dressing room and Hock was wrapped in a towel, cooling off on a low bench. "He had a hundred in the Navy and fifty-odd bootlegs in Europe and Africa."

"That's it. Aken," said Steve. "Beat a Negro light heavy. Last year. I should have known him. Saw the fight."

Sailor Hock neither affirmed nor denied. He seemed disinterested.

Socker said, "Pat Paule's smart. Ran up his record around L.A. Nothing spectacular, see? The way it is, Steve, the big dough is with the I.B.C., on television. But if you tie up with the I.B.C. they call the turn. You got no rights because they build you and they feel they got to get paid for the build-up."

"I've heard some talk," Steve said.

"Sure. Well, there's Arcel's Saturday fights, but

that's the hard way and nobody but Bobo Olson made it real good. Pat figures to outsmart the I.B.C."

"I don't quite get that."

Socker explained, "Mostly on television you got these boys who look real good to the guy at home. They get the build-up. Flash boxers, who throw punches that can be seen on a small screen. Elbow boys with personality. People write letters, they like 'em."

"You mean fighters have to make like ham actors for television?"

Sailor Hock looked at him with contempt. He grunted, "Listen to the square. Is he for real?"

"Nice sort of kid." Socker jerked a thumb toward the pale-eyed youth. "Like a murderer." He turned on Hock. "Keep a civil tongue in your head, tough boy."

The pugilist leaped to his feet. "Don't yak at me, you old has-been, or I'll pop you one on the kisser!"

Socker swung without hesitation. His big hamlike fist slammed against the base of the smaller man's brain, sending him forward. His knee came up and struck the hard chin. Then Socker grabbed the falling body with ludicrous gentle care lest permanent damage occur.

He said to Steve, "He's real good, see? A tiger."

"A jerk," Steve said.

"That's what makes him good." Socker laughed, stretching the pug on the bench, covering him with towels. "The I.B.C. has got a problem boy, see? People like him fine. Georgie Appleton, a colored kid, a rough, tough kid, a hitter. There is only one trouble with this boy. They can't get anybody in the ring with him."

"I thought they owned a lot of fighters."

"It ain't that simple. They don't want one of their flashy boys killed. They don't want Appleton knocked off, either. They want Appleton to knock off somebody else a few times, then they will throw him into it with the champ, for grabs."

Steve said, "It's too complicated for me."

"You got a loose grand ain't working?" Socker said.

"For what?"

"I lay it on a certain guy, see? He gets around, talks up Sailor Hock, puts it out that old Socker's got a bum, a real bum, and what ex-pug hasn't had a dozen? Socker thinks his bum can whip anybody, even Georgie Appleton. So they let Sailor in there with him."

Hock blinked, rolled off the bench, coming to his feet. He started a right hand for Socker's head. Steve caught him, wrenched him off balance, slammed him against a locker, pinned him there, towering over him, grinning down at him. "Save it for Georgie Appleton, boy. You might get hurt around here."

"Nobody puts the knee to me and gets away with it," stormed Hock, spitting out words as though they hurt his throat. "Not for marbles, money, or chalk!"

Steve loosed the voice of authority he learned in Army camps. "Blow that out your barracks bag! If I'm investing dough in you, I want you in one piece."

Hock glared from one to the other of the bigger men. For a moment he was like a caged animal. Then the film washed from his eyes and he relaxed and Steve let him sit down again on the bench. Hock said dully, "You gonna put up the dough? Then I listen."

In the office, Steve wrote a check for a thousand. They heard the shower running and knew they were safe from listening ears. Socker chortled, "We'll get maybe three to one. Fives on a k.o. We spread it among half a dozen bookies. This'll be a score they won't forget!"

"I believe you," Steve said. "This fight I've got to see."

Socker sobered. "No private bets until ringside. If it got out you were taking the odds around town it would hurt us."

"You mean Jack Barr or Sid November?"

"Yeah."

"You've learned something?"

"I been told."

Steve leaned forward. "Told what, Socker?"

"To lay off. A couple hoods, real polite, told me to stay away from the Murphy thing. They were November's boys."

"November, Jack Barr, and a couple of men named Lebella and Bogardus," Steve said slowly.

"I hate to admit it, but Barr is tied to the mains," Socker said. "Not to November, you know that. But in the gambling business there's always a tie-up. Lebella and them got wires to everyplace. Even Jack isn't able to cross those wires."

"He's such a nice guy," Steve said.

"Lots of nice guys in the business," Socker nodded. "Steve, I can't get anyplace on Legs. But a certain Jersey cop tipped me that his ma is ready to talk to the fuzz. She might of found out something. I better not go over there, the way it is, though."

"I'm going over tonight." He was thinking of Jack Barr and of Fay and wondering how far Barr was into it and how it would affect Fay.

"Keep it quiet," Socker said worriedly. "Don't let it get in the papers again. Next thing you know, they'll be hotting us up."

Someone was coming into the gym. Socker went to warn Sailor Hock and get him unobtrusively away and Steve changed for a workout. He could not stop thinking about Fay and Jack. He wished he had met

Fay before she got tangled up with Jack. He wished a whole hell of a lot of things, he told himself, savagely punching the heavy bag. Better he should begin doing something about them.

13

It was dusk when Virginia came to the apartment and he had already mixed Martinis in the shaving mug. He took hers to her as she sat in the low chair under the light and said, "I forgot about getting a driver's license. I'm sorry."

She looked quizzically up at him, accepting the cocktail glass, sipping at the pale, potent drink. "Don't be sorry. We can get there in a cab."

He called Madison 5-4000 and told them to send Sol Mintz to him and returned his attention to the girl. She was serious; there was something on her mind. He turned on the radio, but the music was all pop stuff at that hour and unsuited to their mood.

She said. "Are we going to eat in Jersey?"

"There's some delicatessen stuff from your friend Cohen in the refrigerator," he suggested.

She was apathetic. He found himself trying to bring her out of her low humor, smiling anxiously. She seemed to watch him with detachment and it began to annoy him. He was ready to quarrel with her when the bell rang and it was Sol downstairs waiting. He said, "So we'll eat in Jersey."

They went silently down to the cab and Sol squinted at Virginia, looked hard at Steve, and asked, "What's it now?"

"Back to Mrs. Murphy," Steve said. "Only you're invited to dinner in Jersey if you know a good place."

"I should know from eating in Jersey?" Sol was insulted.

They were in the taxi. Steve said, "Lots of people eat in Jersey."

"Not me," Sol said. "Why should I eat in Jersey? What kinda tsimmis you trying to raise with me? You wanta go to Jersey, O.K., ten bucks and what's onna flag. Eat in Jersey, never!"

Steve waited until the cab was headed for the Lincoln Tunnel. Then he asked, "Sol, have you had your dinner?"

"O.K., O.K.! So I eat early."

"Sol. Where in Jersey is there a good place to eat?"

Virginia giggled. Sol regarded her severely in the rearview mirror. "You wanta dance, I should take it? Soft lights, sweet music?"

Steve said patiently, "Sol, we want to eat."

"In Newark, maybe?"

"You know we don't go through Newark." Virginia had caught onto the game they played and was enjoying it.

"You couldn't grab a samwitch? I got to wait while you eat?"

"With the flag down, you'll wait all night in a snowstorm."

Sol sniffed and pretended high dudgeon. They ran past a truck and slid to the toll booth. Steve gave Sol the money and received no response. When he leaned back, Virginia squeezed his hand, smothering a smile. Sol and his antics had broken the strange restraint between them.

They came out of the tunnel onto a clover leaf and Sol twisted the wheel hard and they ran west off the main road and turned up a narrow lane. In five minutes the hurly-burly and the racket of the big artery were gone, so that their ears rang with emptiness. There was a low building with a neon sign that read, "Harry's Steak House."

Sol parked and said sullenly, "Harry's a sort of cousin of my wife. I hate him to pieces. But steaks he has got."

Virginia and Steve went inside. It was a long, dimly lighted room with rough pine furniture and red-and-white tablecloths and a beagle-faced waiter and Muzak very quietly seeping through the aroma of good cooking.

Virginia asked, "How come red-checkered tablecloths always signify good cooking?"

"They really don't, but the nose knows," Steve said. There were few customers, prosperous, weary-looking men, and in a far corner a couple of obvious refugees from the race track. He selected a table removed from those occupied and they seated themselves.

From the kitchen came a large, florid man with an amazingly bulbous nose. He rubbed his hands together and cried, "Sol brings me only the best people! So nice to serve you, Mr. Galloway. It'll be maybe the steak with mushrooms, sirloin, finest cut?"

Steve looked at Virginia. Then he said, "Whatever you suggest, Harry. Bring us the works and a bottle of wine."

Harry breathed hard on them. He was a garlic-user. "I got a red wine from France, it will make you sing. It even looks good. It is the finest red wine—"

"Bring it," Steve said. "We'll take your word for it."

"Tomatoes I got for salad, grown right in my back yard. A pound apiece they weigh. Celery from Florida, you should taste it." He hesitated. "You want a shrimp cocktail, something?"

"Just steaks," Steve said.

He finally left them, his hands nearly smoking

from the rubbing he had given them. Virginia was grinning in frank amusement, he saw. He laughed and said, "Sol warned us not to eat in Jersey."

"Characters, characters, never anything but characters," she said. "You never meet just plain people anymore."

The waiter brought the wine, but Steve ordered two Martinis and they let the bottle rest in an ice bucket where it had no right to be in the first place. He wanted only to keep Virginia in her present humor. The two racetrack characters finished their meal and walked clear across the room out of their way and stared and for a moment he was irate. Then he grinned, cooling off.

"Pals of yours?" he asked the girl.

She looked coolly at the men as they paid their tabs. "If I ever saw them I've forgotten them. I run to more conservative men."

"What was the matter with you earlier?" he asked suddenly, without intending to.

A shadow deepened her eyes, then she shook her head.

"I was being stupid. I'll tell you later—maybe."

He nodded. "Just so you're all right now. I like you to be yourself."

"Thank you, Steve."

"I mean you're different. You make so much sense." He had meant to keep away from personalities between them, to talk of Sam or Moscow or anything but himself and the girl. He heard his own voice, somewhat inane, go on: "It's been eleven years since I talked to American girls. But I never remember one like you."

"You mean because I can read lips and don't like to wear panties?" she asked mischievously. "Or because I run after you and like Martinis?"

"And other things, most remarkable," he told her.

"Let's stay out of that department." She was laughing and relaxed and the steaks sizzled in the kitchen and the music hit a good beat, and they looked into each other's eyes and were gay and Steve felt very young, much younger than his years.

They ate. The food was superb. Too much of it, and too much accompanying self-praise from Harry, but they enjoyed it. Even the wine was good, and they had a second bottle. Virginia seemed to have completely recovered her spirits, and when they went out she began to tease Sol and the taxi rolled along toward Mrs. Murphy's house and Steve leaned back, replete with food and unable to think about anything except his filled belly.

A heavy sedan passed them, dangerously close, and Sol blistered the air with language that made Virginia straighten and frown, until Sol apologized weakly and she had to break down and laugh. It was a short ride, but Sol missed the turning in the dark and they had to retrace their course slowly, Sol's spotlight slicing the gloom of the unlighted neighborhood beside the dump.

They found it and Sol swung his wheel. There was a roar of engine and a squealing of tires. Sol's spot was still on. It picked out fleetingly a man behind the wheel of a heavy dark sedan, hat pulled low, intent on making the turn back toward New York. Sol braked and Virginia was thrown against Steve and they wallowed helplessly a moment while the cab tilted on two wheels, then heavily thumped back and slewed to a stop.

Sol had no words. When he turned his lips were working and his hatchet face was pinched with rage and frustration. He croaked, "Couldn't even get the number. Didja see the crumb at the wheel?"

"Couldn't make him out," Steve said.

"In Harry's joint. That's the kind of people he gets. Couple of bastardly hoods."

"In Harry's? The race-track types?" Steve jerked upright. "Step on it, Sol. Step on it!"

The motor caught. Sol slammed the cab down the street and Steve was out and running before the brakes had completely stopped it. He was at the darkened door of Mrs. Murphy's cottage, shouldering it, knowing it would be unlatched, knowing what he would find.

When he clicked on the lights and looked at her the steak inside him was no longer a comfort. He managed to choke out, "Virginia, stay in the cab!"

Then he reeled to the corner of the little porch and retched, vomiting through rage and impotence and utter hatred of ruthless violence and its perpetrators. Not a war, not a life led on the edge of the underworld had cured him of his detestation of murder, of the surging desire for vengeance, man's cry against the injustice and brutality of man. He wept, and the taste of vomit was not as bitter as the taste of wild, mounting rage.

He felt Virginia's hand on him and mumbled, "Don't go in there."

"I sent Sol for the police," she said. "Steve, those men heard that fool Harry yowl out your name. They had time to make a phone call. Then they raced past us."

"I'd know those men again, anyplace." He wiped his mouth, spat, shuddered.

"You won't see them until this has blown over," she said. "They'll go undercover. You see how it is, Steve? We were followed. Word was flashed ahead that we were heading for Jersey. The Jersey mob was looking for us. Two of them were in Harry's."

"You think Sol ..."

She said, "I wouldn't know. More likely Harry's is a regular stop—good food, all that. It's nothing for the syndicate to have men anyplace they might be needed. When we started for Mrs. Murphy's, they knew. They beat us here, barely got away."

"Sol missed that turning. He could have done it on purpose, to give them time."

She shook her head. "Sol seemed too scared, really scared. But we'll check him."

Steve looked at her in the darkness. "You know an awful lot about how it had to be. You're a smart girl, Virginia."

She said, "I've done a lot of thinking and remembering what Sam taught me. And—I've got Sam's little red book."

"What? Why didn't you ..." He paused. He said slowly, "Now I get it. You had to steal it from Moscow. That's why you were so quiet this evening."

"You're pretty smart yourself sometimes, Steve." Her voice was low. "Now I'm going in there."

"No!"

"Yes. I need to see it. I've been holding back, unwilling. Now I've got to make myself see what can happen."

He followed her, taking her arm. They stood in the doorway, squeezed tight within the frame. There was reflected light from the kitchen lancing across the tiny, huddled body, illuminating the crushed head, the twisted neck of the remains of Mrs. Murphy.

"Like killing a chicken," she murmured. "No more thought, no more effort. Two big men, twisting the neck of a small woman, smashing her skull with a blackjack. A moment's work, then back into the car, a quick getaway, a report to the bosses, a plane ride somewhere, anywhere. Smoking their fat cigars, digesting Harry's steaks, playing canasta, probably, or reading the *Racing Form*."

"It was the same way with Sam."

"Yes, it was like that with Sam."

They stood stolidly until the police came, not entering the house, just looking and thinking. Sol was voluble with the officers, his hands waving, the surface of his cynicism cracked. A lieutenant named Carraway was polite, a big man, well spoken.

When the morgue wagon had departed with its pitiful burden, Carraway sat and listened. They told him everything that could help the New Jersey end. They did not mention the red notebook, although Steve decided to divulge their belief in the tie-up between the Murphys and the death of Sam Goulding.

There was a pause. Then Carraway asked, "Have you been to the New York police?"

"No," Steve said.

"I see." Again a pause. "The New York end is none of my business. In a way. If you're right, and there is a connection, then it is my business, with theirs. It opens a thing."

"Politics?" Steve asked.

"You can call it that." Carraway's intelligent face was bitter.

They were alone. Steve went to the door, made sure no one was within hearing distance. He came back and faced Carraway. "I told you about Sam because I wanted to level with you. If you want to forget it, officially, that's good with me. New York won't reopen the case unless there's pressure, and if we put on the heat you know what will happen. They'll all take cover."

Carraway nodded. "Unofficially, I admit it. They're too big."

"Legs was murdered because he was blackmailing

someone and they were afraid he'd talk. His mother found some evidence and agreed to talk to you and they killed her, but not until I headed this way. Therefore they feared what she would say to me more than what she might tell you. Does that make sense?"

Carraway said, "I figure it that way."

"Then we may suppose that she was going to tell me something about Sam Goulding, or about Flaming Arrow."

"You may also suppose that they're onto you," Carraway said.

"I thought of that." He looked at Virginia. They would be onto her, too.

"You'll need protection. You'll have to go to the New York police now."

"Not unless you insist," Steve said carefully, unwilling to offend Carraway, yet knowing he would not consult the police as yet. "I'd like a little time. Not much. Not enough to compromise you. I could report to you by phone. You see, Lieutenant, I'm not trying to save my life. I'm trying to avenge a couple of deaths."

"The girl?" Carraway nodded toward Virginia.

She said, "Sam was a father to me, too."

Again there was silence. Then Carraway nodded heavily. "Officially you merely found the body and have no idea who might have done it. Could have been a thief. We'll play it that way. I can keep the heat off for a while. You're looking for bad trouble, you know that."

"Three people have been killed," Steve said. "We'd be pretty stupid if we didn't know."

"I think you're stupid enough." He got up, a heavy-set man with a slight trace of whisky in the veins about his long nose. "So am I. I used to be a hot boy when I first got on the cops, a real hot boy. I've cooled off some in twenty years. But you know what? A guy never quite gets over wanting to be a hero. And even a cop doesn't get this kind of chance too often."

"He could muff it."

"He could, he could." Carraway sighed. "Maybe I'll muff it. I can't promise anything except to go along a while."

Steve said, "That's good with me." He had an inspiration. He said carefully, "Look, Carraway, I was going to hire a private detective to look into the Jersey end of this."

Carraway glanced instinctively at the window. He said, "Thanks. No checks, though. You can send some cash to Six-fifty-four Southwood Drive. Use regular mail. And—I'll try to earn it."

They left. Sol had nothing to say for three miles. Then he slowed, turned, and stared at them. "Looks bad for me, huh? Harry and all. Missin' the turn."

"We'll know if you're in it," Steve said coldly. "It'll show, sooner or later."

"I told you I hate Harry. Now we'll go back there."

"Carraway will check Harry."

Sol shook his head. Five minutes later he was swinging into the parking lot of Harry's place. He was out of the cab, Steve on his heels. They went in the back way and Sol slammed open the door of an office off the kitchen.

Harry was eating one of his own steaks. Sol was across the room and had him by the throat before Steve could make a move. The big man tried to get up, tried to ward off his assailant, but Sol clung like a leech. His voice pounded, shrill, shaken. "Them two hoodlums. Who are they? You gonna talk, you dirty *goniff*, or am I gonna kill you, you should be dead years ago?"

Harry managed to pry him loose, gagging, trembling, appealing to Steve. "Mr. Galloway, what's with him?"

Steve said, "The race-track boys who were eating when we came in. Was there a call for them before we got here?"

"Yeah, there was a call for 'em. So what? Guy named Smith took the call."

"Smith, eh? Very imaginative," Steve said, holding Sol off with one hand. "They made a call out, then waited until we left. Any ideas?"

Harry looked frightened. "They stick you up or something?"

"You know 'em," Sol shrieked. "Give, you fat slob!"

"They been in here before, sure. I heard one call the other Hotsy or somethin'. A couple hoods, sure. They pay, so what?"

"Hotsy and Smith." Steve tugged at Sol. "Come on. He doesn't know any more."

Sol insisted, "I'll get more outa him. He couldn't tell the truth if he tried, the slob."

"Come on," Steve said. "I'll believe you're on the level. Let's go. I've still got things to do."

He had to carry the struggling small man to the taxi and shove him behind the wheel. Sol kept repeating, "You see? With him, it's always trouble for me. That no-good-nick ..."

When they were finally rolling toward New York, Steve asked, "Why do you hate Harry so, Sol?"

"He gave me the knockdown to my wife!" Sol snapped.

Virginia giggled and the tautness began to ease and Steve felt his muscles relaxing, realizing that they had been tense for hours, that he was emotionally exhausted, that he was hungry again, that he needed a drink.

Virginia said, "Your place, Steve. We need to talk."

"Yes, we need to talk." He was grateful for the girl's presence. He marveled at the way she took things, the way she responded to moods and events without losing equilibrium. He patted her hand and felt the reassuring pressure of her fingers and began again to gain confidence.

He had felt little of it since the sight of Mrs. Murphy's body. He had talked, he had tried to think, but underneath he had been far from confident. The scope and strength of the syndicate had partially stunned him, he now realized. It was necessary to readjust values, to re-examine procedure. He had been a fool, rushing in, all boy scout plus Superman, ready and eager to take on all corners to avenge the death of Sam Goulding. The police of the nation could not cope with the combination of gamblers and gangsters that was loosely known merely as "the syndicate." What chance had Steve Galloway?

The apartment seemed safe and snug and the cold meat and potato salad were delicious and filling. Steve looked at Virginia's slim, exciting legs and then looked quickly away as she removed the soiled dishes, fussed in the kitchen. He was getting accustomed to her and liking it and it was no good. Where was romance, where the pitapat of heart, the strumming of lyres, the deep sigh of lovers, the night walking, the poetry? Some of this he had felt through knowing Fay; he expected more of it.

When she came back into the room she was holding the notebook, looking at it, her eyelids lowered, her mouth turned slightly down at the corners. She sat down opposite him and he waited.

There were tears in her eyes when she looked up.

She said, "At first I was sad because of deceiving Lou. Now all I can think of is Sam, lying there in the street like Mrs. Murphy. I'm glad I looked at her, Steve."

She extended the notebook and he took it from her. It was vest-pocket size, about two and a half inches by four. It didn't seem to have seen much use, and less than half of its pages held entries. At first he was confused by Sam's crabbed shorthand, but after a few moments he sensed the key.

He said, "N-o-v. That's Sid November. Sam was on his tail for some reason, did you notice?"

"I can translate it," she offered. "I've studied it."

"It would save time. I can check later."

She said steadily, "Sam had been drunk off and on for weeks. Then he had enough of that, but he played drunk for another little while. He heard that Sid November was down heavy on Flaming Arrow. See the entry connecting them, 'Nov' crossed by the arrow?"

It was as Virginia said. Steve stared at the crude symbol and for an instant recovered the image of Sam, his round, strong face, his deep-set blue eyes, the cottony hair, the seamed, tanned skin, the ready genuine smile. He could smell stables and liniment and oiled leather and hay and feel the tickle of forked loose straw in his nostrils and breathe the air of early morning and hear the whinny of a thoroughbred.

Virginia was saying, "You know if Sam had hocked his diamond we'd have the ticket in the office. There's no mention of it in the notes. Only data on a deal concerning November, which I can't make out. I don't think anyone can. Now look at the last note in the book, Steve."

He turned to the final page containing an entry. The writing was shaky, almost illegible. He made out, "Legs ... Jersey ... Nov ... Mrs. M. O.K.... Synd. deal

... Lou get to Steve."

"Lou, get to Steve," he repeated.

"Can you make out the rest?"

"No." The old man had needed him and Lou had his address. He stared at the girl. "Why didn't Lou wire me? Where does Lou fit in this deal?"

"I don't know. It worries me."

"He's scared. He has to know something about the syndicate, being Sam's lawyer. Just being Moscow, he would know something."

"He'll never talk. You couldn't make him."

That was true. Steve considered. Moscow had suppressed Sam's notebook. To the police it meant nothing, evidently, except the memos of a horse player. But it had to mean something to Moscow.

He said, "Learn what you can from him. You'll know how to handle him better than anyone else. It looks as if we should start looking for Sam's diamond. If we find that, we'll have his killer."

"Maybe. It was a valuable stone. It could have changed hands several times by now."

He nodded. She was right again. "I'll work Barr and Socker."

"And Barr's girl?" she asked blandly.

He shot a quick look at her. She answered it frankly, opening her eyes wide, unflinching. He said, "Why not?"

"No reason. On the contrary," she said sweetly. "Don't misunderstand me, Steve. I think you should get what you can out of those people. It's the only way we'll ever learn about Sam."

"They led me to November," he said defensively.

"I thought Socker introduced you," she murmured.

"You know what I mean." He could not keep the heat out of his tone. "Barr got me into the poker game."

"And slapped November down. You think that was an act?"

"You saw how they acted yesterday, like strange bulldogs."

"I was watching Fay Fowler at the time," she said demurely. "She was very uncomfortable—when she wasn't whispering to you."

"You see a whole hell of a lot, don't you?" he flung at her.

She rose and picked up her hat, adjusting it. When she lifted her arms every line of her body came into bold relief. She was extraordinarily symmetrical, lovelier than he could ever quite believe. He watched her, regretting his hasty words.

She turned, smiling gently. "Good-night, Steve. I'll get a cab."

"It's after midnight," he said ungraciously. "I'll see you home."

She was moving toward the door. "Just an old-fashioned boy. You've been away too long. Girls go home alone without thinking anything of it these days."

He caught her before she could manage the latch. He said, "I like it the old-fashioned way." He fought down his pique, smiling.

For a moment they stood motionless. Then she laughed a little. "We're not sleeping together tonight, Steve. But you can take me home. I guess I like that."

14

Senator Joe McCarthy and the two newest alphabet-bombs were all over the papers the next day and poor Mrs. Murphy received scant notices.

He must remember to have Carraway arrange for

a decent funeral, Steve thought. He put bills in an envelope and mailed it to the Jersey cop, going out to the mail chute in the hall in his robe. When he re-entered the apartment his telephone was ringing.

It was Jack Barr. "Hiya, gambler. Tried to get you last night for a game."

Steve said, "Had a date with a female woman type. What about tonight? We could play here."

"I'd like to see your place," Barr said. "Got room for six?"

"Yeah, but no room for November to fall down after you hit him," Steve said. "Make him promise to be good if you bring him."

"I'm not about to bring him, see him, or play with him, the bum," Barr said emphatically. "I can get a bunch without him."

"Make it early."

"Seven o'clock. Say, Steve, I got a tip for you."

"Yeah? I don't bet horses."

There was a moment's pause. Then Barr said incredulously, "You don't what?"

"I never bet horses." Steve kept his voice natural, laughed a little. "Just don't care for the races, that's all."

Barr said, "I never heard of a gambler who didn't bet horses."

"I've been away, remember? I don't like 'em, Jack. Too many angles." He was very careful now. "Of course, if you're on the inside, it's different."

"I wouldn't know any horses by their first name," Barr said quickly. "Anyway, my tip's on a fight."

"That's different," Steve said promptly. "Fights I like."

"They just set up a bout between Georgie Appleton and some new kid from out West," Barr said. "This Appleton is murder. You'll have to give some odds, but get down on him."

"Who's the short-ender?"

"Hock, Hack, something like that. It's a push, Steve. This Appleton is great."

"Thanks, I'll take a look at him."

"Look, schnook, I'm telling you! I know fights, pal, don't I?"

"O.K., you know fights," Steve said. "Thanks, anyway."

"See you at seven, boy." Barr hung up.

Such a pleasant guy, Steve thought. Giving me the word on Appleton. They must have moved fast, making the bout. Guess it was pretty well set when Socker got into it.

He called Socker. He said, "Barr's already getting down on Appleton. He let me in on it."

"You didn't bet him?"

"I'm not that dumb. Will you come over here, Socker? Something bad happened last night in Jersey."

"Shhhh!" Socker hesitated, then said, "You shouldn't gamble with them Jersey boys. And don't talk about it—they're murder. I'll see you later, Steve."

Socker broke the connection. Steve frowned. Had he been wrong to talk to Socker on the telephone? Surely his wire wasn't tapped.... He remembered the board downstairs and the girl in attendance. Socker was being overcautious; he had inherited a private outside line with the apartment.

He thought about the gamblers, the ones with whom he would be dealing directly, even tonight, here in his own home. A strange breed, from his direct experience. Restless, always seeking a new interest, like kids looking for sensations. They had everything running for them in such a way that there was no risk,

yet they were always switching around, looking for
different angles. Right now it would be the fights,
especially with Georgie Appleton in there, and of
course they had that one figured for the edge. Always
the edge, even when they looked for new thrills.
Destroying their intent, bloodsucking the two-dollar
long-shot player, laughing at the suckers—and in the
end negating their search for adventure. A witless lot,
in many ways.

And he was one of them. He had lately been an oil
man. He had learned a lot about it, too, and it had
paid him his million. But he had never really enjoyed
the labor, the effort of organization, the actual
drilling and sweating. Only the excitement of
wondering if it would come in had kept him at it, the
gamble of his money and time against the stubborn
sands.

It was not pleasant to face this, as he went to
answer his buzzer.

He admitted Socker and explained about the
telephone. He said, "However, you're right. We've all
got to move carefully. They got Mrs. Murphy." He
told the story.

Socker shook his head. "They're onto you, Steve.
You better buy that gun."

"I'll get one today," Steve said. "How do we keep
track of November now that Jack won't bring him
around?"

"I'll check," Socker said reluctantly. "I can't ask
no more. They warned me. And Steve—don't go
betting them on the fight. Not even undercover."

"It's a chance to hurt them," Steve said.

"How can you hurt them? You take a million
from them. They got another million pourin' in the
next day. Don't be a sucker, Steve."

"Barr hasn't got it going for him like that."

Socker said, "Look, you can bet him ringside all he can handle, it don't matter. But we got to spread the other money. Listen to him, con him along, but don't lay him money, Steve."

Again Socker was right. Steve moved restlessly. "I want to get at them. November is the key man. Let me get November alone in an alley and I'll know the score."

"That's about it," Socker said.

"Then let's work it that way. Make me a date with November, somehow, anyhow. I'll handle it from there before they hurt someone else."

Socker shook his head. "You'd have to kill him. Otherwise he'd run to the mains and then it would be you. Or me."

Or Virginia, Steve thought at once. He should not have taken Virginia to the football game. He should never be seen with her. She was Moscow's secretary and they had to know about Moscow. It was snowballing around him and he did not like it.

Socker said earnestly, "You got to go slow. This is no chicken mob you're up against. You got to go slow. You got to play Jack Barr and his pals and then you got to make up your mind. When you're ready to work over November and then knock him off, you can move."

Steve shook his head. "I couldn't kill him without knowing he was the one that did for Sam."

"If you kill him you got to run," Socker added grimly.

Neither spoke for several minutes. Then Steve said quietly, "I know what you're thinking. That I'm crazy for even trying. That the cops should take care of it."

"No. I wasn't thinking that." Socker looked squarely at him. "I was thinkin' that you're lucky. Awful lucky. I was thinkin' about how much better it

would be for a horse player like me if he didn't think
the syndicate had every race rigged. I was thinkin'
that maybe you could go a long way into them. Not
to the top. But deep enough and loud enough to bring
in some other people."

"It would be a nice thing to do for Sam."

"It might break you. They might knock you off."

"And that's a gamble," Steve said. "I can't seem to
live without a big gamble. I might as well figure to go
all the way with one."

Socker nodded. "O.K. I'll look around. You want
to start puttin' out some dough on Sailor Hock?"

"Can you cash a check on the quiet?" Steve wrote
in his pocket checkbook. "I'll give you two. Each for
twenty-five thousand. What odds as of now?"

"Fours." Socker chuckled. "They'll go down
ringside, but nobody knows the Sailor yet. Pat Paule's
in town, he already bet his wad."

Steve asked thoughtfully, "No chance for a
cross-up?"

"With Hock, sure. I wouldn't trust him across the
street. But Pat Paule's decent, and he knows me. I'm
bettin' five gees for him."

"We might have to scare Hock."

Socker said, "Money counts with him. I'm laying a
couple grand of this for him, too."

"You reckon he can beat Appleton, honest?" Steve
laughed. "Wait—don't say it. You believe he can. But
you say Appleton's got a k.o. punch. So anything can
happen."

"That's right. It's the price," Socker said jauntily.

When Socker had gone, Steve shook his head.
There it went again along the old lines. He was
betting fifty thousand dollars and probably a lot more
before it was all over, because the price was right.
And he would love it, every minute of it, and if he did

not bet such a large amount he wouldn't get the kick out of it.

You're a gambler, Galloway, he told himself, and not even a very smart gambler. What right have you got to criticize someone else?

Murder was another matter, however. He thought of the crumpled, still body of Mrs. Murphy and of Sam Goulding dead on First Avenue. If he could stick it into them deep enough to hurt, if he could get anywhere near the top people, it would be the best thing he had ever done in his bootless life.

Jack Barr listened to Freddy, sullen, stubborn.

"He was over in Jersey to see the Murphy woman. You know that. The broad was with him, Moscow's secretary. November moved fast and I don't like it any better than you do, but it had to happen."

"Killin' old dames!" said Barr. "Christ!"

"You didn't kill her. I didn't kill her. The point is this: November moved ahead of you and the mains know it. They expect you to do something about Galloway." He raised a hand. "All right, they don't want trouble. Not with a guy like Galloway. They want action of some kind."

Barr said, "I'm sticking close to him."

"You tipped him on the Appleton thing," Freddy pointed out. "What are you, queer for this guy? You can't help yourself?"

"It's funny," Barr admitted. "You got to like him. He's—regular. He lays it on the line. You saw him get November told, after I slugged the slob. He's got moxie."

"You keep playing with him, Lebella and Bogardus will have something to say about it."

He wanted to fight, he wanted to argue, he wanted to hit Freddy in the face. He had always fought and always won and this was a spot on which he had never thought to find himself. He said four dirty words, grabbed his hat, smoothing its curved edges, adjusting it carefully even in his rage.

Freddy merely looked sad, defeated. It was no good cursing Freddy or Lebella or anyone. Not even Sid November. He stalked down the street, automatically acknowledging the friendly greetings of the people he had known all his life, not knowing where he was going, wanting only to get away.

It was because of Fay. He had been carefree and invincible before Fay. He dimly perceived that he had been weakened by his love for the girl, by his desire for a normal life in another clime. So long as he stuck with what he knew, with these people who liked him and understood him—with Freddy—he was on safe ground.

He caught a cruising hack and went down Madison Avenue. He had to see Fay. It wouldn't do any good, his problem still would remain unsolved, but he could not do without seeing her.

It was still warm in the Las Vegas sunshine. Lebella wore a Hawaiian shirt loose about his lean middle, sitting back in a deck chair, watching the girls in the pool of the Falcon Hotel. Bogardus reclined beside him, smoking a fat Havana cigar. The new Falcon stretched before them and behind them, all tinted glass and redwood galleries and sloping tile roofs, four separate structures connected by breezeways, with a row of bungalows to boot, each one different in design but attuned to the symmetry of the whole. It was a triumph of architecture, everyone admitted; possibly a touch on the antiseptic side, but functional and good to look at. And the casino would pay off the mortgage in five years.

Lebella said, "You hear from Sophie?"

"Called this morning. Everything's fine. Marie's gonna have the baby tomorrow, next day."

"Well, it ain't your first grandchild."

"I started young," Bogardus said lazily. "So did Marie."

"She's a beautiful girl, your kid."

"Never gave me trouble. I got to give her credit. All the way through school, no trouble." He chuckled. "Y'know, she went to church, nice church in New Rochelle. Episcopalian. Like Sophie. Nice preacher, guy about our age. He had a daughter. What do you think?"

"She got knocked up," Lebella said.

"Yeah. By a sailor on leave." Bogardus frowned, not relishing Lebella's spoiling of his story. "You talk to November?"

"Not yet. Thought I'd wait till I saw you."

Bogardus puffed on his cigar, mollified. "I don't know what to say, Ossie, I really don't."

Lebella made a gesture with one languid hand. "You got something like this goin' for you, it's hard to think about things like that, ain't it?"

"It sure is. Here we sit, lookin' at forty million bucks' worth of legit gambling joint, and a piece of it ours. It ain't like the old days on the West Side."

"Even the taxes I don't mind," Lebella said. "Much."

"Wait'll they get more people in Nevada," Bogardus said. "Then we'll organize, all of us big investors. We'll get the taxes down. Not enough citizens now."

"The fix back home is bigger," Lebella admitted judiciously. "I guess we got no kick comin' on the tax."

"You know what?" Bogardus looked a trifle

shamefaced, but defiant. "Sometimes when I know the tax we're payin' I feel good. Like a real, you know, business guy, doin' his duty." He laughed self-consciously. "I'm talkin' like a mark, huh?"

Lebella rose to the occasion. "No, you ain't, Al. If I was to tell you the truth, I gotta admit I felt the same way myself."

They sat and contemplated their stations in life as good citizens. The sun dipped and a breeze came off the desert and Lebella frowned, feeling cheated. He enjoyed the sun biting into his thin arms. He said, "How you look at this business with this Galloway?"

"I know how we would both of looked at it some years ago," Bogardus said moodily.

"Don't never let Sid hear you talk like that," Lebella warned. "I got a little trouble with Sid in that direction."

"It's good there's one like Sid left. I admit we don't want that old stuff, we can't stand that heat from Washington, all that. But I'm glad we got one torpedo left."

"You got a point there. Now—what about Jack?"

"There is only one way to look at it about Jack," Bogardus said. "We give him our word. He cleans it up about Galloway, he gets what he wants."

Lebella sighed. "O.K. Check."

"It's our policy, Ossie," Bogardus said persuasively. "We done real good keepin' our word about stuff like that."

"Him and that Freddy. The way they walk around."

"I know, I know," Bogardus said. "But Jack's been a real good boy for us, lots of times. And we give our word."

"Sid would like to have him. Sid don't like bein' muscled."

"We got no guarantee Sid could take him," Bogardus argued. "Look what could happen. A real heat-up. And don't forget those cops. Cassidy and Kline."

Lebella waved a hand in defeat. "Yeah. He brought them in. I got to give Jack that."

"*Honest* cops," Bogardus said.

"Two fine boys. You know about Cassidy and the church?"

"He gives half of everything he takes from us to the priest," Bogardus said in awe. "It's on the level. Kline told me."

"Half! Imagine that! You got to give that boy credit."

"Jack gives them a lot, too. Him and Cassidy was kids together. You got to hand it to them for that."

Lebella said, "I'm glad you reminded me. It makes me feel better about Jack."

"We got nothin' to worry about," Bogardus said comfortably. "Sid will check on Galloway because he don't like him. He'll keep tabs on Jack for the same reason. We got two honest cops on our side. The Goulding thing was an accident like, anyway."

"That's right. Nobody wanted to hurt Sam. He was a good man, old Sam. I always liked him."

"Me, too, I liked him."

They nodded in unison, smiling benevolently, thinking about how much they had liked old Sam.

Then Crane said, "You seen that broad with Galloway? She was Sam's kid before he died."

"She was? I thought she was Moscow's secretary."

"Sure, only Sam was takin' care of her. Then she went with Moscow."

"That young broad? Sam and Moscow?"

"You can't never tell about broads."

"Now it's Galloway. She got a change there,

anyway."

"I been thinkin' about that one ever since I seen her with Galloway," Bogardus said. "It's been too long since I had a steady broad."

Lebella said, "You mean you broke up with Alice?"

"She went commercial on me," Bogardus said. "Asked me. Always askin'. Like I didn't give her enough."

"Maybe you didn't give her enough." Lebella snickered.

"That I know," Bogardus said ruefully. "And I didn't mind her gettin' it here and there, so long as she kept it quiet. But askin' for dough alla time, I couldn't take it."

"Well, if somethin' should have to happen to Galloway, you can mouse in," Lebella said. "She's cute, all right."

"Better than cute," Bogardus said soulfully. "A doll. A livin' doll."

The sun went out of sight altogether behind a purple, distant mountain. The two men rose and went inside, toward the bar, where a white-coated man lifted a cocktail shaker and agitated it to white frostiness. They were very happy men in late middle age, secure in their power, satisfied that all was well in a near-perfect world.

15

All through the poker game Steve hated believing that the pleasant man across the table was in any way venal. Besides Barr, there were Slidell, Freddy, and two sharpshooters whom Barr had brought along to make it more interesting. Steve's luck ran smoothly, and he was a large winner at midnight.

Barr lost over a thousand dollars. He played his cards right, never pushing them, coolheaded. But he lost pot after pot.

They were breaking up early by agreement. It had been a pleasant game and Steve suspected that the two sharpies were not high players. Freddy, ever the banker, began to cash in the chips.

Barr said suddenly, fingering the remainder of his stack, "Anyone for high card?"

Fred paused in his counting, staring up at Barr. The two strangers laughingly declined, but lingered to kibitz as Steve reached for his winnings and said, "Cut 'em, gambler."

Barr pushed five hundred into the center of Steve's table. Steve put a five chip beside them. Barr picked up the deck, shuffled it, gave it to Steve for a cut.

The deck lay with its edges tight. For one instant Barr hesitated, and Steve could see the pulse in his temple lift its beat, and he knew with the gamester's instinct what was in Barr's mind. Luck was a fickle lady, to be wooed by daring. Her devotees fear one thing more than any other, to be barely beaten with consistency. Barr was tempting her now, praying to her a little, asking forgiveness for an unknown trespass.

Barr touched the deck, lifted a portion, faced the card. It was the king of spades and his face lightened, again for only a brief instant, just long enough for Steve to perceive and recognize his hopefulness.

Then Steve flipped over the next card. It was the ace of hearts.

Freddy's breath hissed out like steam from a cold radiator. The sharpies murmured, shifting their feet.

"Try again?" Barr asked, almost begged.

"Double or nothing?"

Barr shook his head, grinning. "Not the sucker

trick. Just for another five cees."

Steve nodded. This time he did not need to watch; he could feel everything that Barr was feeling, know every sensation he was experiencing. He saw the square hand cut the cards, read the ten-spot of diamonds. He quickly selected his own card, knowing what it would be with sharp prescience, half sorry for his opponent.

Barr stared at the jack of clubs in Steve's hand and lifted his shoulders. He murmured, "Not my night, not my night at all."

"Topped him twice," said one of the strangers. He looked at Barr, shook his head. "Better lay off, Jack, for a while. Once it hit me and I was ten months winnin' a bet."

Barr did not answer. The two men drifted out and said good night to Steve at the door. When he returned to the den, Freddy had the new chips all stacked in the leather box and Barr was looking at the pictures on the wall, whistling under his breath, unperturbed.

"For a guy don't bet horses, you got strange artwork in here."

"They came with the place," Steve said. Freddy had put the clean, crisp bills that were his winnings in a neat pile. "Look, how about a bite to eat?"

"It's an idea," Barr said. "I'm starved. Might as well get something back from you."

Freddy said, "I'm for bed, Jack. We broke up early so we could sleep some."

"Taking a trip?" Steve asked. He could not imagine any other reason for retiring early in their circle.

"A little business," Barr said offhandedly. "Freddy is a great sleeper. Go on home, Freddy. Hit the pad."

Freddy arose, hesitated. Then he said, "Yeah. I'll

do that." He went to the door, turned, and said, "Don't take any wooden marbles." He stared at Barr for a moment, then left.

Steve produced salami, rye bread, butter, and a container of coleslaw. He put cheese and mustard on the table, and two bottles of cold beer. Barr sat slumped, watching with amusement. Steve laid out knives, forks, napkins, platters.

"Hey, you'd make somebody a good wife," Barr said.

"Never tried that. Did you?" Steve sat down and spread butter on the bread, added coleslaw. "I like it inside the sandwich. Strictly a New York trick I've learned from Mr. Cohen."

"I was raised with it," Barr said, picking up his knife. "Guess you missed American food while you were abroad."

"I'm adjustable," Steve said. "I was happy to get back to it."

"I did my service in Florida." Barr made a thick sandwich, surveyed it with pleasure. "AWUTC at Drew Field in Tampa. Mosquitoes, humidity, and rum with Coke. Strictly local dames with fat accents. Nothin', brother, nothin'!"

"No games?"

"Now, you know there were games," Barr said. "How did you make out?"

"Good."

"You always lucky?" Barr bit into his sandwich, making his question offhand.

Steve deliberately withheld his answer until he was certain that the man across the table was waiting with more than ordinary interest. Then he said slowly, "Like everybody. Sometimes I'm hot. You know."

"You get real hot, though. You got nothing particular going for you. No percentages, nothing like that."

Steve forbore to reveal his past connections with establishments in Hawaii and other places. "I got into this oil deal."

"But before that. You had to have a roll to promote the oil drilling."

"Oh, sure." Steve dismissed it lightly. "Have some more of that slaw. Cohen makes it with his own lily-white hands."

They ate and drank the beer and Steve brought out two more bottles. Barr lighted a cigar. He seemed in no hurry to leave. The beer was sharp and mellow at once and Steve was wide awake.

Barr said, "If you were going to stick around, there are lots of things going. You ought to have connections."

Steve shook his head. "I'm a loner. I like to play poker, bet a fight now and then, shoot a little dice. That's all." He looked hard at Barr. "How would connections help me?"

"Well, you know—the law, all that."

"And slobs like Sid November?"

"Well—I guess you're not worried about November much."

"Maybe I ought to be?"

Barr did not meet his eye. "He carries some weight. I had a little trouble getting players tonight."

"Oh?" Steve raised his eyebrows.

"The word gets around," Barr said. He seemed unhappy but determined to talk about it. "The high players are always careful, you know that. You and me together are marked dangerous."

After a moment Steve said, "I'll have trouble getting a play, then? What would you advise, Jack?"

"There's always Vegas, Reno." Barr laughed. "Miami is hot."

"You mean I should get out of town? You must be kidding!"

Barr shrugged. "It's none of my business. You and me sort of hit it off. I figure, you want a good play, you can get it better someplace else for now. In a few months you come back, it's all forgotten."

"You talk as if I did something bad," Steve said. "How come November swings so much weight? What about you and him?"

Barr said deliberately, "He's a fink. You saw how I handled him. I've got no use for the ground he walks on. But he carries weight. I'm thinking about taking a trip myself. Getting married, you know."

"I gathered as much," Steve said steadily. "You and Fay."

"That's right." Barr's voice softened. "She's a great gal. I want to take a long trip. Maybe a couple years. Rio—Paris—the works."

"Sounds nice." He sipped at his beer, his heart pounding at the thought of Fay gone, married to Barr. "I just got home, Jack. If I can't get a high game I'll still live a little. Hope you have a wonderful honeymoon."

"You ought to see Vegas," Barr said. There was the beginning of a desperate note in his voice. "Do you good. Wide open, all legit."

"Legitimate? I hear the syndicate controls most of it."

"So what? The percentages are good enough for the syndicate," Barr said sharply.

"Of course I don't know anything about that," Steve said. "What does he make with the syndicate?"

Barr tapped ashes into a tray. He looked at his wrist watch. "I couldn't tell you. I'm sort of a loner, too. And right now I better get some of that shut-eye Freddy was talking about."

He picked up his hat in the living room, stroked it with appreciative fingers, put it on with his customary care. He said, "Thanks for the use of the hall. If you want to go to Vegas or Reno I can give you some names."

"Thanks. I'll let you know," Steve said. "See you at the fights?"

"Oh, yes! I've got four ducats ringside. You want to bring that cool dame—what's her name? Butler?"

"Virginia? I don't know. Maybe," Steve said. "I'll bring someone. Dinner?"

"Great," Barr said. "See you before then. Good night, Steve."

When the door was closed, Steve sat in the low chair and stretched out his feet. Barr had been warning him to get out of town; there was no doubt of that whatsoever. Why?

Because of the Murphy thing, because of Sid November. Barr was in it up to his neck.

They were completely aware of Steve's angle, then. They knew that he was somehow connected with the Murphy business. Soon they would learn of his relationship to Sam Goulding; they seemed able to track down any information they desired. They already knew about Virginia, they had to know.

"They," he repeated aloud. "Who the hell are *they?*"

November and Barr and assorted thugs. Lebella and Bogardus and a couple of dozen like them from Chicago, Miami, St. Louis, Los Angeles, San Francisco, Boston, New Orleans. Who had given the order to kill Sam? Who had executed him?

So far it all pointed to November. Steve was too astute to believe, however, that any one man, on his own, struck down Sam on First Avenue. The drugging of Flaming Arrow was a syndicate trick to make a big score by bringing in a long shot. Legs Murphy had been in on it, and Legs was dead. Sam had learned of it and Sam was dead.

Mrs. Murphy could only have guessed something, and he had very nearly witnessed her death.

And Barr had warned him to get out of town. It was decent of Barr. But it put Barr right in there, with knowledge of events that Steve must have. Involving Barr, it involved Fay. If they were to get married and leave the country ...

He didn't want to think of that. But lying in bed he had a bad half hour when he could think of nothing else.

He was awakened by the insistent ringing of his door buzzer. He switched on the bed lamp and it was four o'clock. He flung the white burnoose about him and went sleepily to the door.

The night doorman was white-faced, supporting a swaying, bloody figure, saying, "He—he keeps calling your name, Mr. Galloway. I hope it's all right. The poor guy ..."

Steve leaped, taking Socker in his arms. He needed the doorman's help to get him to the bed, stretch out the heavy form. He shuddered at the sight of the broken features, the blood at the base of the brain, and said sharply, "Get that doctor downstairs. Quick!"

The doorman fled. Steve stood staring down at his friend. Both eyes were closed beneath lumps of swollen flesh. The lips were beaten to bloody pulp. The broken nose had been mashed flatter than ever. The serious injury was at the back of the skull, he realized, and knew then it was similar to the injuries that had been fatal to Sam and then to Mrs. Murphy.

There was a faint pulse. They had underestimated

the bull strength of the old fighter and his will to live, he hoped. He stood helplessly, his heart pounding, his fists clenching and unclenching, waiting for aid.

The doctor was named Chalmers, and he was alert despite the hour. He took one look at Socker and turned to Steve. "A hospital case, Mr. Galloway. Would you care to explain?"

"He came here for help. He's a friend. That's all I know," Steve said. He added on impulse, "However, I wish you'd go to work here and now."

"Of course. But this sort of beating must be reported to the police."

"Not if it would be dangerous for the patient," Steve said.

"Dangerous? You mean—he's believed to be dead?"

Steve nodded. "Please, Dr. Chalmers, attend to him. We can talk later."

It would give him time to think. He paced the floor while the doctor went to work. Socker had asked one question too many, of course. They had tried to kill him. Perhaps they had succeeded.

They would try again, too. Was a hospital safe? Others had been killed while lying on a hospital bed. He had to think of a way out, a way to keep Socker from them. He went to the telephone. He dialed Information and asked for a number in New Jersey. In a moment he had a sleepy Lieutenant Carraway on the wire.

He quickly related what had happened. He asked, "Could you handle it if I got him over there?"

After a moment Carraway said, "I can handle it. The expense will be considerable, Galloway."

"Spend what you have to," Steve said. "I'm coming over with him. Can you talk to my doctor here?"

"I can try," Carraway said. "This is pretty risky business."

Dr. Chalmers came into the room, drying his hands. Steve beckoned him to the telephone.

The doctor looked disturbed, then doubtful. Steve could hear Carraway's insistent voice. The doctor hung up and looked questioningly at Steve. "The Lieutenant said you would explain fully."

Steve took a deep breath. "Socker was undoubtedly investigating a crime in which we are interested and in which the police are not. Gangsters beat him up. To ensure his safety until he recovers, I want him over the river, in a private hospital."

"He has a bad concussion. He must have nursing twenty-four hours a day. Moving him means an ambulance."

"Doctor, you will be serving justice if you arrange for this," Steve said urgently. "I wish I could tell you the entire story. Socker's life will be in danger until I can settle this matter."

"It's very irregular." The doctor scowled.

"I know that. I'm asking you to take a chance. I'll gladly pay all expenses if you feel you should ride the ambulance until we get to the hospital—anything you say. But I want him out of New York, secretly."

Chalmers said reluctantly, "This is way out of my line. I'll expect you to have a doctor waiting in Jersey, every precaution taken. I'll ride over with you."

Steve was already doffing the burnoose, going for his clothing. "You'll never regret it, Dr. Chalmers. I'll fill you in on the ride. I know you'll agree we're doing the right thing."

He was lucky that the doctor was young, pliable, he thought. He could tell him enough to lull his fears. The main thing was to get Socker safely stowed away until he could recover. And talk, he thought, tell him who had beaten him.

There was no talk from Socker that night, not during the ghostly flight in a heavy fog through the tunnel and on to a small hospital, on the outskirts of Teaneck, not through the tender ministrations of the resident physician and Chalmers and two nurses, not through the hours past daylight while Carraway waited with him and admitted that he could learn nothing more of Mrs. Murphy's death and nothing new about Legs Murphy. Socker was in a coma.

When they had done all that was possible, Chalmers returned in the ambulance to New York and Steve repaired with Carraway to an all-night diner on the highway for coffee and conversation.

Carraway said, "He'll be safe here. I'll hire a man to watch."

"Hire a good man," Steve said. "And when he talks, try to be there. Call me no matter what time it is. If I'm not home, leave word at the switchboard of my apartment. Don't give your name. Leave a code message and I'll understand." He wrote down his private phone number and the apartment-house number.

Carraway said, "You think he got onto something?"

"I don't know. Maybe not. He was warned not even to ask questions," Steve said. "These people don't fool around."

"Puts you in kind of a spot," Carraway suggested. "Maybe I could take a leave of absence, move in with you for a while."

"Thanks. I'd rather have you on this end. I meant to buy a gun, but I forgot about it."

Carraway said, "You got a gun. No serial numbers. Picked it off a character last week. It's in the car." He shook his head. "Could I ever get in a jam, playing ball with you like this!"

"It would look bad. But how would you go after this thing? You know they'd laugh at me in any police headquarters."

"That's why I'm going along. I didn't like what they did to Mrs. Murphy, not at all. Now your pal."

"There was Sam, in the beginning. On First Avenue. The same deal, Carraway. A blunt weapon at the base of the skull."

"Yeah, you got a slugger. Two sluggers, I'd say. Hold 'em and hit 'em. No ballistics angle, nothing. Smart."

"Oh, they're smart." A thought struck Steve, and he started. "I wonder how smart." He was thinking of the two checks he had given Socker. Fifty thousand dollars. He had no way of learning whether Socker had spread the money around. He said, "I've got to get back to town."

Carraway said, "Don't you want to stick around today, see if he comes out of it?"

"I'll depend on you." He had to start learning things. He had scant idea where to start.

Carraway drove him to Newark and he took the tube, getting off at Hudson Terminal. He caught a taxicab there and went directly to the bank. His checks had been cashed.

He walked across town to Lou Moscow's office. Virginia stared at him, whispering, "Where were you? I called."

"Lunch," he said. "Meet me at Costello's." He went into the inner office.

The lean lawyer looked older, somehow, his face yellowish, his eyes dimmed behind the spectacles. He had papers for Steve to sign, and he was curtly businesslike.

Steve said, "I want a half million in cash spread

around in a few banks. And I want some information."

Moscow's back was to the window. He shaded his eyes with one hand and said disinterestedly, "All right. Just as you say."

"What exactly did Sam tell you the day he died?"

"That he had a lead on the Flaming Arrow deal. That he would call me again."

"Why should he tell you later—not at the time he called?"

"I've wondered that myself."

Steve said slowly, "Why don't you tell the truth, Lou?"

"If you think I'm lying, why trust me with your business? Why don't you get out, go to someone else?" Moscow's voice was flat, weary.

"I don't think you're scared to handle my business," Steve said contemptuously. "You're just scared of Sid November."

Moscow lowered his hand, looked scornfully across the desk. "Sid November is a nothing. Nobody is frightened of him."

"Of the men behind him, then."

Moscow sighed. "Ignorance is a wonderful thing, sometimes. Especially in the young. You come back here, all full of what you're going to do about Sam when it's too late to help him. You start tossing out money, trying to throw your weight around. You expect me to fall in with whatever your feeble brain schemes up, whatever wild scheme. You're a fool, Steve. A damned fool."

"And you're an old coward. All right, I won't argue." Steve reached for his hat. "See that the money is available."

He paused at Virginia's desk, jerked his head at the rear office, and said, "No help. See you at noon.

They got Socker."

"Dead?" She mouthed the word, wide-eyed.

He shook his head. He gestured and went out.

He found himself walking up Madison Avenue. He slowed his pace, debating with himself. Fay had known Lebella and Bogardus at the football game, therefore she had some knowledge of what went on. Would it be worthwhile to try to get some information from her?

He wanted to see her. It was stupid. Last night Barr had been definite about their wedding plans. So they were attracted to each other; Fay admitted that by implication at their every meeting. She was going to marry Barr.

He had to learn whether Socker had placed the bets, or had been robbed before he had the opportunity. He had no idea how to go about this. He had hoped for help from Lou Moscow, but that avenue was hopelessly closed. Fay could not help him there.

He made up his mind, hopped into a cab, and went over to Eighth Avenue and mounted the stairs of Stillman's Gym. He paid his admission and stood in the rear of the hall, orienting himself. The two rings were occupied despite the early hour.

He realized then that the colored boy buffeting his opponent with such savage satisfaction was Georgie Appleton. He moved closer, found a chair, and sat watching.

Appleton was a hooker, but he could throw a straight punch hard to the head. In close he arched his body and lowered his shoulder, driving his right glove upward under the heart. If the other man pulled back the same punch would find the chin or head. He seemed to take masochistic pleasure in the counterpunching of the boy against him, his bullet head darting to and fro like that of a cobra in action.

Appleton was ugly, smooth, and smart, he decided. His manager of record, a thin man in a gray jersey, conferred with him as the round ended and the colored boy laughed and nodded. A buzz went around the small crowd on the chairs, but no money was wagered as far as Steve could see. The wise guys were laying off, figuring it a cinch for Appleton, a build-up fight prior to throwing the champion to the tough Negro boy.

Appleton left and Sailor Hock came into the gym, followed by a ruddy man who must be Pat Paule, his manager from the West Coast. Steve sat quietly, watching the workout.

Hock looked good, but not too good. He went two rounds with each of four men and was scarcely breathing at the finish. Steve had seen enough by then.

Hock was under wraps. He had shown none of the stuff that Steve had seen against Socker. The bout was even enough.

Even, but no better, he decided. Well, Socker had said as much. Only the price was right and that was what counted.

He sought out Pat Paule, introduced himself. Hock was in the showers. Steve asked, "Do you know how much money Socker spread around?"

Pat Paule looked doubtful. "I don't think he got started. He didn't give me the office."

Steve bit his lip. Then he said, "Socker's badly hurt. I've got to take over."

Paule said in a low voice, "I know you were putting up the capital, Galloway. Anything I can do?"

"Don't try to get in touch with Socker. I'll give you money to bet for you and Hock, so we're sure you're taken care of. What I want is the name of every bookie you know, everywhere in the country. We've got to spread the lay or we'll lower the price."

Pat Paule said hesitantly, "I ain't guaranteeing we win, Galloway. You see Appleton?"

"I saw him. I only want to know Hock's right."

"Hock's right," growled a voice behind him. The Sailor had come in barefooted and was toweling himself, glaring at Steve. "I told you once. You put up dough, that's enough."

"Somebody else could put up more dough," Steve said calmly.

Before Hock could answer, Pat Paule said quietly, "Sailor's mean, Galloway. Real mean. But there ain't that much dough."

Steve wrote a check, handed it over. "Ten thousand. See that you bet it. Send me the slip, some proof."

"That's a cinch," Paule said, grinning. "I'll get you a list of the bookies right quick. Today."

Hock was staring at the slip of paper in Paule's hand. "Ten thousand? *Ten?* How much *you* layin' on it, Galloway?"

Steve looked into the small, hard eyes. "More than you ever dreamed of, Sailor. This is either a big score or a shutout."

He went out, leaving manager and fighter thoughtful and silent. He was working blindly, but he thought he had chosen the proper way to impress them. The less they knew from now on, the better. It was an even gamble as far as the fight went, but he could get four to one and he meant to get a lot of it before the price sagged.

He made it to Costello's, under the old Third Avenue El, at noon. Fay had brought him here and he had liked the solid Irish cooking, the busy but genial atmosphere, the phonies and the working newspapermen from Forty-second Street, the newsboys who wandered in and out, and the characters impossible to categorize. And he had at once loved the best of all possible barkeepers, Tim Costello. "Take a hangover to Tim and get absolution," they said, and it was the truth.

As he sat in a booth beneath the varnished Thurber whimsies on the wall he was suddenly aware of lack of sleep. He touched his unshaven chin and ordered a stinger as Virginia entered, looked hesitantly about. He got up and called to her. She was wearing the sweater in which he had first seen her.

She stared at him and asked, "Any word from Socker? Where is he? What happened?"

He told her, glad to be able to put it all together, beginning with Barr's warning and going through to his venture with Pat Paule. Her face reflected a dozen emotions.

She said, "Steve, this shows you're in danger. How did Socker get to your place? They may have dumped him there a warning. They may be after you next."

He tapped his chest. "I'm wearing a thirty-two automatic right now, courtesy of the Lieutenant."

"You think they'll give you a chance to use it? You've got to be careful, Steve. Real careful. You couldn't get anything out of Lou, could you?"

"Only criticism," he said bitterly.

"That's my fault," she said. "I tried to question him. He's no fool. He put you and me together. It made him furious. He's changed since you came back, Steve. He's—unhappy."

"He's scared."

She nodded. "I'm beginning to wonder about him. About him and Sam. And the syndicate. There's something wrong."

"He'll never talk," Steve said discouragedly.

"Now he's sore at us, that makes it even worse."

She brightened. "I can help you one way, Steve. I know a lot of bookies around the country. I was with Sam, you know."

"Start writing them down," he said promptly. "I'm using Socker's name, but he'd be known to those who were Sam's pals."

She was already making notes in a firm hand. She was using the back pages of Sam's little red notebook, he saw, and again his heart was wrenched by memories of the man who had saved him from a drab existence in an institution and had given him so many good things.

He said, "Talking of danger, what about you?"

She shook her head. "Not while I work for Lou."

"How can you be sure?"

She looked up at him. "I'm not sure. I just believe that. If it's not true, what are we going to do about it?"

He could not answer that. She couldn't very well move in with him. Or he with her. To hire protection was unwise and probably dangerous. Yet it stayed in his mind and worried him.

"I'm going to clip them if Hock wins," he said. "They can't be broken, but I'm going to make them hurt. Then we'll see."

She thought a moment, watching him sip his stinger. The waiter returned and they ordered the stew. She said, "What if Hock loses?"

"I never figure to lose." He would try something else, he knew. He would keep trying until something cracked open. "Socker warned me not to bet Barr until ringside. But I'm going to take a big bite at him there."

The stew was delicious and he found himself starved. He had another stinger with it and one atop it. Virginia did not take a drink. They sat a few moments and then she had to return to the office. He paid the tab and walked out on Third Avenue with her. He put the list of bookies in his pocket and said, "I'll call you later. If I can stay awake. I never was one for going without sleep."

"It's all right," she told him. "Call me when you can."

He watched her hips swing away from him and he wanted her, suddenly; he almost called to her. He made himself walk in the opposite direction.

He found himself on Madison Avenue, but now he did not want to talk with Fay. He had to go home and begin placing his bets and check on Socker and get some sleep and be careful not to drink anymore, because he was feeling it now and this was no time to allow anything to interfere with his efficiency.

He had a sudden picture of Socker's beaten face and the blood on him and his rage burned dangerously high, but he fought it down.

Play it cool, Galloway, he told himself, signaling a taxi. If you don't play it cool you'll wind up stone cold on a morgue slab.

16

The apartment seemed closed in, the walls too close, the air too well washed by the ventilating system. Steve called Miami and asked for a name provided by Pat Paule via messenger service and made his voice casual, placing a thousand-dollar bet that he represented as emanating from a group of long-shot players. He laughed with the pleased bookie and concluded, "I'm taking my commission, so what the hell?"

"Is there more of it?"

"Not enough," Steve said. "I'd handle it myself, but I'm top-heavy from other things. May get you another grand."

"Shoot it to me, pal. Any friend of Socker's ... Say, what's Sid November doin' about it?"

"Taking what he can get."

"Good man, Sid. Always got the dope."

"Yeah, fine," Steve said. He hung up.

He called again, this time to Los Angeles, using one of Virginia's names. He had placed over a hundred thousand dollars' worth of Hock money now, and it was four o'clock.

He found difficulty in laying a large bet. There was California money on Sailor Hock. The bookie was earnest. "You might be smart layin' it off, bud. Tell November, huh? I been meanin' to call him. This Sailor is no bum."

"I'll tell him," Steve said. "Thanks." He hung up. Only five hundred to the L.A. man. He put it on his list. Could be a bad thing if the West Coast was shut off. He tried Portland and it was better there. Hock had drawn with one of their tigers and they thought California was a crazy place anyway.

Pat Paule was no slouch. He had indubitably put a halter on Hock in Portland.

Chicago was great. He was able to get ten thousand spread around among the cocksure Midwesterners.

His buzzer sounded. He went to the door, opened it cautiously, fell back in astonishment.

Fay Fowler said, "I sneaked past the doorman. May I come in?"

She moved into the room and he thought of how often he had imagined her coming here, wanting to see him, and how it would be between them and how wonderful. He stammered, "Fay, this is great! Sit down. Have a brandy."

She accepted the brandy. He had shaved and was wearing the silk burnoose and sandals.

He said, "I'll change."

"It's all right. I can't stay long." She did not sniff the liquor. She drained it and he poured another, reinforcing his own glass, at a loss for words. She said, "Jack doesn't know I'm here."

"That's all right," Steve said inanely.

She looked at him over the rim of the glass. "We keep repeating that it's all right. It's not."

She sat gracefully, feet together, her face shadowed in the approaching twilight, the long planes of her body evident in a smooth-fitting gabardine suit over a severe white blouse that only accented her femininity. He could not take his gaze from her.

"You're going to be married," he said thickly.

"That's right." She regained her offhand pleasantness for a moment. "Am I to be congratulated? No—don't answer that."

"You're not in love with Jack?"

She set the glass down abruptly. "I was in love with him. I want to know if I love him now, enough to marry him."

"You—you think I have the answer?"

She arose and walked across the room. Her finely made body seemed to float upon the slender stems of her legs. He felt desire like a blow at his throat and struggled with it.

"I was strong, I thought I knew the answers. Everything was going to be fine," she said, half to herself. "He was going to get out and we were home free."

"Home free," he echoed. "Nobody's ever home free, is he?"

She wheeled to face him from the far end of the

room. "You know Jack's business. You're a gambler, too. Why can't he just cut loose from those people? Why can't he do as he promised me?"

"Well, there are angles," he said cautiously.

"You're not mixed up with Lebella and Bogardus and Sid November."

He shrugged. "I'm an outsider, a newcomer."

"If I knew more about it," she went on. "I don't know enough. Jack doesn't tell me. He just keeps saying we'll get out and be married and go to Rio and live happily ever after. He believes that. He's like a child repeating a fairy tale."

There was nothing to say. Steve folded himself in the voluminous robe, waiting. She walked toward him, paused, reseated herself in the low chair, lifted the brandy snifter nervously.

She said, "Yet he's no child, not in any way. How can a man, a strong man, allow himself to be tangled up with people like that?"

"Business," Steve said vaguely. He did not know what to say, truthfully. The strong appeal the woman had always exerted on him was never more evident. One more drink, he thought, and he would know what to do. He lifted the brandy, sternly refrained from drinking it. The acrid odor partially cleared his mind. "I don't know what to say to you, Fay."

She stared straight ahead. "You could tell me why you're here, in New York. Why Jack thinks he has to watch you, be afraid of what you may do."

"Jack thinks *what?*" He tried to sound amazed, unbelieving.

"They won't let him get free until he makes sure you won't cause trouble. What sort of trouble? What's it all about? How could you be involved when you've been abroad for eleven years? Who's lying to me, Steve? Who—and why?"

He said, "Now, wait a minute, Fay. Let's take it easy."

"I don't want to take it easy," she said passionately. "I want to get things settled. I've gone along for a year, running the shop, sleeping with Jack—" She broke off, shaking her head. "I didn't mean to tell you that. Not that you haven't guessed. I don't want you to think he bought me or anything like that. I loved him. I think I still love him." The words poured forth. "Only you came along and started to make a pass at me and—I was always able to laugh them off, feeling nothing. But I couldn't feel nothing about you. I can't quit on Jack, he needs me, but I want to *know*. Why can't you let me know? Am I a child, a moron? How can I go away with a man, bear children, without knowing?"

He was shaken by her nearness to hysteria. He said, "Fay, what can I tell you? This must be tough for you. I'm sorry."

Instinctively he went to her, patting her shoulder. She flinched away for a brief moment, then rose so that she faced him. In the half-light her face was pale; her eyes shone like candles in darkness.

"I've got to know," she half moaned. Her arms went about him, tight. Her hands clawed, digging through the thin silk of the burnoose.

He felt her lips against his, and everything in him responded to this girl he had desired on sight. His arm circled her waist, lifting her bringing her close. Breathless, she turned her face, whispered, "Tell me, Steve. Tell me what it is, the trouble, how it will come out. I'm frightened. I'm so scared!"

She moved against him, half willing, twisting her hips. She stared into his eyes.

She asked, "What is it to be? Tell me, Steve!"

He read honesty in her and indecision and

sincerity of purpose. He had a blinding instant of recognition of her as a tortured woman, coming to him for surcease. He could imagine Jack temporizing, unwilling to tell the whole truth, yet trying to ease his own discomfort by half confidences better left unshared.

She felt the change in him. She relaxed, standing loosely in his arms. "You can't share it, either, can you? I'm to be closed out."

He found his voice. "I wish I could tell you, Fay. I wish I could do lots of things. Right now, it had better go as it stands."

She stepped back, smiling ruefully, struggling successfully for control. "You're not any help, are you?"

He understood her. "Not much, I'm afraid. Let me say this: I've a good reason for being here, doing what I am doing. If Jack is worried, it's because of the people he does business with. I'm not hounding Jack."

She was adjusting her jacket. Her grace of movement made it a gesture in which there was nothing gauche. Her smile became steady. She said, "I'll take another brandy now. Better now than five minutes ago, I might add."

He poured into both glasses. "Yes. You're right. It wouldn't have been any good. Not with you and me."

She lifted the brandy. "To our purity."

He scowled at her. "No. I won't believe it's funny. Damn it, some things aren't funny."

"It's safer to believe that they are," she said sweetly. "I came here to test us out, you know."

If she wanted it that way, he thought, there was nothing he could do but play it straight. He tried once more. "Fay, I was ready to fall in love with you. Maybe I am in love with you."

"But Jack is your friend? You're going to tell me that?"

"I'm not going to tell you any such ridiculous thing," he said angrily. "You came here because you were worried about you and Jack and about me. I couldn't take advantage of it."

"Take advantage?" She was punishing him now. She sipped the brandy. "Are all you big, brave gamblers alike? All juveniles?"

He held tight to his temper. He caught a glance from her, tried to catch her gaze, failed. Either the brandy or his heightened senses whispered to him that she needed an out, that she had to seem the sophisticated lady or again break down.

"I guess you're right." He hoped he sounded rueful, attempting to match her mood. "Idiots unable to face facts."

"No one could have treated me better than Jack. If only he would come clean, all the way. And now—you won't tell me."

"I can't, Fay. There's nothing to tell." He hesitated, then ventured, "Probably it has something to do with Sid November."

"Jack always handled him. With contempt."

"That's all I know. November doesn't like me. Those two men—Lebella and Bogardus. They have something to do with it, don't they?"

"Of course."

He almost asked her then. He almost mentioned Flaming Arrow and Sam Goulding. Instantly he knew it would be a mistake. She would question Jack, as she had tried to question him. He had no way of knowing how this would affect Jack, because he had no idea that Jack even knew Sam. Jack was a high gambler and hooked in with the syndicate, but was he a murderer?

He said, "Well, that's Jack's business. I wish I could help. Can I take you to dinner, Fay?"

"No thanks." She finished the brandy. "I'll go along now. I'm meeting Jack later." At the door she hesitated, then looked directly at him. "Thanks, Steve. Thanks for everything."

She was gone. He put his back against the door and wiped one hand across his chest. It had been close, too close.

Yet, he wondered, had it really? The telephone rang. It's Virginia, he thought. It must be Virginia. I hope it is. If it isn't, I'll call her!

It was St. Louis, and he put up eighty-five hundred dollars on Sailor Hock.

Then he called Virginia. The wire was busy.

He tried the hospital near Teaneck. Socker's condition was unchanged, they understood about Mr. Galloway, they would let him talk to the special male nurse. A rough man's voice assured him that Socker was still unconscious and that a watch was being maintained.

He dialed Virginia's number. She answered and he said, "How about dinner?"

"I'll be ready in half an hour," she promised. "Any news?"

"I'll save it." He hung up, shaking his head. He would not tell her about Fay. It would serve no purpose. He went into the bedroom and began to dress. He looked at the smooth, unrumpled bed and wondered at himself.

He had wanted Fay as much as he had ever wanted a woman. He had invested her with delights that probably did not exist. Why hadn't he taken her?

Was it because in doing so he would have felt that he must take her into his confidence? Because she could never be, to him, a casual conquest, but always a precious being set apart from others? Was it because of some squeamish scruple about Jack Barr?

He shook his head at his reflection in the mirror, tying one of the expensive ties he had bought from Edgar. He had no measuring stick to apply to his conduct. He was slightly bewildered, but he felt that he had acted according to a sixth sense. Without volition, he told himself wryly, he behaved better.

Downstairs he caught Sol Mintz at the cab stand and for once the little man was without caustic comment. Part way downtown a red light stopped them and Sol said, "You got no call to be sore on me."

"I'm not," Steve said. "You're in the clear."

"What about that business in Jersey? That old lady? The cops?"

"Let me worry about that."

"You are using another hack?"

"No, Sol. I'm not using another hack."

The light changed. Sol drove a while silently hunched over the wheel. There was the drone of late traffic, the rumble of the subways always in the air, the whistle of a traffic policeman. Steve said, "You were right about the noise. It's always with us."

"So it's noisy."

Sol's feelings were undoubtedly hurt. Steve was amused, then a bit concerned. They went through Washington Arch and made the stop on Sullivan Street and he selected a five-dollar bill from his clip. He leaned forward and extended it to Sol. "Buy a house. Buy a brick house on account of they last longer than a wooden house."

Sol did not accept the money at first. "This where your broad lives? You ain't takin' her out? I couldn't wait?"

"I thought you didn't like to wait."

"O.K., O.K., I said it. But for you I'll wait."

Steve put the money back into the clip. "All right. Wait."

It was quite dark now. He went quickly across the sidewalk and up the steps and into the vestibule of the house.

He was aware of two things at once. He had forgotten his pistol. There were two big men in the darkness of the vestibule.

Even as he struck out they pinned him, one on each side. They were strong and practiced. He kicked out and they managed his legs, lifting him off balance, tying him in close. A blow across the mouth stung and rendered him speechless.

He did not quit. He was thinking of Virginia now. If they had been upstairs ... He lashed out his left leg and caught a shin with his heel.

A slicing judo cut nailed him at the nape of the neck. That was the spot where the blunt instrument landed, he remembered. He tried to twist away, but one of them managed a hammer lock, bending him forward with a grasp upon his left wrist and elbow. He knew better than to fight it, the way the big man exerted pressure.

A hoarse whisper began in his ear. "Wise guy, this is a warnin'. Just a warnin', to letcha know we can take you or the broad any time we get ready. We got word for you. Take a trip. Take a long trip. Don't hurry, you got a little time, nobody's worried about you. But get the broad steamed, get outa town. Her too. You got maybe two weeks, the boss says. Maybe not, if you keep nosin' around. Now go outside and tell that cab not to wait, understand? Tell him you changed your mind."

They loosed him. He started to swing, but stopped, knowing there wasn't room in the vestibule to fight men of this bulk. He tried to see their faces, but they wore felt hats with pulled-down brims and they kept cannily in the shadow. He remembered now that there was usually a small bulb burning, realized that they had turned it out. He pulled himself erect, his head spinning, his arm aching sharply.

He went to the door, opened it. He could run now, but where to? It meant leaving Virginia upstairs and the two thugs downstairs. He said, "Cabby! Come up here, will you?"

Sol came up the steps, squinting, trying to see past him. Steve moved to let the corner street lamp hit him, hoping he was disheveled in such a manner that Sol would take note. He said in a voice louder than his natural accents, "Here's your fare, cabby. I've changed my mind, you needn't wait."

For an instant he feared that Sol would not understand, then the little man took the five and made careful change. He pretended to return a small tip, slipped the four bills into Sol's hand.

Sol turned, muttered, "G'night," and went back to the cab. Steve went back into the vestibule.

The hoarse voice said, "Done like a little man. O.K., Galloway, you've had your warnin'. Go have your fun."

Steve said, "No use asking you who sent you? Or why?"

"Listen at him," gurgled the whisperer. The other man had not uttered a sound. Nothing could be seen of them but their bulk and spread of shoulder. "He don't know who sent us. He don't know nothin'. Galloway, you better keep it that way. Just don't know nothin'. Go ahead up, we'll wait."

He had to ring Virginia's bell, open the door on the release button, go inside. The moment he had closed himself in they drifted out onto the steps and were gone from view.

No use to follow, he knew; they were taking every precaution that he should never recognize them. The only chance was that Sol had thought it through and was circling the block, and this was something it was best not to learn now. He went up the stairs, cursing himself for a careless fool.

Not that the gun would have been any use. They had him too quickly to allow anything like that. But he should not have walked into a dark place unprepared. He was not hardened to the battle. It was difficult for him to believe it could happen here, in New York. Abroad he would have accepted it, moved with the care he had learned in dangerous places. Here at home he allowed himself to be taken like any greenhorn.

He went into Virginia's apartment and she stared at him. "You're white as a sheet, Steve. What happened?"

He had to tell her, for her own protection. Her lips closed firmly and she heard him through, one foot tapping the floor. She cried, "I wish I'd known!"

He had found her whisky. He gulped a big slug and smiled at her. "What would you have done, tiger woman?"

She turned and with amazing speed she had opened a drawer of a wall secretary. She spun, a .32 revolver in her hand. She said tightly, "I can use it, too. Sam taught me."

He went to her, taking her hands, removing the revolver from her grasp, putting it away. He said, "Why, you would, wouldn't you?"

"If they ever try that again I'll kill them!" She did not wilt in his arms. She stared up at him. "I have trouble sleeping. Sam, Mrs. Murphy, Socker—they haunt me. If I killed those men I could sleep again."

"I believe you," he said. He did believe her and it shocked him. At the same time he felt a small thrill, as when a brave deed is performed, or a parade marches by.

"You feel the same way."

"Yes," he said. He shook with anger. "Do you think I should call in the cops, Virginia?"

"They'd be picked up, if they were real unlucky, for simple assault." She shook her head. "No police yet, Steve. Later, maybe."

He kissed her and she clung to him with such fierceness that he almost forgot Sol, dinner, everything. He managed to say, "Let's go out first, darling."

She pulled away, staring at him. "You called me darling. That's the first time you ever did, Steve."

He batted his eyes foolishly. "You are a darling. You're the greatest. You're a whole hell of a lot of wonderful things."

She grabbed for a hat and pulled him toward the door. "Now we've got to get out of here fast if we're going to eat. And I'm starved."

Sol was waiting two doors away. They got into the cab and he jerked away from the curb like a racing driver. Steve said, "Hey, what's the idea?"

"I seen them mugs," Sol hurled back.

"O.K., take it easy. They're not hanging around for me to see them."

"They're scared of you? Ha!" Sol turned a corner, looked fearfully behind him, skidded onto Fourteenth Street. After a block of watching, he slowed down.

Virginia said, "Let's eat at Luchow's."

Steve gave Sol another five. "It wasn't the two we saw at Harry's, I know that."

"Them punks!"

"You'd know if you saw this pair again?"

Sol looked gloomily straight ahead. "I should get into a shmear like this. Yeah, I'd know 'em. Gorillas from 'way back."

"You've seen them before?"

"Plenty like them." He fiddled with the gearshift, his hands shaking. "In court I'd never say I knew them. You ask me, O.K."

"If you ever see them again, call me," Steve said. It was hopeless, of course. The worst part of it was that now he knew that no two particular killers were used by the syndicate. The beatings, the use of the blackjack at the base of the skull, these were merely their version of the ice pick utilized by Murder, Inc. Their trademark.

He took Virginia's arm and they entered Luchow's to the strains of "The Blue Danube." It seemed to him that the string quartet had been there forever and all the waiters were familiar and the smells of the dark, heavy furniture and the customers slowly consuming great quantities of potato pancakes and sausages and the gravied specialties of the house. They took a small table in the outer room, next to the men's bar, and Virginia's seriousness matched his.

After they had ordered he said, "It's getting close to a finish. They ordered me out of town. They also ordered you out with me."

She nodded. "It has to be that way."

"I'm scared, Virginia."

"I'm scared, too. They could have had me tonight as easily as they took you."

He nodded. The waiter brought tall shells of Pilsener beer, pale and delicate. He was thirsty and his head ached. "They'll do it next time. They know about you and me."

She tasted the beer, nodded, took a deep draught. "I'll quit tomorrow. I can move out in an hour."

"I hoped you'd do that. What about Lou?"

Her face darkened. "Lou's been making cracks about you. He's so nervous he jitters. I can't get anything out of him, so there's no use staying around him."

"Where will you go?"

She smiled. "Not far from you. You don't think I'd leave you with the sack, do you?"

He looked at her, fumbling with his napkin. "My place?"

"Why, Mr. Galloway!" She laughed aloud at his embarrassment. "That was a great invitation to the dance, wasn't it?"

"Nuts," he muttered. Twice in one day, he thought. What the hell is the matter with me? How did I get mixed up with two women who are able to make me feel like a damned schoolboy?

"When I leave Moscow they're going to start looking for me, just in case," she was saying. "They'll check the planes, probably. Maybe I ought to take one—say, to Puerto Rico."

"Puerto Rico?"

"They're not likely to check through. It's a chance we could take. I don't mind a round trip. I think I might come back a señorita."

"Now wait, let's not get theatrical," Steve said impatiently. "You quit Moscow, you move into my place at night. Don't answer the phone, stay out of sight. It won't be for long. Puerto Rico!"

She said meekly, "I was just thinking out loud, Steve."

"Pack a bag tonight," he said with sudden inspiration. "They'll think we're scared and that you ducked town."

She finished her beer with gusto. "All right. If you say so." She assumed a demure smirk. "Will I be safe with you, Steve? You know what I mean—safe?"

"No!"

"Then let's hurry."

17

In the second-floor conference room of the Uptown Political Club it was hot and the air was fetid with cigar smoke. Jack Barr fidgeted, staring across at Sid November.

Freddy was behind him, watchful, and Freddy was carrying heat tonight, under his arm and in his hip pocket. The slim, dandified friend of his youth would use it, too, if he had to. November was flanked by Slide Gabrowski and Horse Koenig, but Freddy could handle muscle men every day in the week and twice on Sunday.

November said, "Don't be a sucker all your life, Jack. Your dame went up there and spent over an hour with him. He's got to go."

Barr said, "If she went up there it was for a reason. You wouldn't know about that. No use trying to explain to you."

"Whatever." November shrugged. "Am I saying anything wrong? I'm just telling you. I talked to Vegas. Galloway has got to go."

"All right," Barr said. "What about it?"

"You know the deal. We're giving him some time. Like Ossie says, we don't want trouble. If he don't blow town, you've got to set him up."

Freddy spoke from the background. "You crumb, are you giving orders again?"

The heavy-set muscle men moved, looking hard at Freddy, then at November. November motioned them to subside and said, "I tell you I talked to Vegas."

Barr said, "So you tried to scare him? I've got

news for you. Galloway won't scare much."

"We figured that."

"I can talk to him." He had already tried. He
knew it was no use. The strange reluctance to go
against Steve rose in him. "I'll talk to Vegas myself. It
wasn't smart to muscle him."

Gabrowski laughed hoarsely. "He took it real
good, though. Real good!"

"He would. He's smart," Barr snapped. "Maybe
you should have finished him. If he ever catches up
with you he might get even."

November shook his head wonderingly. "I don't
get it. How come this guy is such a hero? Because he
busted you a few inna gym? Because he beats you out
of a few bucks? What's so great with this character?
Slide and Horse didn't have no trouble with him."

"Put it down I've got a hunch," Barr said.

"That kinda hunch'll get you nowhere,"
November warned. "Look, Jack, I'm tryin' to be a
pal. We had our differences, O.K. This is big. You
know what's happened to other organizations when
something was turned up on them. It costs. It costs
plenty, and some poor guys hadda fry, too.
Remember Lepke? Whoever thought they'd get
Lepke?"

"All right, Sid. *All right*." He got up from the
table. He was linked with it and he couldn't squirm
loose. He knew why he envied Steve now. Steve had
what he wanted, freedom. Steve was loaded and he
owed nothing to Ossie Lebella nor Al Bogardus or
any of the overlords of any syndicate. With the
acknowledged envy came the first twinge of
resentment. Steve had it all and Fay recognized it and
went up to see him, to talk things over.

He motioned Freddy to the door. He looked back
at November and said, "I don't like any part of it. I

never did like it. You know that. I'll talk to Vegas and see you around."

He left the room. November wiped sweat from his brow. He waddled to the door, waited until he heard the sound of Barr's Cadillac pulling away. He returned and reseated himself. His kerchief was soaking wet.

He muttered, "If he knew the whole score ... But I can't tell him about Socker. Where the hell they got Socker?"

"Geez, Sid, everybody's been lookin' for him. You know how he hauls off and takes trips where the nags are runnin'. People think he just went on a vacation. He ain't in a New York hospital."

November glared at him. "You know what? I'm just liable to get rid of you crumbs. You blew it with Socker and you blew it bad."

Gabrowski's face twisted as though he would weep. "Geez, Sid, you wouldn't, would you? We're your boys, Sid, remember that. Where you gonna get somebody like us? Geez, Sid, we're takin' chances too."

Horse Koenig's voice was a high whinny. "We take care of things for you, Sid, you know that. We do just like you say."

Plenty they had done for him, and without the knowledge of Lebella or Bogardus. He had been able to maintain his position through them. If he dared, he would have put them on Barr, but there was always Freddy with his rods, and if they weren't smart enough to know it, he knew it, and he knew the danger of starting civil war in the organization. Now that he had banished Charlie Goode they were his only standbys, but he did not mean to let them know it.

He said, "If Socker turns up alive, you're dead.

That's all I got to say."

"Geez," wheezed Gabrowski. "How could he live? We give him the business, like always. Nobody else never lived."

Horse whined, "If we hadda leave town we'd miss the fight."

"Yeah, geez, Sid. And I got a broad over in Brooklyn, I couldn't trust her with a snake."

"I wanna see the fight," Horse moaned.

November sighed. It was hard to manage, sometimes. The Goulding matter was too close to home. Legs and the old lady were Jersey cases and he never went across the river. He had taken both killings upon himself and so far it was all right. If Socker had turned up a corpse, that would have been all right, too. Nobody cared about a broken-down dead fighter, a horse player to boot. Even if Galloway were to die, who would complain? It was all in knowing who had connections, he thought, watching the two big men, enjoying their trepidation, letting them sweat it out.

The broad, too, she could be handled. A few jabs in the veins, where the junk really gets them, a few months, maybe only weeks, and she'd be hooked. That would be no trouble. Galloway had no family.

Moscow? No problem. Never any problem with Moscow. Old men always cling to life at any cost.

It had to be clean when he made his move. If Barr could be set up at the same time, so much the better. But it would have to look as if Galloway killed Barr or something like that, because the mains would be sore, and there were Cassidy and Kline. That was it again, Barr had connections.

Barr had to go, some way, somehow. He remembered the blows he had taken and again reached for his handkerchief. He was ill every time he thought of it. Oh, yes, a year, ten years, Barr had to go. Even if he got out, if they let him quit, there would come a time. He had to see Barr get it. He would never be a whole man again until he saw Barr getting it.

"The treatment," they called it. He had originated it and even the mains had admitted it was good. The beating, the mace to cave in the skull, it was all his. Cleaner than ice picks, and better. It was what everybody hated, a beating. Then death.

He growled at his companions, "You got everything covered?"

"We got guys working, they don't even know what they're doin'," Gabrowski said quickly, eagerly. "We got private eyes hired, they don't know who they're workin' for. Everything is like you say."

"You're sure Galloway didn't spot you?"

Gabrowski said, "Sid! You know how we work. You know how it is. We didn't even take a cab, in case he should holler cop. We *walked* away!"

November grunted. "O.K. Stick around. You know where to call me."

"You goin' undercover, Sid?"

"While we wait for Galloway to move."

"He couldn't prove nothin'. He asked who sent us, the dumb cluck."

November said, "Face it, he's a sharpie. He sees me, he asks a lot of questions. Barr's got to work on him. He don't know from Barr. He thinks Barr is his chum. When we know something I'll be showing around."

"You ain't going to miss the fight?" Horse was horrified.

November asked querulously, "Is that all you ever think about, that fight?"

"I got four cees bet around," Horse said. "I like to

see Georgie shellac 'em. Georgie beats up on 'em good."

November nodded. "I got to get some action on the fight. Out in the sticks. California, where the suckers grow."

"I hear there's Midwest money," Horse said. "Here and there, like you say. Long-shot players."

"All right, blow," November said. "You know where to get me. Same place." Not even Lebella and Bogardus knew about this spot, he added to himself. He would have to leave an indirect trail so that they could reach him after Barr checked in with them. He watched the two muscle men go out, pondering, testing every thread of his weblike schemes. He was reaching pretty far, but he had a bridge behind him, to South America, if things went wrong. He chuckled. Barr had put that idea in his head. He wondered if Rio de Janeiro was big enough for both Barr and Sid November.

The Cadillac moved slowly through the uptown traffic, Freddy silent at the wheel, Barr slumped beside him, looking straight ahead through the windshield. A red light caught them and Freddy stirred.

He said, "What do you think Fay told Galloway?"

"She couldn't tell him anything," Barr said listlessly. "She doesn't know anything."

"Then why did she go up there?"

"I don't know. I don't care. They're friends. He buys stuff from her. Maybe she delivered a package and had a drink."

"Could be." Freddy nodded. "She's on the level, all right. That's not what's worrying me."

"You worry too much."

Freddy let the car drift ahead on the green. He

said, "Look, Jack, I got to worry. It ain't right, the way it's going. You can call Vegas all you want, things are still screwed up."

"I know." His voice sounded dull, even to himself.

"You got to snap out of it," Freddy said. He was coaxing now, deadly serious. "You're letting Sid take the play away. You never went for anything like that before."

"I'll handle him when I have to."

"You know better than that. You got to get off first, stick him, keep him off balance. Maybe you got to k.o. him."

Barr said, "I want out, that's all I want. When the Galloway thing blows over, I'll be through with it."

Freddy beat a clenched fist on the wheel. "I tell you it can't be that way. Things don't blow over. Lebella and Bogardus have given Sid the word. Galloway has got to go."

"You want me to knock him off? Have you gone crazy, Freddy?"

"Certainly not!" Freddy's voice pounded at him. "But there are ways of taking care of him, making him sick of New York. He's smart, but I can rig a game so he won't know what hit him. You can turn Fay against him."

Barr cut in. "But why? Why all the fuss? Just because they think he's connected with Legs Murphy in some way ..."

"Jack, I gotta tell you. Since that guy has been around you been goofing." Freddy had lowered his voice now. He had never been more earnest, Barr realized. "Even Sid sees it. Galloway topped you. Don't interrupt, Jack, listen to me. He topped you that first day, in Socker's gym. He topped you since. I never saw anything like the way he outcarded you the other night. It's uncanny. I know how you feel.

Another thing—Fay never even looked at another guy
until he came along."

"Never mind Fay."

Freddy waved as though brushing away an insect.
"I know Fay's not a cheater. Not that. Just that she
likes the guy, likes to be with him. She never talked to
me like she does him, and she knows I'm her pal, I've
always been on her side. It's not Fay. It's him. He's
poison for you, Jack."

There was no reply short of stupidity. Galloway
was poison to him, any way you looked at it. Freddy
was right. Fay was right, too. Fay was seldom wrong.
Steve was a good guy, he was tough, he was friendly
and warm and you had to respect him, as Fay did.

He was beginning to feel the heat, the big heat. He
said, "He's going to the fights with us. I think I'll lay
off until then. I got to admit you're right, Freddy."

Freddy sighed with vast relief. "As long as you
admit it, we got nothing to worry about. You and me,
kid, if you'll let me operate, we can top anybody. First
Galloway, then Sid November!"

"After Galloway I get out," Barr said stubbornly.
"We run him out of town—that's all."

Freddy hesitated, then said slowly, "I got to tell
you something, Jack. You remember when you told
me Galloway played football at Trinity College?"

"Sure. What of it?" He knew what of it. He knew
what Freddy had done; he had checked through,
which Barr had failed to do.

"There's several Trinity colleges. I contacted them
all. He played football, all right. No scholarship stuff,
he was loaded, he had an angel sent him through."

"Nice for him."

"Yeah, it was a nice guy did it for him. Sam
Goulding."

Barr slid down until the back of his head hit the

leather upholstery of the seat. "That does it, then."

"Lebella and Bogardus and November are right. We're wrong."

"Not you. Only me," Barr said. The last prop had been taken from under him. He could no longer defend Steve.

Freddy said, "We'll be doing him a favor if we shake him down. Maybe we can frame a small thing on him and put him on the lam. Better that way. Sid wouldn't do it that way."

"Right," Barr said.

He felt worn out with it all. He wanted to see Fay. Would she tell him about visiting Steve? He would never ask. He couldn't ask, let her know she had been watched, allow the slightest suspicion that he had caused the surveillance. He couldn't let anything like that come up between them.

Freddy said, "After the fights, then? Maybe start it that night?"

"Yeah. I'll be thinking. You've got it about right. We'll have it ready at the fights."

Freddy said happily, "You're a great kid, you know it? I thought you might be sore at me. Checking on Galloway and all."

"You're my right eye, is all, pal."

His head hurt. He wondered what had become of Socker. The gym was closed and there was no note on the door. Socker usually told everyone when he was going to make a trip around the race tracks.

He had some collections to pick up from the numbers boys and the madams of the uptown houses. He had to clear a new peddler for the junk setup, a thing he had always despised, but without which he could not control his territory. He had to see Fay later and he could not prevent his mind from whirling in a circle.

18

At noon, in his office, Lou Moscow crouched behind his desk and stared at the girl who stood facing him. He tried to speak, produced a croak, swallowed, and began again. "But why? I can't get it through my head why."

Virginia said coolly, "I'm leaving town. I want a change."

"Where are you going, my dear? You can't just go off like that."

"I'm not telling anyone where I'm going."

"You must tell me! I'm practically your guardian!"

She seized upon the fallacious statement with unerring accuracy. "Lou, you're a lawyer. You know very well you're not my guardian. You have no right to question my coming or going."

"No right?" He spread his hands imploringly. "I've the right of an old man who loves you and fears for you, Virginia."

"And interferes with my life." She wondered if by goading him she might learn something useful.

He sat bolt upright, a slight flush spotting his pallid cheeks. "Galloway! He's turned you against me!"

"Oh, my sainted uncle!" she said.

"Nothing but trouble since he came home. You're different—everything's different. Digging up that business about poor Sam ..."

She broke in. "I don't get it, Lou. You were all hot against Steve for not doing anything about Sam. Now he's a heavy for looking into it. Why don't you tell Steve what you really know?"

"I know nothing!" He was becoming flustered and

angry. "I only know that if you leave me, you're ungrateful. I need you. You know I need you. My affairs need attention from someone I can trust."

"You can't trust me," she said. "I want to know the truth about Sam."

He drew a deep breath, spreading his hands on the desk. He sat a long time, his head down. Then without looking up at her he said, "I'm sorry, Virginia. I've tried. I've done what I thought best. I do love you. God bless you."

She waited, but he did not lift his head. She went quietly out and took her few possessions from her desk. She packed them in a small bag she had brought for the purpose and quickly hid them in a filing cabinet drawer that was never used.

She hesitated, then left the office and rode down in the elevator and mingled with the crowd going to lunch. She walked to Fifth Avenue, moving without haste. She turned north, looking into show windows, trying to learn if anyone was following her.

She crossed the street with the light, timing it so that she was the last pedestrian to reach the curb at Forty-fourth. She went swiftly into the Guaranty Trust Company's entrance on Fifth, walked straight through and out the side door, onto Forty-fourth.

She crossed the street and ran toward Sixth. In front of the Harvard Club she caught a taxicab, headed east on the one-way street. She sank back into the cushions and told him to take her to Grand Central Terminal, reversing her tracks.

She got out on Vanderbilt and ducked into the station. She went to the pay locker she and Steve had rented last night over his objections and removed a bundle and took it into the ladies' rest room.

She was having fun now. There was a big streak of ham in her, she thought, hitherto unrevealed. She unlocked and entered a pay toilet. She daubed dark pancake make-up on her face, neck, and hands. She tied a cheap, gaudy kerchief from a chain drugstore around her hair, binding it up. She donned horn-rimmed spectacles, altered her lipstick, thickening the line, spreading it. She applied false eyelashes and rouged her cheeks.

She took off her high-heeled slippers and slipped on a pair of black ballet slippers. The final touch, however, was her favorite. She donned a white maid's apron, tying it about her slim waist. She put away her compact and mirror, stowed her shoes and the other articles in a shopping bag of colored string.

She let herself out and a couple of women glanced at her and one asked petulantly, "Are you the maid? I need some change."

Virginia rolled her eyes and drawled, "Yes, ma'am." She went out of the rest room carrying her bag and walked out the Forty-second Street exit and caught a taxi and rode to Sixth and Fifty-seventh. She got out there and minced toward Central Park South.

The doorman to Steve's apartment regarded her suspiciously, but was taken in by the apron, as she had expected. She sauntered through the servants' entrance, then cut quickly for the service elevator before the woman in charge of the cleaning force should intercept her.

She rang Steve's buzzer, and when he opened the door and stared inquiringly at her she crowed with delight. He dragged her inside and slammed the door and she paraded for him, taking little short steps that completely disguised her gait, swinging the bag, taunting him with his objections of the night before.

She ended, "And there was a man at Forty-fourth and Fifth who was staring around and I know he was following me. There's another man across the street now with a newspaper. He's got one eye on this building."

"I've already checked him," Steve said. "I admit you were right, darling. The getup is terrific."

She twitched her bottom at him. "Want to corrupt the poor serving maid? Just like the old melodramas!"

He grabbed her and hauled her down on the divan alongside him and dabbed at the heavy lipstick with his handkerchief. He said, "I like the other dame better."

"You're no fun," she complained.

He kissed her hard and she subsided, sighing contentedly. He said, "We're going to get into bad habits."

"What are bad habits?"

"Any kind," he said.

"You're not very smart sometimes," she told him.

"I got another hundred thousand bet around," he crowed. "The worst I got was three to one. That's almost a quarter million."

"All that money on a fight!" The idea sobered her. "Suppose we lose?"

"Suppose we get a little careless and they knock us off?" He shrugged. "All I know how to do is stir them up. When I begin taking their ringside bets they'll know."

"I wonder if that's right," she mused.

"We can't hide you out forever. I called and Socker hasn't talked yet. He may never talk again. I've got to make them come to me."

"They're going to come to you quick enough if you don't leave town," she said.

"Their way." He nodded. "I want them hurt in the pocketbook and maybe too angry to be careful. I want Sid November to come to me."

"And Jack Barr?"

"And anyone else," he said flatly.

"If only Socker could tell us who got him."

"I wouldn't wait," he confessed. "It's no good waiting. If I was sure, I could find November, I could blow off the top. Then we can tell the police and let them take over."

She nestled against him. "I know I should be thinking about it, worrying about it. When I get used to being here it will be easier."

"What about Lou?"

"He sort of collapsed. Like deflating a balloon. He swears he knows nothing about Sam's death." She shook her head. "If things got very tough, I'd call him."

"Don't do it!"

"I would. I know I could. But he's scared, Steve. It would have to be awfully tough to make me call him. He's a frightened old man."

She did not add that he loved her not as an old man, that she had seen it clearly at the end, that she had purposely not gone in to his office to say good-by because of that. It was better for Steve to go along his way. There were several things it was better that Steve should not know at this particular time.

She crawled closer to him, knowing it was dangerous to let herself go this far but unable to resist the woman in her, the clinging to her man that is so much a part of womankind, the part-mistress, part-mother role that came with daily contact, with sleeping together like couples should, with using the kitchen together and knowing when each used the bathroom and learning the details that between man and woman are part of the strongest bond of all. Habit, he had said.

He was pretty clever, sometimes, whether he knew it or not. Habit, the strongest force in all the world.

She hugged the word to her even as she hugged the
man, feeling him respond.

He awakened before she did in the morning and
turned to look at her. One arm was thrown up and
her breast, young and firm, was exposed to the chill
air. He found himself tenderly covering it. He didn't
remember ever, having done this to such a tempting
breast before.

He frowned, examining her sleeping face, looking
for flaws, afraid he would find none. Her mouth was
wide, but it wore a half-smile that was so appealing
that he turned away, angry with himself.

He slid out of bed and went into the bathroom
and scrubbed his teeth. Better not to think right now,
this was emergency, he had to keep moving, to act as
if she were not here, to go about his daily routine and
let himself be seen by those that watched. He had
already been to Socker's gym and looked properly
puzzled at finding it closed. Now he had to walk in
the Park for exercise, then get over and calm down
Pat Paule without revealing anything more about
Socker.

He had to see Jack. And Fay.

Yes, he had to see Fay. There was no getting
around it, they would think it strange if he did not see
them, both of them. Dinner, perhaps, and never mind
if Virginia had to eat alone with the television for
amusement; this was serious business. Not that she
would complain. She never complained.

He went into the dressing room and slipped into
one of the new suits and put on one of the new hats
and then he saw her in the mirror, naked, relaxed,
smiling sleepily from the doorway. She went without
clothing as naturally as a baby on a beach, and at first
he had been mildly shocked, but now he liked it. She

said, "You look too pretty to be allowed out alone."

"You're pretty, too," he told her. "And you're not allowed to go out and don't forget it."

"Don't you forget to send up some books," she said. "And to tell the cleaning people I'm your sister. And to watch yourself, Steve, all the time."

He kissed her and she snatched up his burnoose and wrapped it about her, following him into the living room. He called Teaneck and after a moment the rough-voiced watchdog came on and rasped, "Nothin' yet, but he's gainin'. The doc says maybe soon the crisis will be over."

"You tell that to Carraway?"

"The Lieutenant's here every day," the voice said respectfully. "He don't miss no tricks."

Steve thanked the man and hung up. He shook his head at Virginia, and she frowned, hugging herself inside the robe.

"If he could only tell us what he knows. I'm sure that will be it, Steve. They wouldn't have gone after Socker without a real good reason."

Steve said, "I'm going out now. Remember not to answer the phone. There's plenty of food and I'll bring in some more."

"Spaghetti," she said. "I make real good spaghetti. I'll need some chopped meat, garlic, green peppers—"

"I probably won't make it for dinner tonight," he said uncomfortably. "Got to see Barr, or it will look funny."

She hesitated for only the flicker of an eyelash. "That's right. You'll know about his part in it, too, if you see him. You can tell about those things, sometimes."

The telephone rang. He answered it and Lou Moscow's voice came to him, low-pitched, lifeless., "Steve? Have you seen Virginia?"

"Virginia? Isn't she at work?"

"No." Silence for a moment. Steve gestured at Virginia and she wriggled a bare toe at him. Moscow said, "She's gone away."

"That's funny, she didn't say anything about it to me last time I saw her."

Moscow's voice grew fainter. "Well, young girls ... you know ... I'm a little worried."

"You think she went off with a man?" Steve said.

"No! Oh, no, nothing like that. Not Virginia!" Steve raised his brows at her and she regarded him solemnly, sensing the trend of the conversation. "She'll be all right. Your bank called. You've been betting a lot of money?"

"I've been doing lots of things. Including being warned to leave town by a couple of hoods," Steve said flatly. "Same crowd that knocked off Sam, I imagine."

Moscow's voice went up a few notes. "What? What did you say?"

Steve repeated it slowly. He ended, "I just thought you might be interested."

"You—you don't think they're after Virginia, too?" Moscow quavered.

"Who knows? Maybe it'll be your turn next."

There was a long silence. Then Moscow said, "Let them come after me. Let them!" The wire clicked; he had broken the connection.

Steve said, "That scared him from another angle. You may be right, Virginia. If he thought you were in danger, he'd come through."

"If I could only answer the phone, and not be me!" she said. "He may call back, ready to talk."

"Let him stew a while. You take it easy. Play it cozy with the cleaning people. I'll lay a little loot on them for insurance. It won't be long—the fight's

Friday night and things will pop then."

She nodded. He kissed her again and went out of the apartment. All the while he was explaining to a hard-faced matron who didn't believe him, giving her money, urging her to keep silent about his guest, and later, as he pored over the pocket books in the corner drugstore, and returned to send them up by the same forewoman of the house-cleaners, he was thinking about how good it had proven to be living with Virginia. He had quite a bit of trouble banishing her from his mind as he walked through the Park.

He walked briskly, missing the exercise to which he had been long accustomed. He went toward the reservoir, and it was not wholly by coincidence that he saw coming toward him a toiling figure on a bicycle followed by a trotting runner.

He waited until they had come up to him and then called, "Pat!"

Pat Paule recognized him and stopped and Sailor Hock jogged in place, scowling as always. Steve said, "Hoped I might catch you."

"Something's fishy, ain't it?" Paule asked worriedly. "Where's Socker? How bad is he hurt? Why didn't he call me?"

Hock said in his aggressive, insulting manner, "If you're pulling anything, Galloway, you better never let me catch you."

Steve said, "You've got to keep your mouths shut, both of you."

"We come all the way here by playing it cagey," Paule said steadily. "We ain't about to blow it now. You can't blame us for worrying."

"That's why I'm here, where we can't be overheard," Steve said. "Socker got clobbered."

Hock looked pleased. "Serves him right."

"By the people who would like to see your can

beat off," Steve told him harshly. "By the syndicate. They thought they killed him, but he was too tough for them. I've got him hidden."

"What did he say? Who did he name?" Paule demanded.

"He can't say anything. He damn near died."

Hock said, "You think this guy's lyin', Pat?"

"Shut up," Paule said. His brow wrinkled. He stared at Steve. "You laid the money on us, O.K. But that's chicken feed to you. What's the story, Galloway?"

"All I want from you is the best this bum can do." He ignored Hock now, speaking directly to Paule. "If you win, I'll sweeten it by another thousand apiece. You've got everything going for you. If anybody comes around talking business at the last minute, remember that. Beat Georgie and you've got a title bout and the dough in the bargain. Lose and you're out on your butts."

"We didn't come here to lose," Paule said. "Socker promised to see us through it."

"I'm taking his place," Steve said. "If he regains consciousness and can talk on the phone, I'll put you through to him. If not, just go ahead the way it was planned."

Hock snapped, "I don't buy this jerk, Pat."

Steve turned on him. "Never mind buying me. Worry about Appleton. You're one of those tough guys with a big mouth. You know what Socker did to you. I'd just as soon try the same. I've got thousands riding on you and I'm beginning to wonder if a loud bastard like you can lick a good boy like Appleton!"

Hock started forward, his fists held low, feinting for Steve's head, ready to throw a looping punch to the groin. Pat Paule seemed scarcely to move, but with one thick arm he blocked Hock away, sending him spinning. He said, "Brains you haven't got, Sailor. Leave the thinking to me." He looked hard at Steve again. "You're going to start betting hereabouts at ring time?"

"Plenty."

He nodded. "Then I'll know what any last-minute crap might be about. Glad you told me, Galloway. Try and lemme talk to Socker. But no matter what, you got a deal."

He shouldered a still belligerent Hock onto the road, mounted the bicycle, and rode off. Steve watched them until they were out of sight. Sailor Hock was a snake, but he felt he could trust Paule.

It was ironic the way everything now hinged on the night of the fight, which had been set up by Socker, who would never see it. He walked along the drive, wondering if Socker were in pain, wishing he could do something for the big man, wishing Socker could talk.

He had not been followed into the Park, he knew, or if he had, the man had been long since lost. He came out miles above the place he had entered and took a cab and rode down Madison Avenue and got out at Fowler's and went into the shop.

Edgar greeted him, frowned at his slightly wilted collar, insisted on giving him a fresh shirt. He went into the rear and washed and Edgar chattered on, telling him that Fay would return in a moment, that she had a luncheon date with Jack, "such a wonderful boy, really, a gay one and so *good* to everybody, but queer for hats, don'tcha know."

When Fay came in she was alone, however. She arched her brows at him and exclaimed, "Why, you're a living dude! How well we dress you! Edgar, take a bow."

Edgar actually did, too, a low bow, and then

flitted to the nether regions to gloat over the compliment.

"Some lad," Steve said. "Nicest girl I ever met. How about dinner tonight? You and Jack, if you like."

He saw Jack come in the door then. Fay turned and called, "Just had a dinner invitation, Jack."

Barr smiled, extending a hearty hand. "Hiya, gambler. You buying?"

"It's about time," Steve said. "I'm overdue to spring."

Jack said, "You bringing your lovely date, the Butler gal?"

"She's out of town," Steve said carelessly. "I'll stag it if you don't mind."

"Out of town? Too bad. She was special business," Barr said.

"She was, she was," Fay agreed. "You shouldn't have let her get away, Steve."

They were watching him closely, both of them. Steve shrugged and pretended interest in a single necktie spread on a velvet background.

"I might dig you up something," Barr said.

"With a spade?" Steve grinned. "O.K., if she's alive."

Fay said quickly, "Let's not. Spoil me a little. Let me have two handsome men, you should excuse the expression."

"Where will we meet?" Steve asked.

Barr said, "You want to go first class? Or just eat good?"

"You name it."

"I want to dance," Fay said.

"Where you dance you don't eat good," Barr said emphatically. "Let's make it Salerno's and dance later."

"Spaghetti? Well, all right," Fay said. "First Avenue, Steve, near Fifty-second. No fuss and feathers, but wear your dinner jacket for later."

Steve shook his head. "You two can have the late evening."

"Aha, another lovely?"

"Business," Steve said. He thought he saw Barr frown, but could not be sure.

"A gamble I don't know about?"

Steve said, "Not that kind of business."

He got away from them, aware of strain lying deep beneath the surface. On Madison Avenue he walked slowly, knowing that it would never again be the same with them, wishing he had not made the dinner date.

He stopped short, remembering. First Avenue near Fifty-second. Lucky he had not thought of it in the shop.

Sam Goulding had died on First Avenue near Fifty-second.

Did Fay know about that? She knew something about Virginia, he was certain. She had aided Barr in the questioning about her.

He directed his steps toward Central Park South, hurrying a little. Behind him was something that he had liked but which had gone sour. Spending part of the afternoon with Virginia would take away the bitter taste. He would buy food and champagne and he would get away from Fay and Barr early and ...

He shook his head. He was certainly getting a habit.

19

They were reading in the living room. At least, Virginia was reading and Steve was watching her covertly from behind a magazine and thinking that he was really hooked now, that he would never be able to get used to not having her around. The days of close confinement had not disturbed her one whit; she was serene and incredibly lovely in a simple blue housecoat, her perfect legs crossed, one foot dangling saucily.

Saucy, he thought. That's another Sam word. "A saucy little baggage," he would call a girl, or "a fine figure of a woman." Virginia had known Sam and he had known Sam and someone had killed Sam and that was why they were here together, and wasn't that a hell of a thing all the way around?

Then the telephone jangled and he started, dropping the magazine. The thought flashed through him that on this day, Friday, the day of the Hock-Appleton fight, there was danger in the ring of this telephone. Virginia looked at him and he saw that she felt it too. He let it ring again before he picked it up.

A well-remembered hoarse, vicious voice said, "O.K., Galloway, you been smart, huh? You got the broad up there with you."

He said, "Who is this? Where are you?"

"Fun-ny, *fun-ny!*" mocked the wheezing voice. "This is the word, Galloway. You got tickets for the fight, huh? O.K. Tomorrow you blow. Tomorrow, unnastand? You and the broad. Blow and don't come back!"

Steve hung up with an angry gesture. The obscene, jeering threat of the voice was unbearable. He said to Virginia, "I guess they got to the cleaning woman."

"They know I'm here." She nodded. "We didn't expect it to last. You'll have to make your move now."

"Tonight. If I could only be sure I'd locate November at the fight."

She said, "This is the day. Can't you feel it?"

Her eyes were shining. He went across and bent over her and she hugged him to her and kissed him.

He said, "Remember the first time we were together here? We weren't the same people, were we?"

"You've thought of that, too?"

"Neither of us," he said wonderingly. "Who would believe we could change so much in such a short time?"

"Not me, I wouldn't have," she said. "I like us better this way, don't you?"

"I like it."

The phone again rattled its warning. He grabbed it, ready to pour defiance into its black mouth. Carraway's voice said. "Galloway? You'd better get over here pretty quick."

"Socker? He's going to talk?"

"If he ever talks it will be soon," the policeman said. "Hurry!"

Steve hung up. "Get dressed. I can't leave you here now. We're going to Jersey."

She moved swiftly, without question. He dialed the taxi company and was told that Sol was downstairs in the line, if he hadn't already got a fare.

He threw on his clothes. He had cashed a large check and he put a stack of bills into his breast pocket wallet. Virginia was ready as soon as he, her face pale but composed, and they went downstairs and onto the street.

Sol was there. Steve caught his eye and with two

fingers made a small gesture toward the corner. He did not stop. Sol nodded and started the engine.

Steve said, "Stroll toward Fifth. The monkey across the street will think we're going east. Sol will be waiting, I hope."

The man with the newspaper folded it and began following them. On Fifth Avenue Sol swung the cab into the curb. They were into it and gone before the tail could make the corner.

"Back to Teaneck," Steve said.

Sol said, "I don't like it. I been hearing things."

"Pull in your ears," Steve said. He took a ticket from his pocket and extended it past the meter. "You're seeing the fight tonight. You sit right behind us."

"Fight, schmite, I gotta work," Sol said.

"You're going to this fight," Steve told him. "I'm paying you to attend. Ringside, best in the house."

"You ain't fooling me," Sol said grimly. "Those gorillas. You think maybe they'll be there."

"I know damn well they'll be there," Steve said. "They wouldn't miss it. Appleton is their boy, they've got more money bet than they figured. The odds are down to two and a half to one."

"Your money?" Virginia asked.

He nodded. "The wires must have been hot. They stand to lose a million among them. Most of it will have been laid off on the syndicate people."

She said, "A million won't cripple them. But it will cause a rumpus, that's for sure."

Sol craned his neck to look painfully at them. "Millions, they talk! Fights and millions and old ladies killed and now Jersey again. Why did I have to meet you? I'm gettin' ulcers already."

"Just make some time to Teaneck," Steve said. "If this works out I'll buy you some new ulcers."

There was a doctor in the hospital room and Carraway and a nurse. Socker's face was too thin, his skin too white, and his cheekbones were like pickets on a fence. He managed to grin at Steve, but his voice was a low whisper.

The doctor said sharply, "Not too much talk. Neither the nurse nor I should leave this room."

"You needn't," Steve said, surprised.

Socker beckoned him close, frowning. His words came painfully, slowly. "Let 'em go. My idea."

They went out. Carraway settled on the far side of the bed and looked at Steve, shaking his head slightly, deep lines around his mouth. Steve's heart began to beat a little faster.

When Socker was sure that they were alone, he seemed suddenly anxious. He reached out a hand too thin and too weak, pulling Steve close to the pillow. Antiseptic was strong on the air and there was still a large adhesive patch on the base of the big man's skull.

"Steve, listen close. Get it all."

"Shoot, Socker. I got you covered." He tried to smile.

Socker did not respond. He whispered, "They got your fifty gees. Two big slobs, I don't know 'em. November's men. Steve—I think November was there, at the end. When they maced me."

He made a feeble gesture toward the back of his head. Steve could imagine him fighting, trying to stave off that blow, knowing it was coming, his great heart accepting it, striving to survive it.

The whisper went on: "Tenth Avenue, in an alley—it don't matter about that. Listen, Steve, November goes undercover. Hideout, when things are hot. Place I don't know. But I nearly know. That's why they come after me. Charlie Goode ..."

"Charlie Goode?" Steve had almost forgotten the narrow-eyed man who had hung around with November.

"Sid run him off. Queered him. Goode is sore. Nearly had him talkin', Steve. Told me he's dealin' in a joint in Jersey." He stopped, grinned faintly. "Hell, we're in Jersey, huh? Forgot. Carraway knows the joint. Charlie will talk, Steve."

"I'll get to him."

Socker said, "Steve, they hammered me. I can take it, huh? But they give it to you bad.... What the hell, I'm even. World don't owe me a thing. But it wasn't good, that way, Steve.... Like to be there ... when you get November."

Steve said, "Take it easy now, Socker. You'll be all right. I'll handle everything."

Socker hushed him with a gesture. "Steve, Barr's in it. Liked the guy. Maybe I shouldn't have touted you off him. The syndicate owns him. Owns everybody it touches ... Sorry, Steve."

"I knew." Tears were starting somewhere behind his eyes. He stared at Socker, trying to hold them back. Carraway was crouching, listening, his face furrowed, the odor of whisky strong on him.

Socker said, "My fault. Should've told you stuff.... Tried to do things my own sway. Lost your fifty gees for you."

"We'll get it back. They're betting Appleton."

"Like to see ... fight...." Socker's eyelids drooped. "Be a good one. No cinch for Hock. Be a hell of a good fight...." His voice was no longer even a whisper now. His lips moved but nothing came from them.

Steve stepped back, horrified. A quick look at Carraway confirmed his suspicions. He leaped to the door, wrenched it open. The doctor and the nurse hurried past him.

Steve followed them. The tears were in his eyes now. He felt them begin to run down his cheeks and reached for a handkerchief. He saw Carraway turn from the bed.

They went into the hall. Steve balled the handkerchief and said harshly, "Let's go find Goode."

"Yeah," Carraway said. "I got to like that Socker just seeing him fight for his life."

Chalk up another one, Steve thought, going to the waiting room, where he had to break the news to Virginia, who had also been fond of Socker. Another score for the syndicate killers. Another man, this time dying under his gaze, a friend, a good guy, beaten to death.

Chalk up another, and make it the last, scorekeeper, because this time they pay.

Well, maybe they could add Steve Galloway, before it was over. But they'd have to pick up a tab for a few of them. Sid November. The two thugs who had roughed him up and killed Socker.

Jack Barr? Maybe him, too. Or any other sonofabitch that had anything to do with the parlay that did for Sam, Legs, Mrs. Murphy, and the big man on the bed upstairs.

Carraway had a Mercury sedan in the hospital parking lot. He said, "My own car. Couldn't take an official job to this place. You better catch me up on everything, hadn't you?"

They got in the front seat and Steve went over all that had transpired, down to the telephone call of that day. They drove on the main road northward to a turning, then bumped to a stop at what seemed the rear of a private dwelling. They walked across a yard to a side porch. A large man with a low forehead met them there, stared hard at Carraway, then grunted and stepped aside to let them enter.

It was about three in the afternoon and there were very few customers, just a few in the horse room and the usual dice table devotees who looked as though they might have been at it all night. Nobody paid any attention to them, even to Virginia, when they entered with the house man behind them.

Steve saw Charlie Goode at once. He was behind a blackjack table. He wore an eyeshade and a green billiard-cloth apron and was in his shirt sleeves. When they got closer and could see his face, Steve was shocked.

The man looked fifteen years older than when Steve had seen him last. The close-set eyes were red-rimmed, his mouth was enclosed in deep, curving lines, the color of his skin was bad. His shirt was expensive, with a curling monogram over the pocket, but it was not freshly laundered, and there were spots on his Countess Mara tie. He glanced up as they came to the table. He started, looking at Steve, then at Carraway, then back to Steve. He stared hard at Virginia and his lips tried to smile but his eyes could not go along.

"Hello, folks," he said quietly. "Better take some cards."

Steve bought chips and they lined up at the table and he dealt cards to them. Carraway said, "Socker just died."

"You're Jersey law," Goode said. "Right?"

"I'm not here to make a pinch," Carraway said. "I'm with Steve."

"O.K. I had a little trouble getting a job here," Goode said. "Sid's fire sends awful hot heat." His teeth showed for a moment and the red eyes glowed with hatred. "They ran me off the streets of New York. How do you like that?"

"Who ran you off?" Steve asked.

"Slide and Horse, who else?"

"Sid's gorillas?"

"His. Not anybody's but his. If I could get to the mains ..." He broke off, glancing again at Carraway. "Card, copper?"

"Hit me," Carraway said. He showed only a four spot. Goode hit him with a nine and he winced. "Over."

Goode looked at Steve, who showed a nine. "Try one," Steve said. Goode flipped a card. It was a queen. "Twenty-one," Steve said.

Goode held the cards still in his hands. He said, "Lucky. Real lucky. Yeah, you're the one, all right. Socker was right."

"Right about what?"

"He said to talk to you. He said you'd get Sid."

"You know why I'm after him?"

Goode nodded. "Sam Goulding. Wish I could help you. I can't. I knew Sam and liked him a lot. I can guess and you can guess who knocked him off, but evidence I haven't got."

"Were Horse and Slide working for Sid when Sam got it?" Steve asked.

"They been with him two, three years."

"Who are Hotsy and Smith?" Carraway asked suddenly.

Goode said evasively, "I wouldn't know."

"Jersey boys?" Carraway insisted.

"Never heard of them," Goode said listlessly. He turned to Steve and his eyes came alive again. "It was on account of Barr, you know, that Sid aced me out. When Barr slugged him he thought I should have chipped in. I knew you'd take me, so I didn't. What the hell, Barr and Sid were thick enough a year ago. How could I figure it?"

Steve said, "What about the deal on the horse Flaming Arrow?"

"I wasn't in on it," Goode said bitterly. "Card games, things like that night with you guys, gym stuff, broads. Excuse me, Miss Butler, but that's Sid. I was a stiff for him. Never got the gravy. Just a slob for him. Oh, sure, I got in the games and all. If I hit, O.K. If I lost, he laughed at me. Then this thing."

Carraway said, "If Hotsy and Smith are Jersey boys, you might make a deal with me."

Goode took a deep breath. "You couldn't protect me. Nobody can. I'm saying nothing about anybody but Sid."

"The hideout?" Steve snapped out the words.

Goode dealt cards. His voice dropped almost to nothing. He said, "That's the place to get him. Nineteen-nineteen Riverside Drive. He bought the property under a corporation name. Big brownstone. He got drunk one night and took me there with a couple of broads. Excuse me, Miss Butler. If you go up there, he'll guess it was me told you, but I don't care. I'm counting on you staying lucky, Galloway. It's a gamble, see? I'm taking the odds."

Steve said, "I can stake you. Maybe you better take a plane."

"Where to?" Goode moistened his lips with his tongue. "If you don't get him, you better take one yourself. Back to Saudi Arabia."

"Maybe I will," Steve said. He looked at Carraway.

The cop hesitated, then asked, "Goode, nobody told you this girl's name. How come you to know her?"

"Lou Moscow," Goode said, surprised. "Everybody knows she works for Lou. Sam adopted her, didn't he? Everybody knows it."

Carraway said, "I'm not satisfied, Goode."

"I'm telling you all I know. I'm sticking my neck out for them to chop off my head." Perspiration was on Goode's upper lip. "Sid run me outa town. My town, where I was born and raised. You think I'd peep if he hadn't done that? I'm scared to death now, copper. And I wish you'd all go away."

Steve said, "If there's anything else ..." He slid a packet of bills beneath his cards, shoved them across the green table.

"Horse Koenig, Slide Gabrowski, and Sid. Get them all and maybe the heat will come off me. If it does, I'm paying you back this dough someday. That's my bet."

Steve would always remember his face, drawn and racked with mixed hatred and fear. They walked out of the gambling house and Carraway led them to the car.

Driving back to the hospital, where Sol waited, the policeman said, "We've been meaning to close that joint. I'll leave it open a while just in case."

"It won't be long," Steve said. "Tonight may do it. I just want to make sure of a couple of things. Then I'm going to the New York police and—"

"When you go, you'd better have me with you," Carraway said.

"You could help," Steve said gratefully.

They found Sol half asleep in the cab and Carraway hesitated with his hand on the window frame on Steve's side, looking past him at Virginia. "Don't let her out of your sight, will you?"

"No chance," Steve said.

Carraway seemed reluctant to let them go. Finally he stepped back and Sol started the cab. Steve reached for Virginia's hand and found it ready and warm. He said, "Socker tried so hard to live."

"Yes."

"He never wanted very much to make a big score. Gambling was his fun. He got mixed up in it because of Sam and me. Mainly me."

"We're all mixed up in it."

"They're so smug. So sure of themselves," he burst forth angrily.

She pressed his hand between both of hers. "We'll get them."

"I don't know." It was the first time he had felt uncertain. "Maybe I'm all wrong. Maybe I should go to the police. If you get hurt ..." He could not finish. It was a new sensation, this deep-down fear. He had known no fear of this kind before, ever. It was because of Virginia and he had not ever cared enough about anyone before, He looked at her wonderingly.

She said softly, "Let's play out the hand."

Like a man, he thought, only with more guts than most men. It deepened his fears for her. He was aware that he was squeezing her hand so that it hurt her and loosened his grip.

He said, "O.K., darling. O.K."

20

In the privacy of the office in the rear of the shop, Fay looked across her desk at Jack Barr. She said, "You're really going to frame him? You think you can get away with it?"

"Freddy's a magician at that sort of thing."

She shook her head. "Steve will know it's a frame. You think he'll run?"

"I've got to try it," Barr said stubbornly. "I want you in on it, because he'll listen to you. It's best for him."

"Because Sid November is ready to kill him?" she

asked quietly.

There was a silence in the office. She rolled a fountain pen between her fingers, staring into space, waiting.

Barr said heavily, "It's got out of hand. Sid's acting up. I believe he's got orders about Steve."

"You couldn't go to Steve, join him?"

"Fay, are you nuts? Fight the syndicate?"

"Steve seems to be doing all right."

"Steve's an outsider. With plenty of his own dough. He never had any part of the business."

She interrupted. "Is that the only difference between you?"

He slapped a hand on the desk. "Yes! The only difference. He's a gambler, a high player. So am I. Only he's on the outside and to get my start I had to begin with the mob."

After a moment she said quietly, "Maybe you're right. I guess I'm in no position to judge between you."

"Between us? What do you mean, Fay?"

"Just that. You're my man, Jack. I go your way."

He flushed with pleasure. He said quickly, "Fay, maybe I ought to tell you. Steve's got that Butler girl living with him."

"Is that bad?" She smiled, her eyes steady on his.

"I thought you'd like to know. I want to set up an all-night game, after the fight, and—well, she'll be there."

"How do you know?" she could not help asking.

"Freddy got the wire," he said as casually as possible. He could not tell her that Freddy had bribed a private detective originally hired by November. There was too much he could not tell her, he thought, looking at her hungrily, wishing everything were different, wishing it were over, hoping that Steve could be bluffed, hoping November would not move too fast, before he could get in there and somehow get Steve away.

He had to worry about Freddy, too. Freddy would kill Steve as quick as a wink, because Freddy had smelled out danger with November, with Lebella and Bogardus, with Steve, with everyone—and Freddy got a bit gun-happy when he thought there was trouble big enough to warrant it.

Fay said, "It looks like you, me, and Freddy against the world. Shall we go to dinner, Jack? I'd like a nice meal and some drinks before the fights. Let's have a little fun, darling."

He was smiling tenderly at her and he loved her immensely, and it was all for her, only he couldn't seem to make it clear to her. She had taken it big about Virginia Butler, and that showed it was not a love affair or anything like that with her and Steve. He had never thought that, not really, but it was good to know for sure.

No, she had only liked Steve, just as he had liked Steve. She could afford to keep on liking him, but Jack Barr could not. It was not going to be just exactly as he had told her and he was sorry she had to be there, but he needed her presence to make sure Steve wouldn't get too rough. He wanted Freddy to keep Steve under a gun if necessary and he figured Steve wouldn't start anything with both girls on hand to maybe stop a wild bullet. There wouldn't be any wild bullets. Freddy never threw a piece of wild lead in his life. Freddy could drive nails at twenty paces with that rod of his.

It would not come to shooting, he told himself for the hundredth time. It would be a card trick and then Steve off balance and then they would close in on him and read him the word. They would tell him about

November and what November could do and they
would point out that their way was better. And if
Steve got tough, well, he would have to belt him, and
Freddy and he would put him on a train or something
and get him out of town, with the Butler broad, and
then if Steve came back someone would have to get
him.

He watched Fay put on her jacket and hat and
prayed that it would not be like that. If it was, he
might have to kill Steve himself.

He did not want to kill anyone.

He gave Fay his arm and they went out of the
shop, a handsome couple with their pockets amply
supplied with money, going to dinner, then on to
Madison Square Garden to the prize fights, thence to
a card game with friends.

That's the way he wished it, that's what he
wanted, he kept telling himself.

Sol looked strange in his too tight blue suit and
white collar and neat tie. He parked the U-Drive
sedan that Steve had hired in a crowded garage and
walked back to the entrance to the Garden. His
stomach was on fire. He passed Virginia and Steve,
managing not to look too closely at them, and went
down to his seat. He had never been ringside in the
Garden and he should have been curious and
interested to know who spent that kind of money for
tickets and why, but he was only frightened. He sat
low on his chair and cast darting glances about him.
When he realized no one was paying any attention to
him he braced his spine a bit.

All kinds of people, he thought wonderingly. Some
looked like they could afford it no more than he.
Eight-eighty a ducat, not even a champeenship bout!

The lights were bright as the second preliminary

finished and the next pair of pugs entered the ring. Mink coats, too, plenty of dressy dames in mink. And a guy in a choker! Also a face he had seen in the papers, lemme see now. Jack Dempsey! Sure, with that scowly puss and the sharp eyes, Dempsey, like he always needs a shave.

It was very interesting if you only looked at the famous people, but now the two boys were sparring in the ring and this he did not like.

He had never seen many fights and he did not understand the need for them. Of all human stupidity he considered this the greatest. They should punch each other, there ain't trouble enough already? They couldn't get a job driving a hack?

Between rounds the ringside lighted up again. Two clocks they had, one each side of the ring. Very rich people, one clock was not enough. He glanced to his right.

He froze. There was no mistaking the pair that sat chewing on cigars, eyes fixed on the ring, oblivious of anything but the action in the corners, waiting for the bell to start the boxing again. Big men, coarse faces, hats like they all wore, tobacco ashes on their vests, rolling the cigars between thick lips. He had been bold enough to take a good look at them as they had walked on Sullivan Street, catching them under a strong street light.

He looked away, but he was uncomfortable, knowing they were present, knowing he would have to point them out. He wondered how he would tell Steve without letting Barr know he was passing the information. He did not want to be mixed up in it, not nohow. His ulcer kicked like a mule just imagining what might happen later while he was driving Galloway, as he had been hired to do, knowing he had not ever been scared this much in the

war, because in the war it had been a thing of himself
and the company and the flag that he had sworn in
school to defend and his country and the feeling that
this was right and had to be done and fears didn't
matter. This fear did matter and he would get out of it
if he could. If it were not for the old lady in Jersey and
what he knew about Socker and the fact that he was
making so much money from Steve that he could
almost see himself driving his own hack, a veteran's
license, everything, he would get up and walk, he
thought.

Then he saw Steve and the others coming down
the aisle. His mind began working and he got out a
ballpoint pen and his program and again checked to
the right, counting seats, and he wrote hastily,
printing so that it would be clear. He ended, "See you
at the garage."

Steve hung back in the aisle, smart stuff. Barr went
in first, then the other dame, then Virginia Butler, the
nice one that he knew was nice, that he couldn't help
liking.

He recovered himself, got up, slid out of his seat.
He handed the program to Steve, stumbling against
him, muttering a fast, " 'Scuse it, please," and hurried
up the aisle, losing himself among the ringsiders
coming late to the affair, scuttling out the doors onto
Eighth Avenue.

Steve slid the program inside his own and was
solicitous of Virginia's comfort. He was amused at
Sol's defection, remembering that the little cab driver
had hated the idea of viewing boxing matches. He
looked past Virginia to see Fay regarding him from
beneath her lashes and let her have the edge of the
smile.

The lights went down and the second round of the

fight in progress took everyone's attention and he arranged Sol's program as though seeking the names of the contestants and read Sol's message.

For a moment he did not look up, filling his lungs with air, knowing he must make it casual, that if he overdid it they would take note of his interest, recognize that he knew them. They could know it soon enough, but not now, not until the fight was over and they were wondering what hit them in the pocketbook and where to strike back. He made himself look at the lighted ring where two stocky boys were diligently pecking away at one another, bouncing around in that peculiar shuffling style of the boxer, right foot turned out for balance, left foot toed in.

He felt Virginia stir at his side and glanced down at her and imperceptibly nodded, showing her part of the program. She reached for it easily and followed his example of pretending to look at the names of the fighters. Then she held it in her hand a moment, her lips moving, looking straight ahead, and he knew it had got to her, too.

It was morally certain that when the round ended they could count off seats from the opposite square of people, now black in the shadows beyond the white glare of ring lights, and see the killers of Sam Goulding. And Socker Cane. And possibly of Legs, although Legs, he thought, might have been done in by anyone with a gun. Legs and Mrs. Murphy were cases apart, Carraway's cases. They had been killed hastily, with little regard for the classic form of the regular murders, the murders of the condemned meddlers like Sam and Socker, who had dared defy the syndicate on its own grounds.

He sat there with a quarter of a million dollars riding on the main event and all he could think about were the two killers. He was not positive that they had committed the crimes. He had no legal evidence. He had only the eyewitness testimony of Sol Mintz that these were the men that had attacked him at Virginia's place. He had yet to check their names with those given him by Socker. But he knew in his heart they were the men, and he knew they would be with November, and then he would make sure.

The round ended and he could not prevent his gaze from swiveling to the right. Quickly he counted the chairs.

November was not sitting with them. They were gesticulating with cigars, arguing about the fighters now in their corners, being sponged and given fruitless advice. He stared at them for as long as it took to engrave them on the gray matter in his head.

Horse Koenig and Slide Gabrowski. Big men, well dressed, sitting in good ringside seats, betting their blood money on the fights. He felt Virginia press his arm and tore his eyes away and saw that Barr was trying to get his attention.

He leaned past the girls and Barr said in that new voice, unlike the warm tones he had always used before, "Say, how about a game later? I feel like gambling."

"After the fights?" He had to organize his plans.

"All night." Barr grinned. "I got an idea you can't top me tonight."

Steve's mind clicked once, twice. He nodded. "My place. I'll give Virginia the key and meet you there an hour after the fights."

Virginia said sharply, "You promised me, Steve. Let them have the key. You said I could go with you."

She had him over a barrel. He could have kicked her, but he managed to smile and say, "All right. I've an errand to do—kind of important. Then we'll play.

Freddy be around?"

"Right!" Barr leaned back.

Steve continued to press against Virginia's softness, looking at Fay, at Barr. He said, as though inspired, "Look, Jack, you feel lucky, how about the fight?"

Barr laughed. "I don't want sucker bets."

Steve raised his voice a little. "What's the line right now? I can afford to gamble a little."

Barr said, "Two to one, Appleton, and no takers."

"Lay me ten to five?"

"Dollars?" jeered Barr lightly.

"Thousands," Steve said calmly.

The buzzer sending out the seconds sounded on the dying echo of the word. Barr's eyes widened, then narrowed. Behind them a stout man said, "I'll take that in hundreds if you're onna level."

Steve said, "Put it up with Jack. You know Jack?"

The man slid money forward, panting in his eagerness. "I guess Barr remembers me. Johnson? Out of Chi?"

Barr nodded, taking the money. The bell rang and the fighters went to the center of the ring. He stuffed Steve's money in his pocket with that of the stout man. He was thinking hard, Steve knew, turning over in his mind all the possibilities of what might be known to Steve and not to him, wondering, worrying.

The round was half over when Barr excused himself and pushed past the knees of the girls. In the aisle he leaned close and asked, "Is there a switch? Damn it, Steve, have you heard something?"

"I looked at the two boys train," Steve said. "The odds are right. I like a bet where the gamble is right, don't you?" That was what Socker had said.

Barr went up the aisle. When the lights came on again Steve saw him over to the left of the banked ringside chairs. He was talking earnestly to Sid November.

He fought down the flush that crept up his body, increasing his heartbeat, angering him, choking him. He heard Fay ask, "Aren't you splurging tonight, Steve? Five thousand is a heap of thirty-dollar shirts."

"I knew those shirts cost too much," Virginia said gaily. "You've been robbing poor Steve."

Fay looked sweetly at her. "*Single* men can afford such trifles."

Then Barr was returning. He said curtly, to Steve, "You've got a bet."

Johnson of Chi was apologetic but sweating with importance, breaking in. "There's some people from my home town here. They could get up a pool. If you're interested, sir."

"Get it up," Steve said.

Barr settled in his seat, but without comfort. The prelims ended and the semi-final was under way when the pool came through. Steve took out thousand-dollar bills and the Chicago man's eyes were like egg yolks as he saw the number of them, covering the bets of his friends. He moved to whisper to Barr and seemed satisfied at the jerk of the head that told him there was no fix known to the high gamblers of the city. Yet he continued to sweat, Steve noted with satisfaction.

Barr had no further conversation. Steve wondered how much of his money had already been covered by the syndicate and possibly by Barr himself. He was hurting them, he knew that. Not crippling them, that was impossible. But hurting them—if Hock could win.

Fay said, "Doesn't it worry you, the way Steve throws his money around?"

Virginia answered, "From what I can learn, that's

the way he made it in the first place."

She was smart, not accepting the challenge, not trying to turn away the implication that Steve's actions were important to her. She was cool, she was alert, she was Sam's girl, all right. He wished Sam were here now, somewhere around, to see this. Just the gamble, the way it was going around ringside that there was a high shot taking the odds.

He heard a man say, "No, sir. I'm not laying it. I'm taking it for fifty. Good enough for him, it's good enough for me."

That would make them wince. Barr was saying to him, "Want any more, Steve?" looking at him in that peculiar way that said plainly enough that he was no longer Steve's pal, that he was a wary enemy, that the syndicate was sticking to its guns and Barr could bet what he wanted.

Steve said, "I like the price, I told you. How much?"

"What have you got on you?"

He took out the wallet with its depleted hoard. He said, "Ten thousand and I'll write you a check up to a hundred grand."

Fay pulled back on her seat and he saw her body going rigid. Virginia smiled at her and said, "These single men sure are able to afford their fun, dear. You were so right!"

For the first time Barr lost the outer edge of his composure. He said, "Steve, this is pretty crazy."

"You want the bet?" He met Barr's eyes, no longer dissembling, cold, calculating, staring the other man down.

"I'll take it," Barr said. There was sullen defiance in him and an ominous warning. He stood a moment, nodded toward where November sat. He settled back in his seat, staring straight ahead, his arms folded.

It came into the open, with his signal to November, the sign to the syndicate that they were bucking Steve's bankroll. They would remember now the money from all over the country that had been spread through use of Socker's name. No doubt November had received word of it by today and wondered and tried to add it up. Now he had deliberately let them know.

He saw a weasel-like little man scuttle to where Gabrowski and Koenig sat and saw them stare at him. He was aware of eyes from every direction as the house lights went up. He stood up, stretching, glancing around, letting them take a good look. He smiled at Virginia, bought her a candy bar, passed others along to Fay and Barr.

Fay's eyes were sick. She knew the score, then. How much she knew he had no idea, but enough, he was sure. The last doubt, the last compunction fell away from him.

They began introducing celebrities, Kid Gavilan, Dempsey and Tunney in their new brother act, Tony Galento, Archie Moore, the lightweight flash from the Coast, Cisco Andrade. Appleton was in his corner, sleek and brown and pantherish, dancing, jabbing, ferocious before the event. Hock was hooded inside a white terrycloth robe, his face almost concealed, and Pat Paulo was a Billiken in a gray sweater with "Sailor Hock" lettered on its back.

Pat Paule's face was serene, unblemished by worry, and Steve knew from this that the mob had not tried to move in at the last moment. A restlessness was around ringside as the galleries followed custom by hooting at all the fanfare and whistling for action. A voice howled, "Let's get him outa there fast, Georgie, and we can all go home early!"

Then everyone was down off the canvas-covered

platform except the announcer and the fighters and the handlers and the excitement at long last began to nibble at Steve. He sat quietly, watching Hock, but his pulse was not quiet.

Had Sam imbued him with it, this excitement of the big gamble? He couldn't remember ever having been without it. Not the horses, not being raised around the stables. He had never gone for that. But the dice games with the exercise boys, the card games in which Sam had patiently taught him what he needed to know, the wheel and all its vagaries including double zeros—he had not needed Sam to put this in him. It had been there. He wondered how many people had it, if it was universal, if it only needed a certain temperament and a means of letting it out of the system.

He looked at Barr and recognized it in him. The slight smile at the corner of the hard mouth, almost a sneer, the brightness of the eye, the cocky poise of the shoulders saying that there was a high bet riding and wasn't it great—this was all in Barr as it was in Steve. Possibly not in November or the November types. It had been part of Socker, though, and of course it had been Sam's life.

It was in all big men, he thought. Little men could not afford it. They had no resources upon which to fall back if they lost. They lacked the imagination to recoup a serious loss. If it was in them, they repressed it.

It was the money and not the money, he thought. Money was the power to make bigger bets. But it was more of the spirit, the temperament, the fundamental urge to beat the everyday existence that the gambler could not brook.

They took the robe off Hock and the house grew still for just a second, seeing his face for the first time, the hard, unyielding mask of a face, the slit of a mouth, the little pale eyes, the low, jutting brow. Then Appleton was dancing to the center of the ring, all flash and elbows and fine, sculptured torso, and the yell went up for the local favorite, the killer boy.

The referee was explicit, staring at Hock, foreseeing trouble with this throwback specimen. They touched gloves, they returned to their corners. The lights were down. Virginia touched his hand once for luck and the bell rang loud and clear.

Appleton bounded on steel springs, crouched, using his elbows for protection, bobbing. Hock moved into him with a short left. They came together in the exact center of the ring and the spectators looked for Hock to circle to the right, away from the hooks, the classic style to utilize against an Appleton.

Hock exploded a left to the head, then a right to the body, ducking his shoulder and coming up under, hiding his chin behind his thick neck as he turned. Appleton, overjoyed, swung both hands.

Neither backed up a step. Neither reached out an arm to clinch. Both stood toe to toe, ducking and weaving, curled red gloves going short and sharp, in and out, over and under.

Appleton had the speed of a high-geared racing machine. Blood spurted and a great "Ohhhh" went up as a gash opened over Hock's left cheekbone. Hock moved forward inside the hook and dropped two successive rapid rights to the ribs. Appleton did not retreat; he was knocked back, and for a moment his left hand dropped, only an inch or two, but lower than safety demands.

Hock was in like a tiger, slashing. They were clubbing blows, at the side of the face, clawing with the edges of the gloves, chopping for an eye. Appleton crouched and threw the hook.

It landed with crushing force against Hock's jaw. His legs buckled.

Barr was on his feet with the thousands and Steve heard his yell, "There goes your boy!"

Steve recrossed his legs. Hock was on the ropes. Appleton was on him, swinging punches; he stepped back an instant and his right arm dropped in the flashy, full-arm bolo punch he had borrowed from Gavilan.

Hock moved aside. The telegraphed bolo went aimlessly by. Hock, still disdaining to clinch, peered out of his mean little eyes, saw the opening. He chunked a left hand into it and Appleton reeled across the canvas, mouth open.

The bell rang. The entire Garden audience stood cheering, howling, whistling, clapping hands.

Steve said to Virginia, "Good thing Sol left."

She nodded. Her own cheeks were a trifle pale. "I've seen fights before. Lots of them. But not like this."

"You won't often see one like this," he told her. He looked over at Fay and she was equally pallid, staring at the ring. Barr was on the edge of his chair, his fists clenched.

He wondered how the less experienced gamblers felt now. They had built up Appleton as a superman, invincible. They had seen him draw first blood, they had seen him met by one who laughed at his own gore and swiftly struck back for vengeance. How did they like it?

Not that the fight was over. Appleton was magnificently swift. Hock was a trifle slower afoot, but deft and sure with his hands. It was even as Steven, he chuckled. He was enjoying it.

Again the bell. Pat had fixed the cut and Hock shuffled in, left shoulder turned, and Steve remembered him sparring against Socker and then Socker calmly slugging him in the locker room and then the fun went out of it, because Socker lay dead in a Jersey morgue. He bit his lip, trying to throw off the bad feeling, but it persisted throughout the fight.

The fighters came together and the vast auditorium rocked with the cheers of the onlookers, but Steve sat quiet, his hands knotted, his eyes fixed, only mechanically noting the action in the ring.

Appleton had a target, he was a hitter. He went about his business, which was to knock out the man opposite him. He used his head in close, butting at the wounded cheek, and the referee warned him, but Hock calmly pushed the referee aside and went forward. Appleton chopped at the cheek and Hock seemed to invite him to experiment further.

Appleton landed a combination one-two to the head and left to the body and for a moment it seemed Hock would go down. Then the Sailor was going ahead, boring in, and again the shoulders dropped as they came together and the right hand came up inside, three, four times in a rataplan, the old-time attack to the body, relic of another day.

Hock chucked his left hand up, as though to the head. Appleton's face disappeared behind a red glove, went all awry as the awful punch, with the leverage of Hock's body behind it, threw him heavily against the ropes.

Pinned there, he could not move left or right. Hock never stopped punching. The referee hovered, his head pushed forward, almost into the action himself, estimating Appleton's ability to take the beating.

Steve moved a little, sighing. It was a jungle fight, an animal fight. It brought them all up howling, the crowd with its atavistic impulses, its desires for blood and action. Yet he could only hear Socker saying, "He's real good, see? A tiger."

Appleton was fighting back. The referee moved away, Appleton came off the ropes, boxing, tin-canning, still refusing to hold. His left kneecap trembled once and Pat Paule barked a sharp command.

Hock feinted a left lead. Appleton tried to roll with it. Hock rode behind a right hand from the Bronx, a long, unorthodox overhand right that dropped like a bomb on the side of the jaw.

The Negro fighter buckled. He was going down when Hock moved inside. Two, three lefts went to the head. A right thunked against bone. The referee was between them, shoving Hock away. He had to push the fighter, hold him, then shove him. He kept one eye on Appleton, saw that the boy did not stir a muscle. He grabbed Hock's right arm and raised it high. Still Appleton did not move, and the referee looked for the doctor in attendance.

Pat Paule was in there with the robe, very quiet, showing no exultance, wrapping Hock out of view, talking in his ear. The Sailor seemed reluctant, glaring at the fallen Appleton, grudgingly allowing the photographers to catch him in their flash-bulb lights, his feet nervous on the floor as all the fight fans in the Garden stood and howled mingled hatred and praise.

Barr was adjusting his hat with particular care. He reached into his pocket for the stakes. Steve said, "Hold it until later, at the apartment, Jack."

"You had an inside," Barr said dully.

Steve could not resist. "Socker tipped me the boy was tiger."

"Socker? You know where Socker is?"

"Before he—went away," said Steve. "See you later, folks."

He took Virginia's arm and they moved as quickly as possible to the exit. They ran to the garage and Sol had the rented car ready and drove them away.

"Fights," Sol muttered. "Trouble. Them gorillas, they scare me even to look at them."

Steve took the .32 from where he had hidden it in the car. He said, "Virginia, you'll drive around with Sol. I can handle this."

"Alone? I thought you'd call for help, now that you know."

He said quietly, "You know why Hock won tonight, darling?"

"Why, he was the better fighter. I don't see ..."

"He wasn't the better by that much. You see, Appleton wanted to knock him out. One thing Appleton had in his mind—knock out this man in the ring with him."

"Yes, but Hock wanted to knock out Appleton, too."

Steve shook his head. "Hock wanted to *kill* Appleton."

"I don't quite understand."

"Hock is a simple machine, nothing complex about him. He's a killer. Luckily he began boxing at an early age. Otherwise society would have a dangerous man on its hands. He'll be champion because of that drive to destroy."

"But what's that got to do with you, with us?"

"It's a good example." He was grim, he could feel the coldness in his middle. "When I looked at those greasy thugs, at November, it came to me that I've done nothing but aim wild bets at them, play around with them, looking for an opening. It takes more than that to handle Sam's murderers."

"But not alone, Steve. What about Lieutenant Carraway? He offered to go along, bring in the New

York police."

Steve said, "On what evidence? Look, honey, I hurt them tonight. Broke a lot of their bookies. At ringside they learned it was me. If they killed me, they wouldn't have to pay off."

She was silent, thinking about it. Sol turned uptown and drove swiftly to Riverside Drive.

Steve went on, as much to clarify it for himself as to make it clear to the girl. "I've tried playing it cagey. What happened? Mrs. Murphy was killed. Socker was killed. Nobody even tried it on me. Now I've got to put myself in there. I want to do it."

"All right," she said in a low voice. "All right, Steve."

"You understand it now?"

"I see your side of it." She nodded.

"I don't ask you to agree. I didn't want you in on this."

"I know, Steve."

The lights of Palisades Park came in view across the Hudson River and they could see the spidery outline of the roller coaster. Sol drove carefully, silent, hunched over the wheel.

"If they don't show here. I'll try them another time." Steve muttered. "This is just a hunch. November didn't do himself any good with the bosses tonight. He ought to hole up and try to think his way into the clear."

"Playing hunches." She nodded. "Following your luck. Sam taught us that."

"Partly that," he admitted. "Also trying to think ahead of November."

"And Jack Barr?"

"Jack doesn't know about Socker. I could tell when I threw Socker's prediction at him tonight. I've played poker with Jack, I know his reactions." He paused and then added gravely, "I want to find out just how far into this Jack has been all along."

"You know he's not your friend anymore."

"Yes, I know it."

She seemed satisfied. They came to the block in which the house must be located. Sol slowed and they saw that the house was of the Stanford White era, with a brownstone "stoop" and a basement areaway. Large picture windows adorned the front, overlooking the river, and the doorway was a work of art.

Steve looked at his watch and it was not yet eleven. Hock had done his job quickly and well. Sol whispered "What now? I got to park? I'll get a ticket."

Steve said, "Keep circling the block." He leaned over and kissed Virginia on the cheek. "Here goes nothing, baby. Ride it out with Sol. We'll soon know about a lot of things."

He slid across the sidewalk and into deep shadows. He made his way to the basement area of November's hideout. He had the .32 in his waistband, his hand upon the butt. He leaned back against cold stone, waiting.

It was quiet along the Drive at this hour of the night. The heavy traffic was below, on the West Side Highway. A boat whistle hooted downriver.

Minutes ticked by and he thought of Jack Barr and Fay and Freddy waiting at the apartment. He had been fond of these people. He had been almost in love with Fay. It was a weird, crazy thing, the whole business, beginning with the interview with Lou Moscow, a whirl of mixed emotions and events.

Sol went by once, twice. He was a fool, he thought, to wait here. November was probably trying to marshal forces to pay off the long-shot bettors and alibi to the men above him.

He decided to wait another quarter hour, then take his new-found cold determination back to the people waiting at Central Park South.

A taxi ground to a stop and he pulled back deeper into shadows. November's voice growled, heavy with anger. Footsteps pounded on the paving. He had to risk taking a look.

He sucked in his breath as he saw that the three of them had arrived in the cab, November, Gabrowski, and Koenig. He saw the U-Drive turn the corner, almost stop, then drive past. The hack pulled away and November was on the steps, fumbling for keys.

He came out of the areaway and released the safety on the automatic. He bounded up the steps and said, "That's right, November, let's all go in and we'll have a talk."

The heavy door swung open as the men turned. Gabrowski made a sudden motion. Steve hit him on the back of the neck with the muzzle of the pistol, driving him into the spacious hallway. His foot swung as it had not since his punting days in college, catching Koenig in the crotch, sending him over Gabrowski's sprawling form. He shoved the muzzle of the gun against November's fat butt and said, "Inside."

The sudden attack had stunned them for a moment, he knew. He made sure the latch on the front door was released in case he might need a way out in a hurry, and snapped on a hall light.

The two thugs had staggered up, but they did not look dangerous at the moment. Koenig could not straighten his racked body and Gabrowski was dazed. November was blinking at him in delayed recognition. Steve waved them into a room to the right of the entry hall.

November said finally, "This ain't very smart, Galloway."

"I've stopped being smart for now. Get in there, and please, someone, make a bad move. Give me an excuse."

The room was laughable, but it also made Steve angrier. It was Oriental in the manner of another era, overhung with deep shades of red, abounding in couches and silk cushions for revelry, with a cabinet containing a silver-embossed opium layout and hypodermic needles all in their cases. It expressed all the low taste and viciousness in the vulgar fat man who stood uncertainly eying him. November said, "What you want with us? You come on very large tonight. You musta made a million. What's with you and us?"

Steve waved the pistol at the two men. "Gabrowski and Koenig?"

"Sure. I forgot, you never met the boys. Gamblers, like you and me. They went for the bundle tonight. Lost their shirts."

The two shuffled their feet, wary as cornered animals. Steve said, "Bet my fifty thousand right back at me, did you?"

Gabrowski's mouth opened, but he didn't say anything. Koenig looked his fright through his pain.

Steve said, "You didn't explain to Sid that there was fifty grand on Socker. Nobody ever thought Socker would have that much on him."

November blinked once, but shook his head. "Socker? We been trying to find Socker. He's losin' trade at the gym."

"So they kept the money," Steve said conversationally. "Socker got away and you've been looking for him, all right. Only you had to send your Jersey boys, Hotsy and Smith, on a trip. So you didn't locate him in Jersey, where I've had him hidden out."

They became more dangerous then, realizing that he knew so much. He moved to keep them within range. Their minds were sluggish, even November's, he thought. He knew what he should do, he knew he should keep hitting them until the time came for action.

He said, "I've got some questions to ask and I'm not a cop. I'm not polite anymore, either. If I don't get answers, I'm going to hurt you people pretty bad. Where I've been they know about hurting people."

It wasn't working. They weren't afraid. They had that underworld credo about talking. He began to feel that he had made a mistake.

November said slowly, "You oughta know better than that, Galloway. You want anything outa us, call the cops. I'll call them myself."

"Try it," Steve said. He shifted the .32 toward November. He tried one more shocker. "Socker died today, but he talked first."

He sensed it was wrong the moment he said it. They were not only without fear of him, they were brave. Koenig, from his crouching position of pain, dived at his knees. Gabrowski yanked out a gun.

He fired the automatic once, then he was down and Koenig's weight pinned him and a hand grabbed his wrist. November had moved out of point-blank range, but his curses revealed that he was hit. Koenig struck at him, trying to turn him as Gabrowski shouted, "Gimme a shot at him, Horse!"

He fought to get the .32 into play, but Koenig was a heavyweight and knew how to use his strength. He remembered how they had handled him in Virginia's vestibule, and even as he fought he wondered why his luck had run out now, when he needed it to save his life.

Not luck, your judgment, you stupid jerk, he told himself. Koenig was spinning him. He drove with all his might to turn the hand holding the gun. Your bad judgment, your stubbornness, your lack of plan, your juvenile belief that you could make these men tell you anything.

Socker had warned him. Be ready to kill November, it was the only way. He had thought himself ready to kill, but it was not as simple as that. He was not Sailor Hock, he was not built that way. He should have killed Gabrowski and Koenig first. Then November might have talked....

He was being turned like a fowl on a spit. He exerted his last vestige of strength.

The shot sounded. He was braced for it. He felt Koenig relax.

To his amazement, he found strength to flip the man over. He rested an elbow on the carpet and saw Gabrowski turning toward the door. He shot Gabrowski in the belly, then shot him again, knocking him backward onto the luxurious Oriental rug.

He was on his knees, the gun smoking in his hand, trying to line up the room. November lay across the biggest couch, holding his left shoulder, groaning. That was Steve's first shot.

Koenig was not stirring. Gabrowski writhed, then was still. Steve whipped around to the doorway.

Virginia still held the smoking revolver, the .32 he remembered she had shown him. She said flatly, "You see, I could do it, like I told you."

He looked from her to Koenig. She had shot the man through the back. He said, "Thanks, darling. It was nice shooting."

She said in the same expressionless voice, "Sam taught me."

"They had me," he said. "I wasn't so smart."

"You left the door unlatched. That was smart," she consoled him. She looked at November. "What do we do now?"

Steve shook himself to dispel the numbness, fighting reaction to his nerves. He said, "You'd better watch at the door. Someone might have heard the shots. Although these old places have real walls." He took a deep breath. "Watch the door, angel."

She went back into the hall. He walked to where November lay and deliberately grabbed the bullet-torn shoulder, hauling him to a sitting position. November shrieked with agony and Steve hit him hard, across the mouth, shutting off his outcries.

November blubbered, "I don't know anything. If they did anything to Socker, I don't know it."

"I'm thinking of Sam Goulding," Steve said.

"I don't know from Sam Goulding." Now the fear had come, to mingle with the pain. "What I know about Sam Goulding?"

The iron hardened within Steve. He struck with the muzzle of the pistol, raking it across the fat face, leaving a trickle of blood from a shallow furrow in the flesh. November's mouth opened, and Steve filled it with his fist. He grabbed November's hair, jerked his head around so that Koenig and Gabrowski were in his view. "I'm in for killing them. You think it makes any difference now? I'm going to take you apart, piece by piece, November. Where's your safe? Where do you keep your stuff?"

November's hand went feebly to his pocket. Steve beat him to it, dug out keys. He went around the room once, jerking at the ornate silken drapes until he found a wall safe. November sobbed on the couch, his body shaking like a mound of jelly.

The safe was not designed to keep out thieves,

merely as a hiding place. What thief would dare rob Sid November? It opened as easily as a metal locker in Socker's gym.

He threw papers on the floor—stocks and bonds, insurance papers, of no interest to him, November's cache against hard times. He recrossed the room, tilting a chamois bag on a low table.

From among brooches, loose stones, bracelets, necklaces, the large diamond in its square setting winked up at him, like a friend remembered from long ago. He picked it up and called, "Virginia!"

She came into the room, avoiding a glance at the two dead men on the floor, walking straight and wide-eyed to him. He handed her the ring.

She shed only a tear from each eye. She said, "Yes. Sam's stone."

"Have you got paper and a pen in that bag?" he asked her.

She dug out a pen. Then she paused, reached again, and pulled out a small red notebook, Sam's notebook.

Steve grinned without humor. He put the pen and book in front of November on the table beside the ring. He said, "I want it in writing. Starting with the goofball and Flaming Arrow. Then Sam. Then how Legs Murphy was holding out for more dough and you had Hotsy and Smith shoot him. Then Mrs. Murphy and Socker."

November blubbered, shaking his head. "You got me all wrong, Galloway. What they did, Horse and Slide, I dunno. They were just a couple of the boys. I'm in the clear."

"You and Jack Barr," Steve snapped. "But Socker knew, at the end, it was you that maced him. Did you kill Sam, too?"

"No! I liked Sam. He ... They ..." November

sobbed.

Steve said, "Go outside, Virginia. I'm going to have to operate on this one. With bullets. I'm going to shoot parts of him off, and I wouldn't want you to see."

He lowered the muzzle of the automatic, pointing at the fly of November's trousers. The big man screeched and tried to roll away. The broken ends of his collarbone ground together and he collapsed. Froth ran from his mouth, dribbled on his chin. Steve slapped him to consciousness and pointed to the pen. "Write it."

November did not look up. His head limp on his thick neck, he muttered unintelligibly for a moment. Then he took up the pen and began scrawling.

Part of the tension lifted, but he remembered Barr and Fay and Freddy. He said sharply to November, "Put in it whatever you know about Barr. Write it, man!"

November mumbled, "Jack was in the Flaming Arrow deal. All the way in. The bastard, he never had the guts for it. It was always me, I was always the patsy."

"Who ordered Sam Goulding killed?"

November raised his head. "You think I could do that? On my own? It had to clear, didn't it? Everything had to clear."

"Barr sat in on it, on the decision?"

"You know damn well he sat in on it. Him and that goddamn Freddy, always crabbin' the deals. But they went along. They damn well had to go along. If it hadn't been for you, I'd have fixed 'em! I had 'em where I wanted 'em." The false energy drained out of him, tears ran down his fat cheeks. "You'll get me a doctor when write this? I'm dying, Galloway. The pain ..."

"Write!"

The fat hand returned to its faltering task. The little red notebook was filled when he finished. Steve put it in his pocket. He said, "Call your own doctor, November. After a while the cops will come and get you. Maybe you can explain the boys here and then they can come after me. It'll all wash up in the end." He walked to the door, holding Virginia's arm. He paused and said, "If you're thinking about sending anybody after me, remember about the things you just wrote down. I'm mailing the notebook to headquarters right now. The big bosses won't like you, November, and getting some more of their valuable aides killed won't help."

November did not even hear his last words. They went out of the house and no one seemed to have heard the shots. They waited on the sidewalk to be sure, then walked a few steps until they saw Sol faithfully tooling the U-Drive around the corner.

Steve said, "You all right, darling?"

"I wasn't. Then I saw Sam's ring." She held it out to him. "I picked it up as we were leaving. Was that right?"

"It's evidence he could have destroyed." Steve said "We'll give it to Carraway. I've got to call him right away. He'll know how to handle the police."

She said, "I didn't mind shooting that man. Honestly, Steve."

He put his arm around her. She was shaking like a sapling in a storm. "It'll soon be all over. Keep your chin up, darling."

"I'm all right," she insisted.

He said suddenly, "I love you, Virginia."

"I'm glad," she murmured. "I hoped you would."

Sol pulled in to the curb and they got in the car and headed south. She was like a child in his arms, quiescent, trustful.

He had Sol let them off at a midtown all-night drugstore and went to the phone booths at the rear. He lost track of Virginia for a moment as she wandered from view, then he was talking to Carraway's wife over in Jersey.

"He's not at home," she said. "He went with some of the men to look at the fight on television. He may not be home early, he said."

"Did he leave word for me?"

"No, he didn't." The voice sounded disinterested, weary.

Steve said, "When he comes in tell him to call me at once. It's urgent." He gave the number, making sure the woman got it right. He came out of the booth, perturbed. Carraway had promised him to be ready for an emergency.

Virginia came up behind him and said, "I guess we have to see Jack and Fay now, don't we?"

"Yes," he said. "We have to see them."

He did not mail the notebook, not yet. He wanted it in his pocket when he talked to the people who had been his friends. The cold thing in his middle had not yet dissolved. It was heavy, weighing him down, but at the same time driving him on.

21

Going up in the elevator Virginia squeezed his arm and said, "This is the part you hate, isn't it, Steve?"

"Yes."

"Take it easy," she begged. "Make sure before you start on him."

He said, "I wish Carraway had been available."

"I know." She bit her lip, then shook her head and said, "Just let it come out the way it must. Jack's up there for a reason, Steve. You know that."

"Yes. I guess so." The all-night game had seemed a happy suggestion when Barr had made it, but Virginia had given him pause for thought. There was a lot of money involved and he had been mistaken in not thinking about the money. Barr could not afford to lose as much as he had dropped on the fight. And the enmity had been there, in his last bitter words accusing Steve of having inside information.

He said, "You go in first and I'll cover. If they make a move, I'll let Freddy have it, so help me."

"Don't shoot," she begged. "We've got enough to answer for."

"I should have called the police before we left November's place," he admitted. "I'm afraid it was a mistake not to. But I want it all cleaned up. I couldn't stop, Virginia. I couldn't!"

She said, "Just play it slow and easy, Steve. Maybe the luck will hold."

He kissed her, hard. "You're my luck," he said.

The door to the apartment was unlocked. He turned the knob, pushed the door open, and stepped back to let Virginia go through. He could see Fay, a drink in her hand, sitting on the couch.

He followed Virginia, closing the door behind him. He saw Barr standing beside Fay and looked around for Freddy.

Something hit him from behind and knocked him to his knees. He rolled, trying to kick, but another blow hammered stars into his brain and consciousness from it.

He struggled at the bottom of a well, trying to climb toward a small round spot of light far above him. He was on his knees when his senses returned and his gun was gone. He felt with numb fingers for the little red book containing November's confession.

It was not in his pocket.

He heard Virginia say, "If you hit him again I'll kill every one of you."

He shook his head and regained a blurred section of his eyesight. Virginia was crouched a little and in her hand was the revolver. He got Barr lined up, then turned. Freddy was trying to get behind him and draw a weapon from a shoulder holster.

My luck again he thought. A second or two later in coming to and this would be it. He gathered his muscles and heard Barr cry out and knew the gambler had been watching him. He dived low for Freddy.

There was not much of Freddy. With guns he was fine, but he lacked the heft. Steve hit him and drove him against the wall and nailed him there with one hand while he pronged his index and middle fingers and rammed them into Freddy's eyes. He found Freddy's revolver under his arm and took it from him and threw the thin man across the room. He landed in a heap, both hands to his face, weeping silently.

Steve asked Virginia, "Who's got the notebook?"

She said, "I'll get it." She ran to Freddy, took it from his pocket, held it aloft. The revolver was tight in her fist, her eyes shone, her teeth were white behind her slightly parted lips.

The perimeter of his vision cleared and he saw that Barr had not moved. Fay had turned and was staring at him, her color all wrong, her position strained, awkward. He saw regret in her for an instant; then she turned her face away, toward Barr.

Steve said, "We've stopped being polite, haven't we? I'm sorry. I'd hoped we could keep it decent."

"You double-timed us," Barr said. "You started it."

It was so much like a small-boy accusation that Steve almost smiled. Remembrance of deeds done stopped the corners of his mouth, held them hard. "I didn't kill Sam," he said. "That started it."

"I didn't ..." Barr stopped. Then he said, "You put yourself into it. You couldn't let things ride. You can't win, Steve. The cops are on their way up here."

"Your cops?" Steve shook his head, trying to think clearly. They must have been right behind him. They had found November, had known where to get in touch with Barr. They had got the story from November and telephoned ahead. They had to be friendly to Barr or they would not have warned him of the confession.

Now, if they got the little red notebook, Barr and November both were in the clear. They had only to deny everything.

Then it would be up to Virginia and Steve to explain a couple of dead men. Thugs with criminal records, but citizens nevertheless. Plus a diamond ring that was not strong evidence against anyone now except Virginia and Steve.

How had they worked so close to him? How had Barr been able to outthink him so accurately? This rose to the top of his mind, stuck there like a fishbone in a cat's throat.

He looked at Virginia and saw that her mind was working along the same lines as his. He looked down at the gun in his hand, then up at Barr. He said slowly, "I guess you know Sam raised us. Virginia and me."

"We figured that out," Barr said. His tone altered slightly. "Give me that notebook, Steve."

Steve wagged his head from side to side. "No."

"You'll give it to me sooner or later. Why not now? Look, Steve, maybe we can make a deal."

Fay spoke then. "Make a deal with him, Steve. With us. It's for the best. Jack's not like Sid

November."

Barr said quickly, "Sid must have done things I don't even know about. Give me the book and I'll do everything I can to put you in the clear. Gabrowski and Koenig are no loss to anyone. I think I can fix this all the way to the top."

"The top of the police department? Or the top of the syndicate?" The one question refused to disgorge itself from his craw. How had Barr worked so neatly in his footsteps?

"Both," Barr said. He was not desperate, he was not forcing the issue, he was talking quietly now, offering favors. "Play it smart, Steve. You got the men that killed Sam Goulding. They say Sid's likely to die from loss of blood."

Steve asked, "Were you in the Flaming Arrow deal, Jack? Did you make a score off it? Did you know Sam was catching up on you and the syndicate?"

From the floor, wiping his eyes, Freddy cried, "Don't answer him, Jack!"

Steve went on: "If the cops take the notebook away from me, then I'll know I can't win. But until they do, we'll wait it out. Just the five of us. Nice and cozy. I see you've got the whisky out. How about pouring a couple of drinks? Virginia and I have had a hard evening."

He did not feel brash or triumphant or even confident. Barr poured the whisky with a hand too sure and steady. There was something wrong, something he did not know about.

Barr was saying, "We didn't want to get tough with you. But we knew you were rodded up and Freddy had to try and take you. If we had thought of Virginia carrying heat—But who'd have guessed that?" He grinned admiringly at Virginia. "She's some girl, all right."

Steve managed the drink while holding Freddy's gun ready. Virginia was equally wary and adept. Barr crossed and gave Freddy a highball and the lean man got up, groping his way toward the couch.

Fay spoke again. "Jack never wanted to hurt you, Steve. If you would only go away and leave us alone, it would be all right."

"Don't coax him," Freddy muttered, holding a silk handkerchief to his throbbing eyes.

Barr drank from his glass. He sighed. "No use, Fay. You had him right. He's stubborn."

"You promised," she said in a low voice.

"I tried. You know that. He went roaring after Sid and this is what happened."

They were talking as if he and Virginia did not have the drop on them.

Virginia still was unafraid. He could see that. He moved restlessly, tasting the drink, trying to think it through.

Come on, Luck, he thought wryly. Why quit me now? I won a million dollars tonight; with Virginia's help I partially evened it up for Sam and the others. How am I going to get out of this? I can't shoot cops, even crooked cops. Nobody can make that stand up. They'll arrest me for the shootings, they'll frisk me and the notebook will disappear.

His mind finally cleared. He said, "Virginia! In that drawer. Quick! An envelope." She moved with smooth swiftness. "Address it to the Mayor of New York. Here, put this in it. Stamps in the corner there, see?"

He held out the red notebook. He saw Barr start, saw Fay's face twist into a mask, saw Freddy grope his way off the couch. He waved the gun at them and said, "Tried to talk me out of it. You almost succeeded, at that! Freddy rattled my brains, all right."

Virginia was coming across the room toward him. For one fatal moment she was in the line of fire.

He moved, seeing that Freddy had a hidden gun, knowing what he must do. "Mail it!" he shouted, and Virginia leaped and ran.

He shot Freddy in the right arm. Barr drove into him at the same moment and he lost the gun.

He saw Fay reach for something to use as a weapon. She was loyal to Barr, in the end, and he could not condemn her. He took a driving right to the jaw and then he was fighting for his life.

Barr struck with elbows, fists, knees, and feet. The attack carried them over the low chair and to the floor. Fay would be hovering with the heavy ash tray, he supposed. He swung Barr once, could not rid himself of the clawing, crazy brawn of the man. He doubled one arm and rammed his forearm under Barr's chin. Virginia still had the gun, but she had followed his command, as he wanted her to do.

He crashed a fist over his braced forearm, taking a dozen blows, but getting his knuckles against Barr's jaw. He shoved the shorter man away and looped his right.

Barr went over and down. Freddy was trying to get to his gun with his uninjured arm, calling to Fay for help. Fay was frozen against the wall. She held the bronze ash tray in her hand, but she was looking toward the door from the hall.

Steve looked, saw Virginia, then became still as a statue himself.

Carraway was behind Virginia. He held a drawn revolver. With him was a uniformed officer of the New York Police Department. Carraway said, "Galloway, you're under arrest."

The notebook, in the envelope, was in Carraway's hand. It all became very clear in that instant.

Barr said thickly, "Took you long enough. She nearly mailed it."

Carraway balanced the white envelope. "Figured this was it. She didn't get a chance to drop it." His speech was blurred, his eyes were bloodshot.

"Give it to me," Barr said. He wiped blood from his face, paused and smiled at Steve. "You sure do pack a punch. Sorry it has to be like this, honest I am."

Steve found no words. It was Carraway, then. The cop who knew everything had sold out at the last moment. He had made connections with the syndicate and they had offered him—what? Certainty of promotion, money, security, everything. And an alternative—play with the wrong side and be hounded all your life.

That was how they had stayed so close to him. Carraway knew the address of November's place. He had only to pick up a cop designated by Barr and go through the motions. The New York cop need not know anything except that Galloway was the man he wanted. This one did not look very bright. He had shiny handcuffs ready and was coming across the room toward Steve.

He braced himself, knowing the uselessness of fighting. He saw the cop motion Virginia to move over and stand beside him.

He found his tongue. He said, "Jack, I can't blame you for trying. But Carraway! What a dirty sonofabitch you are! You, the guy that saw Socker die!"

Barr said sharply, "Socker dead?"

"This human hyena didn't get around to telling you that? Yes, he's dead. Gabrowski and Koenig and

November killed him. He lived to talk a little and he put you in there with them, Jack." He turned again on Carraway. "You whisky-soaked, lousy, stinking bastard!"

At his vehemence the uniformed cop frowned and hesitated, looking to Barr. Virginia made a sudden swift move.

When she moved, Steve moved. He flung past the New York cop and slugged Carraway hard on his flaccid mouth. He saw Virginia swing open the door and started after her, reckless of consequences.

Again he stopped in his tracks. Lou Moscow, small and dapper and stoop-shouldered, carrying a large brief case, walked into the room. Behind him were two large men who could only be detectives.

Moscow looked around at them, one by one. He said in dry, incisive accents, "I went in today. The Mayor, the Commissioner, everyone knows about it. About everything."

Steve, alert for trouble, saw that none was forthcoming. The two detectives looked unhappy but determined. The larger said sorrowfully to Barr, "This is bad, Jack. About Socker. And that Goulding thing. I never bought that. You know it. Not that, Jack, not never."

Barr said quietly, "I know, Cassidy."

The other detective spoke to the uniformed cop, who looked dazed, but managed to say, "Yes, sir, Lieutenant Kline." He went outside and stood guard at the door.

Steve bent over Carraway and picked up the envelope. He held it out to Moscow. "Here's a complete confession from Sid November."

"Oh?" The lawyer fumbled with the envelope. He took out the little red notebook, started, opened it, then looked at Virginia. He said, "I see. Yes, I do see indeed." He handed the notebook to Cassidy. "Exhibit A for the state."

Barr said, "This finishes you, too, Lou."

"I've *been* finished. Since Sam was killed. And for other reasons." He could not help glancing again at Virginia. He said, "November went too far."

Virginia was close to Steve, whispering in his ear. "Don't ask how he got here. I called him, from the drugstore."

"You did what?"

"Remember what we said? That if it was real bad, he'd come? He'd already started cleaning his house."

Cassidy was saying in his sad tones, "We're all going to have to go down to Centre Street. This Jersey cop, he sold out, Galloway?"

"Evidently." Steve nodded. "He had ambitions, I'm afraid."

Cassidy nodded. "There's a lot of things!" He looked carefully around. "Yeah, we all go downtown. Freddy needs a doctor. You do it to Freddy?" He looked at Steve with some admiration.

"I shot him."

"It's a mess." Cassidy shook his head at Barr. "Geez, kid, I'm sorry. You almost made it, didn't you? I'm real sorry."

Barr picked up his Homburg, fixed it on his head. "I don't want any sympathy." He hesitated a moment, then said, "It was fun, Steve."

"It could have been fun." Steve was watching Fay. She moved like a woman in a dream. She went to Barr's left, took his arm, pressed it.

Barr said softly, "You'll be all right, baby. They've got nothing on you. Everybody knows you're clean."

They went out together then, not looking back. Fay would have to testify, Steve thought. They would plaster her on the front pages of the tabloids; they would call her "friend of notorious gambler involved in murders." And if November survived she would have to endure his accusations whether they proved true or false.

Moscow was putting a folder filled with papers on Steve's desk. He was saying, "You'll find all your affairs in order. Call Vic Hammerslag of Shafer, Boesser and Hammerslag. Best lawyer in the state." He put up his hand, palm out, a weary little old man with sad eyes that lingered again on Virginia. "Don't weep for me. Should have done this years ago. I wasn't meant to be a shyster for these people. Drifted into it. When they got Sam, I got scared. No good being scared."

They were picking up Carraway. The odor of whisky came to Steve's nostrils. He wondered what had happened to the Jersey cop, if he had turned Judas because of a drunken notion, if he had been frightened like Moscow, if he had planned all along to sell out to the bigger bidder. He would never know about Carraway. Perhaps Carraway did not know about himself.

Virginia and he were the last to leave, with Cassidy. He closed and locked the door of the apartment behind them, held the keys a moment, then put them away, the keys he had lent Jack Barr.

Down in the street the squad cars were overloaded. Sol Mintz poked the nose of the U-Drive into the lights. Steve said, "Can't we drive downtown in this, Cassidy?"

The big cop said, relieved, "Good idea, Galloway. Tell you the truth, I don't want to ride down with Jack. I went to school with Jack. He's a pal of mine. I wish I never had to see him again."

Virginia and Steve had the rear seat to themselves. Up ahead the sirens of both police cars wailed like coyotes against the misty overcast that blanketed the city.

Sol Mintz said gloomily, "Noise, noise. Trouble, trouble."

Steve said under his breath, "Fine beginning for a honeymoon."

"Just so there is one," Virginia whispered. "Imagine me, wanting to be married! It's—it's worse than shooting a man!"

"We'll go away from the noise for a while," he told her.

"A real honeymoon." She sighed, moving closer to him on the seat.

Up ahead rode Fay and Jack Barr, not making the honeymoon, not making it to Rio. There wasn't much difference between them, he thought. Four people, wanting the same things, trying to find a breath of happy air, trying to make it, each in his or her own fashion.

You've been lucky again, Galloway, he told himself. Better let it ride now. Don't press it too far, don't ask for anything more. Sam found you a girl and left her to you. The law will provide justice for Sam and you can thank him in your own way, by never forgetting.

He put an arm around the girl and hugged her tightly to him.

THE END

William Robert Cox was born March 14, 1901 in Peapack, New Jersey, but grew up in Newark where he played football and boxed. His writing career began in 1920 as a sport reporter, and his stories, mostly about tough guys  and sports figures, first appeared in 1934 in such magazines as *Dime Detective, Mike Shayne's* and *Black Mask*. Cox published over one thousand short stories in the next 38 years. He moved to the West Coast in 1948 and began working in television where he wrote over one hundred TV shows. His first novel was *Make My Coffin Strong* in 1954. Cox went on to write many crime, action/adventure, sports and western novels under a variety of pseudonyms, and was working on his 81st novel when he died on July 7, 1988, at his home in Los Angeles.

William R. Cox Bibliography
(1901 - 1988)

Crime Fiction
Make My Coffin Strong (1954)
The Tycoon and the Tigress (1958)
Death Comes Early (1961)
Way to Go, Doll Baby (1967)
Hot Times (1973)
The 4th-of-July Kid (1981)

Tom Kincaid series:
Hell to Pay (1958)
Murder in Vegas (1960)
Death on Location (1962)

Westerns
The Lusty Men (1957)
Comanche Moon (1959)
The Duke (1962)
Bigger Than Texas (1963)
Navajo Blood (1963)
The Outlawed (1963)
Day of the Gun (1967)
The Gunsharp (1967)
Firecreek (1968; from the screenplay by Calvin Clements)
Moon of Cobre (1969)
Gunfight at Razor Edge (1970)
Jack O'Diamonds (1975)
The Sixth Horseman (1987)

Bonanza
2. Black Silver (1967)

Cemetery Jones series:
Cemetery Jones (1985)
Cemetery Jones and the Maverick Kid (1986)
Cemetery Jones and the Dancing Guns (1987)
Cemetery Jones and the Gunslingers (1988)
Cemetery Jones and the Tombstone War (1990)

Buchanan series as by Jonas Ward:
Buchanan's Gamble (1973)
Buchanan's Siege (1973)
Buchanan on the Run (1973)
Buchanan's Manhunt (1974)
Buchanan Calls the Shots (1975)
Buchanan Takes Over (1975)
Trap for Buchanan (1972)
Buchanan's Big Showdown (1976)

Buchanan's Texas Treasure (1977)
Get Buchanan (1979)
Buchanan's Stolen Railway (1979)
Buchanan's Range War (1980)
Buchanan's Big Fight (1980)
Buchanan Takes Over (1981)
Buchanan's War (1981)
Buchanan's Black Sheep (1985)
Buchanan's Stage Line (1986)

Sports
Five Were Chosen (1956)
Gridiron Duel (1959)
The Wild Pitch (1963)
Tall On the Court (1964)
Big League Rookie (1965)
Trouble at Second Base (1966)
The Valley Eleven (1967)
Goal Ahead! (1967)
The Running Back (1967)
Jump Shot Joe (1968)
Rookie in the Backcourt (1970)
Big League Sandlotters (1971)
Third and Goal (1971)
Playoff (1972)
Gunner On the Court (1972)
Chicano Cruz (1972)
The Backyard Five (1973)
The Unbeatable Five (1974)
Game, Set, and Match (1977)
Battery Mates (1978)
Home Court Is Where You Find It (1980)

As Mike Frederic

Frank Merriwell Quarterback (1965)
Frank Merriwell Returns (1965)
Frank Merriwell at the Wheel (1967)

Film Screenplays
The Golden Blade (1953; uncredited)
Veils of Baghdad (1953)
Tanganyika (1954)
Jesse James' Women (1954)

Non fiction
Luke Short (1961)
The Mets Will Win the Pennant (1964)

Black Gat Books is a new line of mass market paperbacks introduced in 2015 by Stark House Press. New titles appear every other month, featuring the best in crime fiction reprints. Each book is size to 4.25" x 7", just like they used to be, and priced at $9.99 (1-31) and $10.99 (32-). Collect them all.

Stark House Press

1315 H Street, Eureka, CA 95501 (707) 498-3135
griffinskye3@sbcglobal.net   www.starkhousepress.com
Available from your local bookstore or direct from the publisher

Made in the USA
Middletown, DE
08 June 2022

66811457R10146